THE FIFT

A *Ben Sign* Crime-Espionage Story

By

Matthew Dunn

FORMER *MI6 SPY* AND *BEST-SELLING* AUTHOR

ALSO BY MATTHEW DUNN

SPYCATCHER SERIES
Spycatcher
Sentinel
Slingshot
Dark Spies
The Spy House
Act Of Betrayal
A Soldier's Revenge
Spy Trade
Counterspy

BEN SIGN SERIES
The Spy Whisperer
The Russian Doll
The Kill House
The Spy Thief

PRAISE FOR MATTHEW DUNN

"Terse conversations infused with subtle power plays, brutal encounters among allies with competing agendas, and forays into hostile territory orchestrated for clockwork efficiency...." ---- *Washington Post*

"Great talent, great imagination, and real been-there-done-that authenticity.... Highly recommended." ----Lee Child, author of the *Jack Reacher* series

"Dunn's exuberant, bullet-drenched prose, with its descriptions of intelligence tradecraft and modern anti-terrorism campaigns, bristles with authenticity.... Save for the works of Alan Furst, good thrillers have been thin on the ground of late. Mr. Dunn has redressed this balance with an altogether gripping book." ----*The Economist*

"[Dunn] makes a strong argument that it takes a real spy to write a truly authentic espionage novel.... [The story] practically bursts at the seams with boots-on-the-ground insight and realism. But there's another key ingredient that likely will make the ruthless yet noble protagonist, Will Cochrane, a popular series character for many years to come. Dunn is a gifted storyteller." ----*Fort Worth Star-Telegram*

"Matthew Dunn is [a] very talented new author. I know of no other spy thriller that so successfully blends the fascinating nuances of the business of espionage and intelligence work with full-throttle suspense storytelling. ----Jeffery Deaver, author of *The Bone Collector*

"Just when you think you've got this maze of double-dealing figured out – surprise, it isn't what you think. All the elements of a classic espionage story are here. The novel moves with relentless momentum, scattering bodies in its wake." ----*Kirkus Reviews*

"[Dunn has] a superlative talent for three-dimensional characterisation, gripping dialogue, and plots that featured gasp-inducing twists and betrayals." ----*The Examiner*

"A real spy proves he is a real writer. This is a stunning debut." ----Ted Bell, author of *Patriot*

"Not since Fleming charged Bond with the safety of the world has the international secret agent mystique been so anchored with an insider's reality." ----Noah Boyd, author of *The Bricklayer*

"Once in a while an espionage novelist comes along who has the smack of utter authenticity. Few are as daring as Matthew Dunn, fewer still as up to date…. Is there anyone writing today who knows more about the day-to-day operations of intelligence agencies in the field than Matthew Dunn?" ----John Lawton, author of *Then We Take Berlin*

CHAPTER 1

The Argentinian spy boat was anchored one mile off the Falklands Islands capital, Stanley. The vessel was thirty three yards long, resembled a fishing trawler, and had a crew of three men and one woman. It had been scouring the western and eastern isles of the Falklands for two months. Soon, it was due to return to the Argentinian port of Rio Grande, where the boat would be refuelled, fresh provisions would be taken on board, and the crew would rest for a few days. The boat had long-range telescopes, communications equipment, and thermal imagery. Its movements around the islands were random. Sometimes it would anchor, other times it would circumnavigate the islands, and sometimes it would only travel a few hundred yards before coming to an unanchored stop. Its purpose was twofold: first, to monitor British military movement on the islands; second, to annoy the islanders. Argentina wanted the Falklands back. It needed to show the islanders and UK military bases that it was watching them. But the boat posed no threat. The British military were aware of its presence; so too the islanders. They thought the boat was a joke. The UK navy couldn't be bothered to send a frigate from Portsmouth all the way towards the Antarctic to clear out the spy ship. What could the boat learn, reasoned the British commanders on the islands? That the Falklands only has a population of just over three thousand? That it rears sheep and exports fish? That a land invasion by Argentina would be met by fierce resistance? But the boat remained on duty, taunting the inhabitants of the islands. It was an Argentinian folly. However, the crew were not without teeth. They had guns. And they were firearms trained to the highest standard.

Tonight, the boat rolled in choppy seas. Two of its crew felt nauseas and were trying to stop themselves from vomiting. Only the captain of the vessel was a qualified sailor; the others were technicians. But, all of them had been taught how to master the boat should there be an emergency. They'd been told to watch the islands, but hadn't been given clear instructions as to what purpose their duty served. To them, the job seemed pointless. They were antagonists, they'd concluded – sent by their government to stir up shit and provoke the islanders and the UK military. Still, they had to do the job, no matter what the job. And they'd been told to kill anyone who tried to get close to their vessel.

It was getting dark and snow was falling. The skipper flicked on interior and exterior lights. He didn't care that it would make the vessel visible to others. He did care that if they remained invisible they might be accidentally struck by another ship. He walked on deck, pulled on a hemp seaman's jumper, rubbed ice off his beard, and lit a pipe as he gazed at the shores of the islands. Stanley was a mile away, its lights easily visible, the only sound to be heard was the slap of waves against the vessel and the boat's frame creaking with each movement. It was seven PM. Soon the crew would take it in turn to take over the night vigil for two hours per person while the others slept. It was a slog, no matter who went on shift first. They always woke up exhausted in the morning. It wasn't just the shift rotations and sea sickness that caused them shallow sleep; they never truly rested because there was always the threat that a British fighter plane would blow them to smithereens.

Still, tonight seemed like every other night. Boring. Lonely. Pointless.

The only silver lining was that tomorrow they'd be sailing back to Rio Grande – earlier than planned because the boat needed some urgent maintenance. The captain couldn't wait to turn on the engines and get home. He'd see his wife and kids for a few days, then motor back to the islands. His family thought he was a hero for doing a top secret job. He thought he was a fraud = a covert operative with no real mission.

He wished something would happen before he left – a British navy attempt to board his vessel; an aerial bombardment; commandos clambering up the sides of the boat; a diplomatic incident that would put his job front and centre of the world's press. Anything to relieve the tedium.

In one hand he held a telescope to his eye. In the other hand he gripped a semiautomatic pistol. It had never been fired in anger. He'd relinquish a month's salary to engage the enemy. The Brits had killed his father in the war. Payback was why he was here. But, so far it seemed he was on a fool's folly. Still, he kept grip of his pistol, willing soldiers, sailors, or islanders to attempt to take him and his crew on.

The pub in Stanley was modest in size and a popular venue for local islanders. It was off-limits to British military personnel who were garrisoned on the Islands' various bases, for no other reason than the military wanted to respect the islanders' privacy and community. "This is their homeland, not ours", the highest ranking officer told new military arrivals. "We are here to protect them. But we are not here to turn their town into a place for drunken squaddies to let off steam." Still, the islanders would have welcomed army, navy, or air force personnel into the boozer. Their attitude was *Britain first; Argentina last.*

The pub had Union Jacks hanging from the ceiling, a tiny bar with six barstools, pictures of the Royal Marines and Parachute Regiment marching across the islands during the war, three corner tables, a wooden floor, a *No Smoking* sign that was ignored by all, an old terrier dog that had lost one of its rear legs after stepping onto a mine that had sunk in a minefield and had shifted sideways with the earth – as the soil does in The Falklands – outside of the minefield, a painting of Margaret Thatcher, another of the current Governor of the archipelago, and an overhead fan that was only turned on in the summer or when the room was too clogged with tobacco smoke.

Sally was working the barmaid shift tonight. She'd lived on The Falklands all her life and had never visited anywhere else. But she wasn't naïve. The Internet kept her abreast of the outside world and she had virtual friends on Facebook who lived all over the world. She was twenty seven, pretty, and took shit from no one. Her father owned the pub. Normally he'd be here cleaning the place or checking the week's takings. But tonight he was out helping a mate to get one of his sheep to give birth, even though the unborn lamb was in the breach position.

Sally cleaned glasses while standing behind the bar. Four male islanders were on the other side of the bar, sitting on barstools.

Eddie Wilson. Thirty three years old. Fisherman. Not married and always hitting on Sally, though she was having none of it. Smoker, but not in the day. Facial skin as tough as leather. Hands that were calloused and as strong as a vice. Black hair that tonight was mostly hidden by a woollen hat. A permanent smell of salt and fish on him, no matter how many times he bathed. And a scar on his jaw from when his boat rolled in a swell, he lost his footing, and he accidentally tore a chunk out of his face with the fish hook he was holding. Wilson had splashed sea water on his face, showed no sign of pain, and carried on helping his fellow fisherman to haul the net containing their latest catch.

Rob Taylor. Twenty nine years old. Farmer on his dad's place ten miles west of Stanley. Due to get married to a local girl next summer. Big guy. Fearless and fit because he had to work fourteen hour days in any weather condition. Quiet. Nothing but kind to his childhood sweet heart. But if men got on the wrong side of him when he was drunk, he'd punch them across the room. Nobody in their right mind crossed Taylor. The story goes that a couple of years back one of his dad's sheep got lost. Taylor found the beast at night, bleating on an escarpment, totally exhausted and scared. Taylor lifted the sheep onto his chest and carried him for miles across treacherous terrain. It was a Herculean effort. Back at the farmstead, the sheep was revived, Taylor jumped into his pickup, drove to Sally's bar and challenged anyone in the tavern to an arm wrestle. No one – not even Wilson – took up the offer. Taylor had that look in his eyes. People let him be when he got like that.

Billy Green. Former Royal Engineer army commando corporal who was stationed here in 2009. Thirty four years old. Stayed on the islands after his tour ended because he'd got a local girl pregnant. Tough guy. Not big, but his body had the sinewy strength of high tensile wire. Devoted father, though he'd never married the girl he'd slept with. Blonde hair. Two missing teeth after he'd been in an altercation with five US Marines in a pub in Newquay – the marines had significantly worse injuries. Fearsome temper. A deckhand on Wilson's boat. An enthusiast of epic cross country runs, when he wasn't hungover. And rumour had it that he'd shot several Iraqis in cold blood when on tour in the second Gulf War.

Mike Jackson. Thirty one years old. Divorced. Short and prone to fat, but with the lung capacity of a race horse. Part-time lighthouse keeper at Cape Pembroke, east of Stanley, part-time fireman, part-time coastal repair volunteer and lifeguard. Wicked sense of humour. Bald as a coot. Never touches strong liquor but can out drink any man on the Falklands when it comes to beer. Church goer. Mouth like a sewer. Always taking the piss out of others, none of whom touch him because he rescued two girls when their dingy capsized a year back, single handily put out a peat fire that threatened to scorch a mile of the islands, and stopped Wilson's ship from sailing perilously close to jagged rocks when its navigation system failed in a storm. But there was a side to him. He'd nearly strangled to death an off-duty local cop who'd cheated him in a game of poker. The cop didn't press charges and transferred to another station.

Now, Wilson, Taylor, Green, and Jackson were supping beers. They'd downed tools for the evening. This was their time. They were extremely close friends; the only friends they knew. Often they wouldn't engage eye contact with each other; rather they'd stare ahead at Sally and just order more drinks while they muttered brief sentences to each other. This was man-time after a hard day's work. It wasn't social. It was solace.

Sally poured them four more pints. "You all look like you've got stuff on your minds."

Wilson replied, "We're fucking knackered, gorgeous. What do you expect? You got any sarnies?"

Sally shrugged. "Nothing special – ham and pickle; cheese and onion; corned beef; tuna mayo."

"We'll have all of them." Wilson swivelled in his chair and eyed the two men sitting at the table behind them. "You alright, Carl, Nick? Got that fence fixed yet?"

The men nodded while drinking their beers. Nick replied, "Yeah, thanks for the wood. You going out tonight? Weather's turning. Bit choppy they say. And a blizzard's coming in."

"Tell me about it." Wilson swivelled back to the bar. "I reckon that Argie spy boat's having a hard time of it, if it's moored up somewhere."

Jackson had just come off his lighthouse shift. "Tonight the fucker's anchored a mile off here." He laughed. "The crew will be spewing their guts up."

"I hope they choke on their vomit." Taylor downed his pint in one go and shoved his empty glass towards Sally. "It's about time something should be done about those cunts."

Sally wasn't perturbed by the language. She was as tough as any man and could swear like a trooper. Plus, the four men in front of her were loyal customers. Even when they got blind drunk, the only time she told them to leave was when it was closing time. Bad blood on islands with as small a population as the Falklands were not only bad for business; it was bad for survival. Islanders relied on each other to help out on small matters and major catastrophes. While they could be obnoxious, Wilson, Taylor, Green, and Jackson and others like them would jump into their cars in a second and come to Sally's aid if needs be. And she'd do the same for them.

She slid four pints across the bar. "The Argie boat isn't doing us any harm. It's just watching."

"Watching us," muttered Green. "How would you like it if a stranger watched you while you were having a shower?"

Sally grinned. "I don't think it's quite like that."

"Yes it is. They're always *fucking* watching. Knowing our private business. Bunch of fucking parasites."

They drank their beers in silence for a few minutes.

Taylor spoke next. "I'd like to bash their heads in, point their boat at Argentina, set the throttle, get off the boat, and wave them goodbye."

Wilson chuckled. "If you bashed their heads in they'd be dead."

"Fucking right."

Sally could tell the men's mood was changing. "Give me a few minutes. I'll get the sarnies." She returned with a large baking tray within which was a selection of the food.

The men responded with genuine warmth, all saying nearly the same thing.

"Nice one, gorgeous."

"Nice one, Sal."

"Nice one."

"Yeah, nice one, love."

They woofed down the food, burped, and thrust their empty glasses across the bar. Sally set to work and poured four more drinks.

Wilson said, "I reckon tonight we should do something about those bastards." His tone of voice and expression were cold.

Taylor. "Ram the fucker."

Green. "Put a hole in it."

Jackson. "Sink it or put the shits into it enough so that it buggers off and never comes back."

Behind them, Carl and Nick could hear their conversation. Carl said, "It's just beer talk, lads. The army has got the boat covered."

Green slammed his glass on the bar. "The army?! I was in the army. What use is the army against a boat that's in water that will kill you in seconds if you swim in it? More to the point – where's the fucking navy? Haven't seen those guys around here for a long time. Nah. To get something done it has to be done by local boys."

Nick called out, "So what's the plan?"

Wilson looked at his three friends who nodded. "Tonight we're going to have as many ales as we can before closing time. Then we're going to sail out and get rid of the fucker once and for all."

Sally placed a hand on his hand. "Get as drunk as you like in my pub. But out there it's dangerous and you're not thinking straight." She winked at him, hoping it looked flirtatious. In truth she was trying to calm him down. "The girls in Stanley would hate it if they lost a good man."

Her tactic worked for a while. The men changed subject and talked about anything that came into their brains. Football. Women. Fishing. Farming. Gossip about neighbours ten, twenty, or a hundred miles away. Vehicle repairs. Property repairs. Shipments of provisions to the islands. Funny stories from their youth. And their concern about some of the elderly on the islands and what the four of them should do to help them via odd-jobs and food runs.

They were good men. Tough and coarse, for sure. They had to be. Their livelihoods and existence were merciless. And right now they were really drunk. But say a bad word about these four men to any islander and they'd pin you up against a wall and threaten to kill you. And they'd mean it. Wilson, Taylor, Green, and Jackson respected everyone on The Falklands. In turn, they got respect back. Loyalty holds the islands together. The four men had loyalty imprinted in their DNA.

Closing time. Four very inebriated men.

As they stood to leave, Carl called out in a sarcastic tone, "I hope you're not going to drive."

Wilson replied, "Of course we are. We're too pissed to walk."

Standing alongside his battered Land Rover, Green said to his friends, "I'll meet you on the trawler. First I've got to make a drive."

His friends frowned. "A drive?" said Taylor.

Green nodded as he looked toward the port. "I'm not going out there unless we have protection. I know a man who's got guns. He owes me a favour. I'll be back with the guns in a jiffy. Or it might take an hour or two. I suggest you get your heads down on the boat while I'm gone. When I'm back, we sail and sock it to the Argies."

Three hours' later, Green was on board the trawler. He'd brought with him five British Browning handguns and two SLR assault rifles, all found on the battlefields in '82. Wilson started the boat's engines and drove faster than he normally would out of Stanley. He didn't care that he was breaking speed rules. The harbour master would be in deep sleep at home by now; and the lighthouse was un maned and automated at night. Stanley had shut up shop for the night. Only the men on the boat were awake.

Wilson called out to Green. "Crack open the emergency rations. We need something for the journey."

Green opened a box and withdrew cans of strong lager, which he distributed to each man. They swigged from the cans, some of the drink splashing down their chests every time the boat struck head-on a wave. The weather was becoming treacherous – snow and wind – but Wilson kept a firm grip on the wheel with one hand while drinking from the other. Visibility was non-existent and the rapid descent of snowflakes played havoc on his drunken eyes. But he knew these waters so well that for the most part he could drive his vessel blindfolded. In any case this journey was easy. Normally he'd drive his vessel fifteen or twenty miles out to find fishing grounds of cod and other species. This was only one mile out and one mile back in.

Green stood alongside the skipper, raised his can, and shouted, "Lads, we're off to war!"

They all laughed.

The Argentinian on duty on the spy ship saw the lights of the trawler draw closer. It wasn't unusual, he reasoned, for a fishing boat to be out at night – often that was the best time to make the best catches – but something wasn't right. The spy ship was lit-up like a Christmas tree. Even in these conditions the trawler would be able to see the Argentinian vessel. And the trawler was travelling at speed, heading directly toward the spy ship. The watchman estimated it was five hundred yards away. But, it was difficult to tell. The snow blizzard was playing havoc with his eyes and despite the months he'd been working this detail at sea, he still couldn't master judging distances at sea and in a part of the world where clear air made something look to be a mile away when in fact it was ten miles away. He waited. The vessel was drawing closer, its bow rising and falling, spray spurting from the vessel's sides.

In Spanish he muttered, "Shit", ran into the boat, went to the captain's cot, and woke the man. "Boat approaching fast. Looks civilian, but I can't be sure. Small. Travelling at speed, straight at us!"

The captain rubbed his face, got on his feet, and shouted, "Everyone up! Ten seconds! Weapons at the ready!" He pulled on his cold weather gear. The others who'd been sleeping did the same. They grabbed their handguns and assembled on deck. The captain looked through a telescope. In a loud voice, he said, "Trawler. Three fifty yards. It can see us. We can see them. Prepare to pull up anchor on my command. Weapons by your sides at all times. This could be a raiding party, disguised as fishermen. If they get too close, you know the drill – shoot to kill and flee."

Wilson gunned the vessel to its maximum speed, aiming it at the spy ship's starboard side. He knew his boat's bow was sturdy enough to withstand the impact. He also knew the spy ship was weak on its flanks. He was twenty yards away. His friends were on deck with their weapons.

Shots rang out and all went to Hell.

CHAPTER 2

Two men resided in the fourth floor apartment of a converted Edwardian terraced house in West Square, Southwark, London. The three other apartments in the building occasionally contained students and London workers. But for now they were empty.

The top floor flat contained two bedrooms, a tiny kitchenette, bathroom, and a large lounge that was brimming with antiquities sourced from Burma, Mongolia, France, Patagonia, and Japan. Three armchairs were in the centre of the room – two facing each other next to a fireplace; the third on the other side of the room. On the walls were paintings, framed military maps of various parts of the world, bookshelves containing academic journals, leather-bound out-of-print works of fiction, poetry, non-fiction, and a diary written by a British naval officer during his voyage to America in 1812. Persian rugs were on the floor. The curtains adjacent to the double window were heavy and crimson. The mantelpiece above the fireplace had candles, oil lamps, a revolver that had belonged to a Boer soldier, and an Arabian dagger that had its tip embedded in the mantelpiece's wood and was vertical.

Today, the fire wasn't lit. It was summer in the UK. Tourist season in London. But the property was sufficiently set back from the hustle and bustle of the south bank and all its trappings. Very little could be heard aside from the muffled sound of traffic. It was an oasis of sorts. A place where the occupants could collect their thoughts. It was also their command centre for private detective work that ranged from mundane and routine to matters of national and international security.

Ben Sign was cooking lunch in the kitchen. Partridge, rosemary potatoes, steamed vegetables, and a lemon and orange sauce were on the menu. Sign was forty nine years old, a former MI6 officer who was tipped to be the next Chief of British Intelligence but resigned because he didn't like bureaucracy and following rules, had joined the service after graduating from Oxford University with a double first, had seen plenty of action, but now preferred to use his mental prowess to solve problems. Tall, a widower, no children, kind but - when needed – had the ability to deploy a razor-sharp ruthlessness, Sign was regarded as the finest spy Britain had to offer. He'd thrown it all away and had set up the private detective consulting business. In doing so, he had the support of the prime minister, foreign secretary, home secretary, and commissioner of the Metropolitan Police. It was lovely to have such senior endorsements. But for the most part it didn't help him pay the bills. He wasn't wealthy and right now he and his partner were working for a client who thought her husband was cheating on her. A tedious case, but it would ensure that the next three months' rent was taken care of.

His business partner and co-lodger was Tom Knutsen, a former Met undercover cop who'd joined the police after graduating with a first from Exeter University. Knutsen's belief that the police would be a place where he could quash his tendency to be a loner proved to be a false hope. He'd quickly realised that mass camaraderie and a uniform weren't for him. His superiors also realised that. He was given specialist training and told to infiltrate major criminal gangs in London and elsewhere. Like Sign, it suited him to work in places where he could be killed if his real identity was established. The thirty five year old was resigned to being alone in the world, with one exception – he was increasingly coming to the conclusion that Sign was the only man he could relate to. Sign was older than him, spoke like an aristocrat even though he was born into poverty, was a man of contradictions, had immensely powerful associates and yet was just as happy conversing with the average man on the street, and treated Knutsen with the utmost respect. Sign could also be a belligerent so-and-so whose vast intellect and cut-to-the-chase attitude sometimes hardened his soft interior. That didn't matter. In a deeper way, Knutsen was like Sign and vice versa. They were becoming friends.

Knutsen was in the lounge, sitting in his armchair, listening to Sign cursing in the kitchen about rubbish cases, idiots negotiating Brexit, the dire state of American politics, the incompetent police detective who'd arrested the wrong man for the murder of a boy in Islington, how long it would take the police to identify and capture the real murderer – who Sign had identified by spending two seconds looking at a newspaper archive, and why the world was run by idiots.

Knutsen called out, "You're having one of your moods."

"I'm bored!" Sign served up the food and brought it in on trays. They ate on their laps in their armchairs. "It's been months since we've had a decent case."

Knutsen shovelled the food into his mouth. The meal was delicious. "Since we set up shop six months' ago, we've only had one decent case."

"True."

Their first proper case – to catch a serial killer forcing senior MI6 officers to commit suicide, purely by the power of suggestion.

Sign looked irritated. "Perhaps I should call my *friends* in government and ask them if there's anything they'd like us to do."

"They'd have called you. They have no use for us at the moment."

"Damn fools!"

Knutsen smiled. He liked it when Sign was riled. "Maybe they've got someone better than us to advise and consult on near-intractable problems."

"Nonsense! I know their advisors. All of them have an agenda to either go into politics or earn a lot of money. Or both. They have the wit to feather their own nests but they don't have the intellect to problem solve for a few bob."

"A few bob?"

"You know what I mean."

They finished their lunch in silence. Knutsen washed up. It was their rule. Whoever cooks, the other washes up.

Back in his seat, facing Sign, Knutsen said, "I've often wondered why you chose me to be your business partner. I don't care one way or the other what your answer is. But I must admit it has intrigued me."

Sign waved his hand dismissively. "MI6 officers hate each other. It has to be that way. We are not selected to hunt in packs. MI5 officers are wannabe spies, wherein in fact they are glorified cops. And mainstream police can't think outside of the rule book."

"I was a cop."

"Technically, yes. In reality you were a lost soul who killed the man who killed the woman you were going to propose to."

Knutsen looked away and quietly said, "Yes".

Sign leaned forward and placed his hand on Knutsen's forearm. "Dear chap, I hired you because you were a solitary hunter who'd lost his way in the wilderness. That was far more interesting to me than hiring tired ex-cops, unimaginative special forces types, or Machiavellian former spooks with egos the size of planets."

Knutsen angled his head. "A pity case?"

"Necessity. I needed the right man for the job." Sign's expression steeled. "It's what spies like me do – find the correct person for the task in hand."

Knutsen nodded slowly. "I just wish we could flex our attributes on something other than divorce cases, financial fraud, and petty street gang crime."

The communal entrance downstairs intercom buzzed.

Knutsen frowned. "Are we expecting a client?"

"Not to my knowledge."

"Amazon deliveries?"

"You know I hate the Internet." Sign stood and pressed the button that opened the communal entrance.

Thirty seconds later there was a knock on the door. Sign opened the entrance. A man was standing in the hallway – late forties, cropped but stylish silver hair, medium height, slight build, tailored charcoal grey suit, highly polished black Church's shoes, and a silk tie that was bound in a schoolboy knot over an expensive shirt with cutaway collars. Sign immediately suspected he was a military officer. The man was holding a leather briefcase.

The man said in a posh but clipped accent, "Sir, I'm here to speak to Mr. Ben Sign. I apologise for turning up unannounced."

"I am Mr. Sign. How did you know I was going to be here?"

The man gestured toward the communal front entrance. "I have men. They told me that you and your colleague Tom Knutsen were at home because…"

"They've been watching my home. Sir – you have my name. If you wish to talk to me in the comfort of my home, I will need your name and position."

The man hesitated. "Colonel Richards. I am commander of all military bases on the Falklands Islands."

Sign gestured for Richards to come in. He patted the armchair used by all clients who visited the flat. Sign pointed at Knutsen. "This is Tom Knutsen, my business partner. You may speak freely in front of him."

"I would rather speak to you alone." Richards sat in the chair and crossed his legs.

"Both of us or none of us!"

The colonel bristled. Clearly he wasn't used to being spoken to that way. He held Sign's gaze. "As you wish."

Sign sat in his armchair and interlocked his fingers in front of his chest. "Are you army or Royal Marines?"

"Royal Marines. Plus I did three years in the SBS before returning to regimental duties and gaining promotion. I struggle to understand why what unit I hark from matters to you."

"I wish to have the measure of you before we proceed. What do you plan to do when you retire from the marines?"

"Sir, could we get to business?!

"What do intend to do when you retire?" Sign repeated.

"I… I have been offered a senior position in BP. Also I'll be sitting on the board of directors for a golf club, a charity, a London museum, and a national haulage company."

"All positions requiring energy and youth. You're retiring imminently. Correct?"

"In two months' time. The Falklands is my last posting. My successor is an air commodore in the RAF."

Sign closed his eyes. "So what brings you to England at a time that presumably is very busy, given you're preparing to hand over the baton of command?"

"I came to London to see you. But what drove me here rests in the Falklands." Richards opened his brief case and withdrew a brown file. "I want you to have this, but first let me give you some context to its contents."

Sign opened his eyes and held up his hand. "If you have a case for us, remember it is our prerogative to decide whether we take it on."

"Oh, I think you'll take this on. It's gold dust. And it could lead to war. In fact we want it to lead to war." He eyed Knutsen and Sign. "Gentlemen – I'm not here to waste your time or my time. You've been recommended to me by the chief of defence staff."

Sign chuckled. "How is the general? Last time I saw him I had to instruct him to stop flirting with Russian agent provocateurs, or I'd ensure he lost his job."

Richards looked unsettled. "I… I…Well, he speaks very highly of you. Maybe he owes you a debt of gratitude."

"He owes me more than that. Now, you came here to see me, but the matter pertains to the Falklands and war. Proceed."

The colonel waved the brown file. "It is winter in the Falklands."

"Yes, Yes! Get on with it."

The colonel composed himself. "For two months there's been an Argentinian spy ship circling the islands. Its intentions seem to be pure observation, though goodness knows what they hoped to spot."

"It's provocation. They knew you knew who they were. They were hoping to kick the hornets' nest."

"That was our conclusion, Mr. Sign. And the islanders knew about the boat. For the most part they ignored it. The vessel kept its distance, didn't interfere with local fishing boats, and was viewed by British military and islanders as a useless piece of junk. But, three nights ago something changed."

Sign looked at Richards.

The colonel continued. "Four local lads – two fishermen, a farmer, and a lighthouse keeper – got drunk in a bar in Stanley. In front of witnesses, they bragged they were going to sail out and confront the spy ship. We know that's what they did because we've been monitoring the spy ship with an RAF drone, ever since it arrived. Via drone feed, we saw the locals' boat get close to the spy ship. But then we lost visual of both boats because a hellish blizzard kicked in. When the blizzard abated, we saw that the spy ship was gone and the locals' trawler was drifting close to where we'd last seen it. We sent one of our crafts out to check the local boat. No one was on the vessel. It was Mary Celeste. Of course, my men did a search in the waters around the trawler, but they found nothing. We towed the boat back into Stanley. Military and local police examined the vessel. There was fish blood on the vessel but it was impossible to ascertain if there was human blood."

Knutsen asked, "Evidence of gun fire?"

"Yes. The boat had bullet holes in its cabin. Aside from that the vessel looked like any other sea trawling boat, with the exception that there were guns on board. We think the guns had been fired on that night. They were scattered on the deck." Richards inhaled deeply. "We assumed at the time that the Argentinians had engaged the drunken idiots, killed them, and taken their bodies back to Rio Grande."

Sign said, "And they boarded the boat and intermingled any human blood traces with fish blood."

"Yes. Or they scrubbed the boat clean of the lads' blood."

Sign clasped his fingers together again. "But, it doesn't end there."

The colonel nodded. "The Argentinian ship is gone. It has not returned. But two nights ago four things did return, washed up on Stanley's shore – the bodies of the four locals. All of them had shots to the head and chest. We had to do an emergency post mortem. There is no doubt they were killed by bullets. And we are one hundred percent sure that the bullets were manufactured by Argentinian munitions companies. They were shot by the crew of the spy ship and their bodies were dumped in the sea. The tide brought them in."

Sign said, "The Argentinian military slaughter four civilians. It's an act of war between Britain and Argentina, but only if you have more proof of what happened other than bullets. Tis a shame your drone lost visual. You should have had men watching the spy ship, not artificial intelligence."

The colonel agreed but didn't say so. It was his decision to deploy the drone. "I want you to investigate the murders."

Sign looked at Knutsen, then Richards. "Why? You have the military police and local police at your disposal. Also, you could probably get detectives from Scotland Yard, or operatives from MI5 and MI6 to fly down. You have expert resources at your disposal."

The colonel shook his head. "The police will look at this as a murder investigation. It is not. It's far greater than that. Potentially this is war. The police can't be involved."

Knutsen asked, "And MI6 and MI5? The police might not have a grip on national security but the intelligence agencies do."

The colonel sighed. "There is a complication, and it's a delicate one. Is this a murder investigation, conducted by the police? Or is this a potential act of war, investigated by MI6? At the moment I don't know. What I do know is two things: first, I need someone to investigate this very discretely; second, I want proof that the Argentinians slaughtered the islanders. That's where you come in."

Sign said, "That makes no sense. We can't investigate a case of murderers who've fled back to their home country, and four dead bodies whose cause of death has already been accurately ascertained."

"That's not why I'm here." The colonel spoke calmly as he said, "Before the drone lost visual we had thermal imagery of the islanders' boat. There was no doubt – no doubt whatsoever – that there were five men on the trawler. Only four are accounted for."

Knutsen frowned. "Who is the fifth man?"

"We don't know. No one knows."

"How did the fifth man escape?"

"He used the emergency raft to get back to shore. We found it two miles away from where his friends were washed up. Gentlemen: I need to identify the fifth man. He wasn't in the pub that night. His evidence will enable us to go to war with Argentina. He will still be on the islands, somewhere. My men and the police can't try to find him. This is too delicate a matter. No doubt the fifth man is petrified. His testimony will mobilise an armada of British ships, an army, and a strike force of fighter planes. Find him and we have legitimacy to knock the Argentinians for six. What say you?"

Sign was quiet for a moment. "We'll take the case. All expenses paid for. We'll take one of your planes from Brize Norton to the Falklands. We'll be in civilian attire but I know how it works on that military route. For the sake of anyone asking, I will hold the rank of general; due to his age Mr. Knutsen will hold the rank of colonel. We are special investigators and are not to be obstructed by anyone in the British military. Understood?"

"Yes."

Sign checked his watch. "Time is against us today. But we can be on the first available flight tomorrow. You will pay us one hundred thousand pounds for this case."

"What?!"

"Half in advance; half upon completion of the job. And you will pay all expenses." Sign stood and held out his hand. "We have a deal, do we not?"

"One hundred thousand?!"

"We have a deal sir!"

The colonel slowly stood, looked confused, then nodded and said in a quiet voice, "Yes, we have a deal." He shook hands with Sign. "I will text you details of the flight times." He nodded at Knutsen. "Good day to you Mr. Knutsen." He nodded at Sign. "And good day to you sir." He walked out of the flat.

Sign opened the file. There was very little inside – birth certificates of Wilson, Taylor, Green, and Jackson; their addresses and employment history; a photo of Wilson's trawler; an aerial photo of the spy ship; the post mortem report on the deceased; a thermal image of five men on Wilson's boat before the blizzard hit the vessel and its surroundings; statements from Sally and the two other people in the pub on the night the four men got drunk and sailed their ship, and a photo of the four dead men on the beach. Sign handed the file to Knutsen. "Take a look and tell me what you think."

After Knutsen had carefully looked at the contents, he asked, "Do we trust Colonel Richards?"

"Of course not. We don't know him. But, I believe he's told us the truth. And he knows that if he tries to spin us a lie, then I will make his pension vanish. He's playing a straight bat."

Knutsen leaned forward and stared at the file. "All this tells us is what we already know. If the spy ship comes back, we could get the SBS to board the boat – Richards will have sway with his former unit – and arrest the Argentinians. We could interview the prisoners and get them to confess to what they did."

"The spy ship won't come back to the Falklands."

Knutsen's mind was racing. "Could you and I go to Rio Grande and try to find the spy ship? It's possible its crew are still near to the boat."

Sign shook his head. "A daring thought, but alas it wouldn't work. Upon their return to Rio Grande, the crew would have been debriefed about the incident. The Argentine intelligence services would have immediately recognised the severity of the situation. They'd have dispersed the spy ship crew and ensured they were as far away from Rio Grande as possible. The boat will have been destroyed."

Knutsen drummed his fingers on the arm rest. "So, all we have to go on is the fifth man. With a population of over three thousand in the islands, that's going to be needle in a haystack territory."

Sign stood. "We must endeavour to find the needle. Mr. Knutsen, tonight I will be viewing Mozart's Don Giovanni at the Royal Opera House. Would you care to join me? It's a black tie event."

"I don't have a tuxedo or whatever it's called by you posh types. Anyway, I've got a date with two cans of beer and the final episode of Masterchef." He grinned. "I'm trying to pick up some tips so that I can cook better stuff than the shit you serve up."

Sign smiled. "A laudable venture." His expression changed. "This afternoon, pack your bags. You'll need cold weather hiking gear and a suit."

"A suit?"

"Don't forget, we are high ranking military officers. We will travel in suits and when we arrive on the islands it will be military protocol for us to be invited for cocktails in the officers' mess in one of their establishments. For obvious reasons you can't travel with your handgun, but I will procure you a pistol when we arrive on the islands."

"Why would I need a handgun? We're not at risk. All we're trying to do is identify the fifth man."

Sign placed his hand on Knutsen's shoulder. "Were it that simple. There is a gun fight between two boats. The islanders lost because they were facing professionals who knew how to kill and vanish. But in that melee, the Argentinians must have realised that there was one islander they hadn't killed. That person escaped, most likely during combat. The spy ship had no chance of pursuing the fifth man while rounds were crossing decks. Probably the fifth man used the trawler as a shield while he rowed to shore as the battle raged. Here's the problem: the spy ship will have been decommissioned, its crew will have been laid out to pasture, but there is still a loose end."

"The fifth man. If he speaks, there's war."

"Exactly. Argentina will send new spies to the Falklands – paramilitary or special forces types. Probably no more than four of them. A greater number would arouse suspicion. And this time they will be on terra firma. They will have one purpose: kill the fifth man. We need to find him before they do. And that, Mr. Knutsen, is why you'll need a gun."

CHAPTER 3.

Four AM.

Sign and Knutsen were in their flat's hallway, their luggage at their feet. Knutsen looked bleary eyed, but alert. Sign looked like he'd had the best sleep in a long time. They were about to embark on a case. This was what Sign lived for.

"Have you ordered a cab?" asked Knutsen.

"We have a limousine. Military. It will take us to Brize Norton."

Two hours later they were in the West Oxfordshire RAF air base, exiting the limousine. They showed their passports to the security gate and walked to the main terminal. Inside were numerous military personnel. Those travelling were in civilian attire – that was the security protocol. Those not travelling were in RAF uniform. Sign had been told by Colonel Richards that an RAF corporal would meet them in the departures section of airport. The place was bustling. Knutsen wondered how the corporal was going to identify them amid the throng of people. Sign was unperturbed. He knew that Richards would have a photo of him that had either been given to the colonel by Sign's senior government allies, or had been covertly taken by the colonel's men outside Sign's home. The photo would now be in the possession of the corporal.

A wiry, thirty-something man in uniform came up to them, big grin on his face, and one hand holding a cluster of small documents. He saluted Sign and Knutsen. "General, colonel: Corporal Bainbridge. I have your tickets. Can I take your bags for you?"

"We'll carry our own bags," replied Knutsen.

Bainbridge led them to the check-in counter. He said to the woman behind the counter, "Two VIPs travelling today, Helen." He handed her their tickets. Knutsen and Sign gave her their passports.

She asked them, "Have you travelled this route before?"

Knutsen replied, "No."

Sign answered, "Yes."

She looked at Knutsen. "You'll fly to Ascension Island. There's a swimming pool there and a restaurant. Not much else aside from military and GCHQ instillations. It'll be very hot, so I hope you've packed your swimwear. You'll be there for about three hours. Then you'll head south to the islands." She smiled. "Different ballgame there at the moment, sir. Its winter and it's been chucking it down with snow. Don't be surprised if your flight is delayed."

Thirty minutes later, Sign and Knutsen boarded the flight. It was a civilian aircraft and was crammed with passengers – some of whom were soldiers and sailors returning to base after holiday leave, others were new entrants to the islands' military facilities. The plane had no first, business, or economy class. Instead, it was like a bus. Sign and Knutsen were however positioned at the front of the plane, both seats either side of them were empty.

Eight hours and thirteen minutes later they touched down in Ascension Island. It had been the staging post for troops and convoys on route to combat the Argentinian invasion of the Falklands. Ever since, it retained a military presence and was a place for planes to refuel. Knutsen put on sunglasses as he and Sign walked off the plan and across tarmac.

Knutsen said, "This is not what I expected. The island looks like a shit hole."

Sign replied, "The island's volcanic. There's not much more here than unforgiving shale and the sound of planes coming and going. Still, make the most of the sunshine."

They dined in a military cafeteria. The food was basic and designed to inject as many carbohydrates into hungry young men and women. Knutsen expected Sign's refined tastes to be repulsed by the fare. But instead Sign polished all the food off and rubbed his belly. "A man must eat whatever is offered to him when travelling," said Sign, reading Knutsen's thoughts. "I've eaten considerably worse in impoverished places where kind souls wanted to feed me their last morsel, rather than take the food for themselves. One must always be courteous."

Close to the cafeteria was a small swimming pool. It was within eye shot of Knutsen's table. He could see six Royal Marine commando trainee officers doing laps, jumping out of the pool, doing press ups and star jumps, jumping back into the pool, and repeating the process.

Sign followed his gaze. "Youngsters on a jolly. It will be bought and paid for by the marines. They'll be following the epic seventy five mile route across the islands that 45 Commando took in horrendous weather and with one hundred and twenty pounds on their back in order to engage the enemy." Sign smiled. "It will be deemed by their officers to be a character building exercise for these young men. The reality is they will be tested and at least one of them will twist his ankle on baby heads."

"Baby heads?"

"Much of the Falklands is covered by inflammable heathland. Some of it clusters into vast fields of uneven balls the size of heads. The only way around these stretches is to climb mountains. These lads will take the straightest route. They will suffer torn tendons or broken bones or both. The others will have to decide whether to casualty evacuate the injured party or press on. They will press on. Look at them – no more than twenty years old. Machismo will take a hold of their decision-making. It won't cross their minds that an injured party may not be able to return to training when back in England."

Knutsen looked at the young men. "How do you deduce all this?"

"Imagination and logic." Sign dabbed his napkin against his mouth. "Let's leave the boys to their pool exercise. I fear, no swim shorts and a dip for you, Mr. Knutsen."

"I wasn't going to take a dip, anyway." Knutsen frowned. "Why hasn't the fifth man come forward as a witness?"

"You tell me."

"He's scared. He may have concluded that the Argentinians may come for him. He may fear local police action against him for the reckless events of that night. Maybe he's in shock. Possibly he's protecting the families of the dead men, not wishing to bring dishonour on their names. I don't know. But I do know he's petrified and won't be easy to find."

Sign nodded. "We won't be welcomed by the islanders. "For them, this is not only a tragedy, it is also an embarrassment. Four of their own got slaughter by Argentinians. We must tread carefully. They will be feeling raw and angry."

Knutsen agreed. "Providing they know what happened and that the men are dead."

"They know. It's a close knit community. Richards wouldn't have been able to withhold this information from them." Sign stared at the volcano. Quietly he said, "Richards wants this situation to erupt, but on his terms. He doesn't want the islanders to take the law into their own hands. I very much doubt the islanders know about the fifth man. Finding him gives Richards control of the situation and organise a strike force against mainland Argentina. But if the islanders speak to the fifth man, Richards loses control. The locals will be baying for blood."

"They'll already be baying for blood if what you say is true. The Argentinian occupants of the spy ship killed four of their own. That in itself is enough to get them hot under the collar."

Sign shook his head. "The islanders know that Wilson, Taylor, Green, and Jackson were drunk that night. They also know that the men deliberately sailed out to provoke the spy ship. The islanders will have some sympathy with the men's actions, but they will also think they were stupid. But the fifth man can put a new slant on events – he can tell the islanders that they were executed in cold blood."

"And that paints a whole different picture."

"Yes. Richards wants to keep a grip on that information. If he can't he loses control of the situation and the Falklands." Sign checked his watch. "We depart in ninety minutes. While we're here I'd like to take a walk and examine Ascension Islands flora. I will meet you at the hanger for boarding."

Two hours after landing in the Falklands, Sign and Knutsen entered the officers' mess in RAF Mount Pleasant. They were here by invitation of Colonel Richards. As they walked toward the bar, Sign muttered to Knutsen, "Keep your cover vague. If someone asks, and they will do, say we're in a *specialist unit*. You were commissioned into the Parachute Regiment after graduating from Exeter University. There are no paratroopers based on the islands at present, so it's unlikely anyone here will know someone in your alleged old unit. But if by bad luck they do, say that you were pulled out of the paras after training and had to undergo selection for *special duties*. That should shut them up. I will adopt a similar cover story, though I can reel off a list of genuine contacts in the military. Attack is the best form of defence and all that. If they start asking too many questions, turn the tables and start asking them questions."

Knutsen replied in an irritated tone, "I was an undercover cop, you know. I spent years gaining the trust of criminal gangs and other shit. I do know how to bluff and lie."

Sign chuckled. "I'm sure you do."

They entered the bar. There were four RAF officers, three infantry officers, Richards, twenty five year old daughter, and a barmaid. Richards whispered in the ear of the barmaid.

In a commanding voice, the barmaid said, "Lady and gentlemen, please welcome General Sign and Colonel Knutsen."

A waiter appeared, holding a tray of cocktails. Knutsen and Sign took their drinks and introduced themselves to the officers. Like Sign and Knutsen, the officers were dressed in immaculate suits. Richards' daughter was wearing smart but unfashionable trousers and a blouse. Knutsen correctly assumed she was used to military life and all the rituals it brought, and that she'd change into something more flattering when she returned to her quarters. She was eying Knutsen, with a slight smile on her face. Knutsen knew the look. He felt uncomfortable. The last thing he needed was a twenty five year old getting the hots for him. Knutsen and Sign made a beeline for the colonel.

Quietly, and out of earshot of the others, Sign said, "Thank you for getting us down here and for the invitation. Tomorrow, Mr. Knutsen and I will set to work."

The colonel was on his third cocktail. His face was slightly flushed. "You were lucky. The snow storm has now kicked in with a vengeance. Flights have been cancelled. You won't get out of here for at least a week. How are your quarters?"

Their quarters being in the officers' section of Mount Pleasant.

"Perfectly serviceable, but not sustainable." Sign looked around the room, taking in everything he saw – framed photos of the queen, of previous military commanders of the Falklands, vistas of the islands, its mountains, and the men and woman in the room. Within ten seconds he'd correctly assessed every person's strength and weakness. He looked back at Richards. "Mr. Knutsen and I desire a cottage to rent, away from the military base. Can you arrange that?"

The colonel frowned. "You have everything you need here – a gym, restaurant, bar, shops, many other facilities. I would think…"

"I would think that I know my own mind." Sign gestured toward the others in the room. "Your facilities are for those men, not men like us. Mr. Knutsen and I must work under the radar. A cottage will be all we need, thank you. Two bedrooms; a log burner or open fireplace; a serviceable kitchen; and mobile phone reception. We will also need a four-wheel drive vehicle that is man-enough to drive over snow."

"I…"

"And we will need all of that by tomorrow."

The colonel nodded. "Yes of course. That can be arranged."

"Arranged by you. I want to keep knowledge of our presence on the islands to a minimum. And tomorrow morning, after we've checked out of your salubrious establishment, we will need to be taken by you and you alone to the beach where the dead men were washed ashore. Are we clear on all matters?"

The colonel had given up all hope of flexing his rank. Sign was too powerful and way above Richards' pay grade. "Yes. Ten AM sharp. I'll knock on your doors and escort you to our vehicle."

"Excellent." Sign turned to Knutsen. "Time for us to mingle. Be careful with the colonel's daughter. She's intrigued by you."

That night, Knutsen struggled to sleep. He got out of bed, put on his outdoor hiking gear, and walked through the military facility. Even though it was two AM, there were soldiers, sailors, and other staff milling about. They ignored him because they were used to strangers coming and going in the base. Plus, even if they suspected he was a high ranking officer, they didn't have to bother with salutes or standing to attention or calling him sir, given he wasn't in uniform and had no tabs on his civilian attire to declare his rank. Knutsen was glad he was left alone. He wanted to clear his head after the exhausting flight and from the two cocktails he'd had in the officers' mess. He walked outside, near to the runway. The strip was empty; snow underfoot was at least ten inches deep. That would change – snow was pouring out of the sky, only visible in the beams from lights on the airstrip and exterior walls. It was bitterly cold; so cold that Knutsen felt that every time he breathed his lungs were being filled with ice cubes. He'd travelled overseas before, though not as much as he'd liked – a trip to India with some pals when he was at university, family holidays to France with his poor parents when he was a kid and before they died, and Metropolitan Police assignments to track British criminals in Spain and other parts of Europe. The trouble was, in his adult life he'd been too busy getting under the skin of the darkest parts of London to find time to go on holiday. Plus, who would he go on holiday with? Six months ago, the woman he loved was killed in the line of duty. They'd never dated. He'd never told her he loved her, though she probably suspected she had his heart. It was too early to think about finding a nice woman who'd be thrilled at the prospect of sharing a hotel room with Knutsen in Switzerland, ride a gondolier with him in Venice, eat crab and shrimp in street markets in Hong Kong, or swim with turtles in the Maldives before returning to their beach hut and making love. Maybe that day would come; maybe not. Right now, Knutsen was at a time in his life where he needed to be distracted by work. He also needed male friendship. By pure chance, Sign had come along. He'd offered him a job and lodgings in West Square. Sign was in almost every respect different to Knutsen. At least it seemed that way on paper. Sign spoke like a man in command of everything around him; Knutsen was quiet. Sign liked classical concerts; Knutsen liked Nirvana and other grunge music. Sign socialised with prime ministers and kings; Sign taught kendo to a kid from the wrong side of the tracks in Brixton. Despite his petty crime record, that young man was now a cop in the Met, thanks to Knutsen. Sign wore suits purchased on Saville Row; Knutsen had one suit from M&S. But as he'd got to know Sign, Knutsen had begun to realise that they had far more in common than he'd thought. They'd both repeatedly risked their lives in undercover operations. They were both reluctant loners who, until recently, had failed to realise the pleasure of companionship, until it finally hit them in the face – both men were surprised at how the recent lodging arrangement in West square had lifted their spirits. They were quick thinkers. Knutsen didn't profess to have Sign's intellect, but you don't get a first class degree from Exeter through want of IQ. Sign was courteous; so was Knutsen. They could talk for hours, or they could sit in their armchairs in silence. Knutsen had often tried to pigeonhole Sign's character. It was an impossible task. Sign was a chameleon and unpredictable when working. But in West Square, Sign was himself. He cooked, he stoked the fire in winter, he wore jeans and a T-shirt, he laughed, he regaled Knutsen with his exploits in MI6 – never from an egotistical perspective, always humbling his magnificent successes. And Knutsen would eat Sign's sumptuous food and tell him about the London Sign didn't know. They were fascinated by each other – not in an emotional way; both men were straight; but in an intellectual way backed up by their life experiences. Key to Knutsen and Sign was that West Square was their safe place. If there was one label that Knutsen could slap on Sign it was that the former MI6 officer was like an older brother – one who'd been separated from birth from him, educated differently, taught how to be posh, and had risen through the ranks of government while Knutsen was playacting a gangster in Tower Hamlets and elsewhere. There was no doubt that Sign's persona was that of an aristocratic commander from the nineteenth century, and yet he was full of contradictions. It always made Knutsen laugh when Sign would rifle through the Radio Times after dinner and say, "EastEnders is on in ten minutes. We mustn't be late. I want to find out whether that woman really is cheating on her husband".

Knutsen trudged through the snow and looked around. He'd never been anywhere like this. The remoteness of the islands and proximity to the South Pole made him feel exhilarated. He stopped walking and closed his eyes. There were some sounds from the military base, but aside from that all was silent. And this was Stanley – the capital of the islands, with a population of approximately two thousand, on an archipelago that's total population was three thousand. Sign had told him that beyond Stanley it was commonplace for islanders to live ten or so miles apart from each other. There the silence would be deafening.

Knutsen opened his eyes. Despite the severity of the cold, the air smelled fresh and pure. Tomorrow he'd see the islands in daylight. But for now the former policeman in him tried to get the feel of the place. Was this a zone where a crime would not go unpunished, because everyone knew each other's business? Or was this a territory where one could easily murder someone, bury the body, and nobody else would be any the wiser? Knutsen wanted to know the answer. He turned and walked back to the barracks. He didn't know if he'd be able to sleep. But he did know that he'd get hypothermia if he stayed out here too long.

CHAPTER 4

The following morning, Sign and Knutsen were sitting in a jeep that was heading west from Stanley. Richards was in the driving seat. No one else was with them. As they drove through Stanley they passed a small supermarket, post office, iron mongers, petrol station, vehicle repair shop, and two pubs.

Richards pointed at one of the pubs and shouted above the din of the vehicle's racket and external weather. "That's where the men drank before they got slaughtered." He carried on driving along the coastal route out of Stanley.

Richards was in uniform. Sign and Knutsen were in hardy outdoors gear and hiking boots. Snow and wind were striking the vehicle. The temperature was minus ten. The vehicle was shaking and skidding so badly that Sign and Knutsen had to grip their seatbelts to stop their bodies slamming against the doors.

Richards stopped the vehicle. "We're on foot now. Two hundred yards to the beach. Watch your footing."

He got out of the vehicle. Sign and Knutsen followed him. The beach was partially clear of snow, due to the sea washing over the rock and sand. But snow and hail was still pouring down, hitting the men's faces with the ferocity of a swarm of locusts. They trudged across the beach until Richards stopped and pointed.

"This is where they were washed up. It wasn't unusual they were so tightly grouped. The tides here can be precise. They were caught in a rip tide and funnelled onto the beach."

Sign asked, "Was there any possibility they were placed here?"

Richards shook his head. "The post-mortem proved they'd been in the water for many hours. They were bloated; their lungs were full of liquid; their gunshot wounds were quarterized by the cold; they had blows to the body that had come after death – most likely due to hitting rocks on the seabed as they were washed ashore; and most of their limbs were broken from the mile-long journey to the beach. We consulted with our naval friends. They confirmed that on that night a man dumped next to the spy ship would have been brought in to this place. It's all to do with currents and weather and other stuff I don't understand. There is no doubt they were dropped in the sea and ended up here."

Knutsen knelt down and touched the sand. "There is proof positive they died from gunshot wounds?"

"Yes."

Sign looked out to sea. "And no sight of the spy ship since?"

Richards followed his gaze. "None whatsoever. We've tripled our efforts to monitor the archipelago's coastline. Plus, we're getting help from the GCHQ post in Ascension. It would be wonderful if the boat came back. The SBS have got ten men doing a three month training exercise in Antarctica. They could be with us very quickly and board the ship. I've put them on alert. But I don't think the boat's coming back."

"I know the spy ship's not coming back." Sign crouched and placed his hand on the beach. "Who found the bodies?"

"Two local teenagers. They called the police. The police called me."

"Why?" asked Knutsen.

It was Sign who answered. "Because word had got out that the men were going to do something silly to the spy ship. The police realized they were out of their depth, that this was probably a military and political matter." He looked up, uncaring that his face was being smothered by snow.

Knutsen stared at him, wondering what was going through the man's mind. Sign was immobile, seemingly oblivious to those around him and the adverse weather conditions.

He lowered his head and looked at Richards. "We need to see the bodies."

Richards frowned. "What purpose would that serve? Neither of you are medically trained, and you have excellent post-mortem reports to draw upon."

"The bodies! Where are they?"

The colonel rubbed snow off his face. "King Edward VII Memorial Hospital, in Stanley. It was where the post-mortems were conducted. Their families want the bodies released in the next day or two. Wilson and Green are to be buried at sea. Their families and friends think that's fitting given they spent most of their working days at sea." Richards smiled. "Let's hope they're not washed ashore again. Taylor and Jackson are to be buried in the cemetery."

"Then we have not a moment to lose." Sign walked toward the jeep.

As they drove to Stanley, Richards said, ""I've secured you a two bedroom cottage. It's twelve miles south west of Stanley, near Bluff Cove. It has Wi-Fi, a log burner, you might have occasional problems with mobile reception though there is a landline, and overall it's a perfectly serviceable property. I picked it because it not only has road access to Stanley, but also the other parts of the islands."

"Where the fifth man may be hiding," said Knutsen.

"Precisely." The colonel drove into Stanley. "You'll have a four wheel drive at your disposal. As you requested, it has no military markings. Petrol is available at the RAF base or at the garage in Stanley – nowhere else, though people help each other out on the islands so if you get stuck a farmer will always donate some fuel. Trouble is, you might be twenty miles away from the nearest farmer if you're driving west. Keep on top of your fuel. And today one of you needs to go the grocery store in Stanley and pick up enough provisions for a week. Don't assume shops are open in Stanley every day. In conditions like this, they close if they can't get their deliveries. Always remember that you have Mount Pleasant as a bolt hole, if things go wrong." The colonel stopped his vehicle outside the hospital. "I don't know if either of you are familiar with this type of climate. It can kill you quicker than a man can make a decision." He looked at the men and smiled. "It's not all bad. Bluff Cove is spectacular. It's where the penguins congregate."

They exited the vehicle and walked in to the hospital.

Ten minutes' later they were in a sterile room containing slabs and freezers with bodies inside.

Richards introduced Sign and Knutsen to the only other person in the room – a female. "This is Dr. Carter. She trained and worked in London, and subsequently worked in Mumbai, Washington DC, and Melbourne. But she's an islander and the temptation to return to her roots was ultimately too great."

"My mother had stage four cancer. I wanted to be with her before the end." Carter had an icy demeanour and tone of voice. On the slabs were four bodies, covered with sheets. She pulled off each sheet. Wilson, Taylor, Green, and Jackson were there. "They were fit men. No signs of any pre-existing underlying illnesses. Toxicology reports show they were ten times over the limit, but the reports won't be wholly accurate because they'd been dead for at least twenty four hours before I set to work on them."

Sign and Knutsen stood next to Wilson's body.

Sign asked, "Can you be certain they died from gunshot wounds? Is it possible they drowned and were then shot?"

The doctor answered, "An interesting question."

Richards interjected. "Why would the Argentinians shoot them if they were already dead?"

"To provoke us." Sign leaned forward to get a closer view of Wilson's wounds.

The doctor said, "There is no doubt they were killed by bullets. I extracted the bullets and gave them to Colonel Richards. I believe they are now with ballistics experts in England. I can give you chapter and verse on how I know they died from bullets, and that any subsequent non-bullet wounds or water in the lungs came after death. But it's all in the post-mortem reports." She looked at Richards. "If you need a second opinion, you'll need to fly someone in asap."

It was Sign who answered. "That won't be necessary." He examined the other bodies before returning to Wilson. "He was the skipper of his boat. He was at the helm. He took a bullet to his arm and another to his chest. He turned to flee. That's when he was shot in the back of the head."

Carter was impressed. "You've seen gunshot wounds before."

Sign ignored the compliment. "Taylor, Green, and Jackson were killed while facing their assailants. They were brave men."

"Or drunken fools." Colonel Richards frowned. "I still don't understand why the bodies were thrown into the sea. The captain of the spy ship would have known that the tides were such that night that the dead men would be washed ashore."

"Once again – provocation." Sign stood upright. "He or she wanted the bodies to be found by you. The captain was smart. He realised the enormity of the event but he also realised the opportunity the situation presented to Argentina. This was a shot across the bow, but it wasn't an act of war unless there was proof. He may or may not have been aware of the drone surveillance, but being an expert in long range spying I suspect he knew that the blizzard was shielding coverage of the incident. So, it was a win-win outcome for the spy boat. Provoke the islanders and Britain, vanish, and the task of the spy craft is complete. And I'd hazard a guess that the crew of the spy boat couldn't wait to get back to Argentina, having completed their thus far mundane task with a bang. Argentinian intelligence services would have embraced them. The killings weren't scripted by the intelligence services there. But in that brief explosive encounter, the spy ship had achieved considerably more than months of the ship slogging around the islands." Sign went to Richards and whispered out of the doctor's earshot. "The fifth man is the fly in the ointment. The Argentinians thought they'd got away with the perfect set of murders. But they only saw the fifth man when it was too late. The fifth man was on a dingy, heading for shore. He was too far away. The skipper of the spy ship couldn't risk pursuit, so close to Stanley. This is the loose end the Argentinians will wish to burn."

The colonel nodded. "And they know that there are two possibilities. First, the fifth man came forward to local authorities, told us that he and his pals tried to commit murder, and supplied us with the evidence we need to go to war. Or, second, that he was petrified he'd be thrown in jail so went to ground. They'll suspect he's laying low. They think he's not come forward."

"I agree. But they won't risk the possibility that he may have a change of heart. And they'll know you will have brought in specialists to hunt him down."

"Which is why you didn't want to stay in Mount Pleasant?"

Sign nodded. "Knutsen and I have to be off the radar." Sign spun around and said in a loud voice, "Doctor – thank you so much for allowing us to intrude on your excellent medical facility. I can see that no stone has been unturned in the examination of these unfortunate souls. I believe that funeral logistics are being attended to. We will bother you no more and will allow you to complete your case. Good day to you madam."

Sign strode out of the room.

CHAPTER 5

Knutsen turned off the jeep's engine and looked at Sign. "Are we sure about this? It's in the middle of fucking nowhere!"

"Language, young man. It will suit our purpose." Sign got out of the vehicle and approached the door to the cottage that Richards had secured them. It was an isolated property, a crumbling disused stone sheep pen was twenty yards from the house, all around it was rolling heathland, the sea was thirty yards away, below an escarpment, and there was not another dwelling in sight. There was no evidence of animal life. The snow had forced all fauna into their nests or burrows.

Knutsen joined Sign at the front door.

"It's locked," said Sign.

"I know. Richards said there's a key in the combination lock next to the door. Shit, shit, shit! He gave me the combination but I can't remember it. All I remember is it's four digits."

"Call him."

Knutsen tried. No reception. "Now what do we do?"

Sign stood in front of the lock. "We improvise and use our imagination. Ninety eighty two – the year of the war." He tapped the numbers in to the keyboard. "No. Sixteen ninety – the year that English captain John Strong is officially recorded as discovering the islands. No. Eighteen thirty three – the year Britain reasserted its rule over the islands after French, Spanish, and Argentine settlements on the islands. No." Sign was getting frustrated. "Two thousand and thirteen – the year the islanders held a referendum on sovereignty and overwhelmingly voted to remain British." The number didn't work. "Damn it!"

Knutsen tried not to laugh as he took Sign's place in front of the keypad. "Let's see if this works." He typed in zero zero zero zero. The safe unlocked. Knutsen giggled. "I can't believe I forgot that code."

"Forgot indeed. Very funny, Mr. Knutsen!"

They entered the cottage. Its thick stone walls protected them from much of the sound of wind and precipitation outside, but it also insulated the cold. Sign prepared the wood burner while Knutsen opened curtains and followed the absent owner's written instructions to turn on the water supply and electricity. Knutsen checked the telephone landline – it was working. But, Richards was right – there was no mobile reception here. Once the fire was lit and the cottage's essential services were up and running, Knutsen and Sign examined the property.

Sign said, "Kitchen – electric hob, not ideal. I prefer gas. Knives are cheap junk and blunt. But there is a steel. I will sharpen them. Pots and pans are as bad as can be; none of them non-stick. But there is a slow cooker. I can improvise with that. Plates – fine. Cups – fine. Glasses – fine. Drawers - stocked with utensils and towels. Okay, I can work with this. Let's go upstairs."

The two bedrooms were intersected with a bathroom that contained a toilet, sink, and bath. No shower.

Knutsen said, "I haven't had a bath since I was ten years old. I'm a shower kind of guy."

"We must improvise. When you go to the store, buy the usual bathroom necessities but add on bath foam, or whatever it's called. Are you squared away on the boiler?"

"The boiler?"

"This is not West Square. To get hot water we need to plan at least twelve hours in advance."

"I'll look in to it."

Sign smiled. "I'll take this bedroom."

"It's the smaller of the two. Are you sure?"

"It has a view of the cove. I'm hoping to see the penguins congregate. Did you know, they get cold, just like us?"

Knutsen sighed. "No I didn't. I'm off to the grocery store in Stanley. Back in an hour or two. Don't do anything stupid while I'm gone."

"Such as?"

"Such as visiting your cold friends in Bluff Cove."

"Ha!" Sign slapped his thigh. "When you're in the store see if they sell seal blubber. It's just occurred to me that it might make a more nutritious and tasty substitute for sunflower oil when cooking."

Knutsen gave him a withering look. "Given what I know about this place so far, don't be surprised if we're having beans on toast tonight."

Ninety minutes' later Knutsen returned. He brought in four boxes of groceries.

"Did you source some blubber?" asked Sign.

"Fuck off." Knutsen placed the boxes in the kitchen. "The shop was surprisingly stocked with a variety of stuff. Alongside veg, herbs and spices, bread, tinned stuff, wine, beer, and toiletries, we've got steaks, chicken, cod, lamb, a joint of beef, mince beef, zebra trout, and brown trout." He started unpacking the boxes. "They didn't have your favourite drop of calvados. So, I bought a bottle of brandy instead. Hopefully your gastronomic skills and palate will be able to make something of it all."

"Splendid, dear chap." Sign placed a hard plastic case on the kitchen table, next to the boxes. "While you were gone, Colonel Richards popped over. He gave me this. He opened the box. Inside was a Glock 37 handgun, cleaning kit, and four spare magazines. Sign expertly stripped it down, reassembled it, checked its workings and handed it to Knutsen. "It's a .45 calibre weapon. You'd be able to kill an elephant with this thing. The magazine holds ten rounds. The gun has been cared for – there's not a speck of dust in its mechanics."

Knutsen weighed the gun in his hand. The last time he'd held a gun this powerful was when he was on an undercover assignment to take down a gang lord. His police partner – the woman he was secretly in love with – was his fellow undercover colleague. They'd married prior to the assignment, purely as a façade to give credence to their fake backstory. But Knutsen was convinced they'd never get divorced after the job. Alas, she was killed when they took down the gang leader. Knutsen had used a gun as powerful as the one he was now holding to blow her killer's head to smithereens.

Sign knew all of this and could tell what Knutsen was thinking. "Sometimes we need a sledgehammer to crack a nut. But on this occasion it is possible we may have formidable opposition. We need to find and protect the fifth man. One shot from your gun, *anywhere* in the body, will immobilise the enemy."

Knutsen ensured the safety gadget was engaged and placed the gun between his belt and the nape of his back. "What about you? Did Richards give you an identical model?"

Sign waved his hand dismissively. "You know I no longer use weapons of any sort. The days of violence are behind me."

"So I'm the dumb grunt shooter, and you're the thinker?"

"Incorrect. You are also the thinker. But you carry the gun because your youth means you are better equipped to deal with trauma. One day the trauma will catch up on you, but not yet. When it does, you will be where I am and will never want to pull a trigger again." Sign riffled through the food. In a strident and jovial voice he said, "You've shopped like a queen." He winked at Knutsen. "Lunch will be baguettes with melted cheese and salad. Dinner will be zebra trout with Parma ham, chives, sautéed potatoes, broccoli, carrots, and a drizzle of white wine jus. It's a shame you couldn't source seal blubber. It would have given a lovely shine to the jus. Regardless, while I'm cooking you can do some target practice outside. Just don't shoot any sheep."

Colonel Richards called the British chief of defence staff on a secure military phone. "Sign and Knutsen have arrived. They've demanded that they stay in a cottage, not Mount Pleasant. I've given them a vehicle and a weapon. Sign won't take orders from me."

"That's because when he was office he was infinitely superior to you. Plus, he doesn't take orders from anyone. Will Sign and Knutsen do the job?"

"I'm sure of that. They've distanced themselves from military command and I understand why. They want to work this in their own way. The remit is clear: find the fifth man and make him talk. They can't fly out of here for at least a week. The weather has grounded our planes. They're going nowhere."

"Good." The chief asked, "Everything is in lockdown?"

"Yes. Local police have washed their hands of the case. The hospital obviously knows about the gunfight but don't know details, and I've told the doctor who did the post-mortem that she'd spend a lifetime in prison if she breathed a word about the dead men, given the military now has jurisdiction."

"What about the dead men's families?"

""I've told them that the men drowned on a routine fishing trip."

"They will be suspicious, given the men bragged that they were going to confront the spy ship."

Richards shook his head. "I gave them photos, showing that the spy ship was nowhere near the men's trawler when they died. Obviously, the photos were doctored and taken days before the incident. But I did give them copies of the real toxicology reports. They know the men were blind drunk, the weather was awful, they fell overboard. The families are angry with the men's stupidity. There's no suspicion."

"And within the military?"

Richards replied, "Only a handful of people know about the incident. I've briefed them and laid down the law about national security, blah blah blah. Most important, I've told them about the sensitivity of the situation and that this may lead to war. Sir – are you making preparations?"

"Yes. To kick Argentina in the balls I will be using navy frigates and destroyers, 42 and 45 commando Royal Marines, 2 Para, navy and RAF helos and fighter planes, and I will position a Trident submarine off Argentine's coast. The end game will not be to take Argentina. We don't want their country. But it will be a massive *fuck off and leave us alone*. Nobody messes with Britain and its piss poor protectorates."

Richards smiled. "The number of civilian casualties will be immense."

"Are you worried about that?"

"No."

"Nor am I. The Argentines should have voted in a better government. So, let Sign and Knutsen do their thing and once that's completed we do our thing. Agreed?"

"One hundred percent."

"Alright colonel. Do your job. Make preparations for my task force to use your islands as a launch pad, keep an eye on Sign and Knutsen, and get me the fifth man. His evidence means I can strike Argentina and ensure they don't touch the Falklands." The chief hung up.

It was evening. Knutsen walked toward the cottage, his gun in his hand. It had been dark for two hours, but that had suited Knutsen because he'd wanted to do his target practice with the only light coming from the multitude of stars that resembled large jewels in the crystal clear sky. Since mid-afternoon, snow had stopped. But it had started again with a vengeance. He entered the cottage, stamped his boots on the internal doorway mat, placed his sodden fleece by the log burner, and rubbed snow off his face and hair. The gorgeous smell of Sign's cooking was permeating the lounge. Knutsen went into the kitchen. "It's getting shit out there again."

Sign was dashing between pots, stirring some, dipping his fingers in another and tasting its sauce, and checking the oven containing the zebra trout stuffed with lemons and encased in clay he'd sourced near the beach. "Food will be ready in ten minutes. That should give you enough time to clean your gun."

Knutsen returned to the lounge, stripped down his weapon, cleaned and oiled it, and reassembled the pistol.

Sign emerged from the kitchen holding two plates of food which he placed on the small table. From his pocket he withdrew knives and forks which he positioned next to the plates. He dashed back into the kitchen and returned with a bottle of white wine and two glasses. "Let's eat and be merry."

After the meal, Sign washed up and prepared two fresh coffees and two glasses of brandy. The men sat by the log burner.

Sign said, "Tomorrow we set to work. This will be delicate. We must enquire about matters that we don't want the islanders to know about, and yet to get to the truth we must speak to the islanders. It is an amusing yet complex spin on investigative procedures."

"Richards has covered up the killings?"

"No. He's blurred lines. It would be impossible in a place with such a small population to hide the deaths of four of its brethren. Richards has given the islanders part truths and part lies. I advised him to do so."

"What's the point? It's not like the islanders are going to raise a militia and invade Argentina."

Sign smiled. "The point is we don't want the islanders growing antagonistic towards the British military. If they knew that four of them had been slaughtered by Argentinians, they'd be baying for blood. A British military delay in action against Argentina would be deemed bad form by the islanders."

"Bad form?"

"You have to remember that we're in a delicate ecosystem. The islanders want the military to protect them. But they also have lives to lead. Every year, the military causes problems to their livelihood – accidental fires that scorch acres of rich farmland, landmines killing sheep, drunken liaisons between squaddies and young lasses, the list goes on and on. In equal measure, the islanders respect and reluctantly tolerate the British military presence. They'd rather the RAF, army, and navy weren't here; and they'd rather they were here. It's a delicate balance."

Knutsen sipped his coffee. "That's a bit of a mind flip."

"It's complicated. Unlike in our colonial days – when, like it or not, we always knew there was the inevitability of self-determination by our conquered countries' indigenous populations – here we are protecting British people who live on the other side of the world. It's hard for them; it's hard for us. We must muddle through. And in our case we must tread very carefully."

"Is Richards treading carefully?"

Sign placed his hands around his brandy, to warm the glass before imbibing. "He's an action man who's past his prime. He still clamours for blood and glory, though he won't be leading the charge. But he can instigate carnage. In his mind it will be his last volley. He wants war – every military person does. This will be his swan song. He *is* treading carefully by engaging us to get the evidence he needs. Thus, he is manipulating us for his own ends."

"You don't strike me as someone who can be manipulated."

Sign took a swig of his brandy. "I am several steps ahead of Richards. I'm several chess moves ahead of the Argentinians and the British chief of defence. No one manipulates me."

"Steps ahead? What do you mean? We haven't even started the investigation."

Sign looked at the fire. His voice was distant as he said, "Some people see what they want to see. That's when they're vulnerable. It's the time when a clever predator strikes them down." He looked at Knutsen and smiled. "Dear chap, we have a busy day tomorrow. Let's lighten the tone tonight. May I suggest we take a stroll to the cove? I wish to show you something."

Adorned with their hardy hiking gear, they strode to the cliff edge. Snow was falling rapidly but the flakes were small. Visibility was still good due to the stars and a moon that was three quarters visible, The air was thick with the smell of grass, heather, and the salty smell of the sea that was washing the beach.

Sign pointed at the beach. "Do you see them?"

Knutsen looked at the beach. There were hundreds of penguins there, not moving, just standing immobile, shoulders hunched, looking miserable.

"It's like Dunkirk is it not?"

Knutsen hadn't thought of it that way. "They want to leave but they don't know how to leave."

"Just like us, the military, and the islanders."

"And yet they embrace this climate because it produces fish they can feed upon. They are hardy folk." Sign put his hand on Knutsen's shoulder. "They hunt where the food chain exists. Clever. We must be equally clever. Come – let's retire to our quarters."

CHAPTER 6

Nine AM. Eight miles outside of Buenos Aires.

Major Alejandro Casero was in a safe house owned by his employer the Federal Intelligence Agency, Argentina's primary spy and security organisation. For the past two years he'd been running a top secret fifteen-person strong black operations unit called Special Projects. The unit was responsible for surveillance in hostile locations, infiltration of large criminal gangs, destruction of material assets purchased with dirty money, and the executions of key wanted individuals. The executions were always made to look like revenge attacks by rival criminal or spy organisations. Special Projects worked off the grid. They were not answerable to the FIA. Even Argentina's judiciary was not aware of its existence. In fact, Casero had a very simple chain of command – he reported to Argentina's president; no one else.

Casero was thirty seven years old. Before joining FIA he was a special forces officer. In large part, he'd been responsible for handpicking the current members of Special Projects. He'd drawn people from the ranks of FIA, military intelligence, special forces, and specialist police units. The people he'd selected not only needed to have outstanding skills; they also needed to be grey men and women who could blend in anywhere. The frontline Special Projects field operatives were experts in unarmed military combat, small arms, explosives, covert infiltration, exfiltration, communications, deep cover, sniper skills, and every other attribute required for an elite assassination unit. They also needed to look and sound the part. Special Projects were masters at disguise. They could pass as a drug gang member from Colombia and could just as easily convince someone they were French, German, or British white collar businessmen. All of them were highly educated. Fluent English, no accent, was a prerequisite for entry into the unit. Within the team, other fluent languages spoken were Portuguese, and most other European languages. They could also vary their accents to mirror regional variants in tone. All of them had mastery of the Falklands Islands accent, which sounded a close match to that of New Zealand.

Selection into Special Projects was merciless, regardless of the gender or age of the applicants. Candidates were put through a month of hell – forty mile mountain walks carrying sixty pounds of weight on their backs, two mile swims in clothing, minimal sleep, escape and evasion exercises with dogs and armed men on their heels, twelve hour interrogations, and daily ten mile runs in sodden clothes and boots. After that, continuation training and selection kicked in. They had to prove that they could acquire all the skills needed to be a Special Projects member. Three months later, the tiny number of successful applicants were allowed into the unit. There wasn't a graduation ceremony or any form of celebration. Casero would simply look at them while sitting behind his desk and say, "You're not in any recognisable unit now. Ditch lovers, husbands, wives, anything that ties you to your old life. But don't think you've got a new family. Special Projects needs brilliant loners, not team players seeking camaraderie."

Now, Casero entered the dining room of the safe house. Three members of Special Projects were in there – Javier Rojo, Maria Fontonia, and Zaia Sosa. They were sitting at the table. Underneath their civilian clothes, they had handguns strapped to their waists and back-up pistols attached to their ankles. Casero hadn't chosen them to be here because they were better than their peers in the unit – all members of Special Projects were exemplary. Rather, he'd picked them for the assignment because they looked Anglo-Saxon.

Rojo was a thirty six year old male. He'd spent five years in the French Foreign Legion's elite parachute regiment before returning to Argentina and joining special forces. He was medium height, had the strength of an ox, shoulder length blonde hair that he tied into a ponytail, a goatee, blue eyes that were penetrating and sexy, and a permanent slight smile that either suggested he knew something others didn't or he had a mischievous inner joke about the world. He was the first person Casero had recruited into the unit. Since then, Rojo had worked cases in Argentina, Chile, Paraguay, Bolivia, Venezuela, Mexico, and the United States. Though he wasn't university educated, he had a razor sharp brain, hidden behind his façade that some interpreted that to be of a cage fighter, others a slacker surfer dude or a guy that had just got out of a long stint in prison.

Fontonia was a thirty three year old female. After graduating with politics and economics at Harvard University, she'd joined the police. She could have made a career of it, rising to the top. Instead, she'd volunteered for the serious crime unit. It was a job that required her to wear Kevlar vests and carry a gun, while she and her assistants stormed houses, ranches, and any other place that held criminal targets. She'd lost count of the number of people she'd cuffed or shot. Despite her magnificent track record of takedowns, at heart she was a superb investigator. None of her arrests and killings would have happened had she not devoted weeks or months identifying the men she wanted to arrest or kill. But, she'd grown bored of the police. That's when Casero had identified her as a potential candidate for Special Projects. When he first interviewed her to see if she was suitable for selection, he was struck by her presence – she wasn't particularly beautiful, but nor was she plain. Brunette, average height, average build. Perfect for blending in. But when she talked everything changed. She spoke with a tone that was mesmerising. Casero knew that he was in the presence of someone special. And that's what he searched for in all of his candidates: something special.

Sosa was a thirty six year old woman. Tall, facially looked a bit like the actress Jodie Foster, and liked to wear dowdy clothes just to stop men gawping at her. She'd obtained the highest grade in her year when studying at Argentina's top university - Universidad de Buenos Aires – and had been snapped up by the Federal Intelligence Agency when she applied to be a field operative. After training and mentoring, she'd run some of the FIA's most sensitive cases, taking her all over South America, North America, and Europe. Things changed for her when a low level FIA analyst had booked her on a series of flights that ultimately took her to Tokyo. She was carrying twenty thousand dollars in cash to meet one of her agents in Japan and pay him the money. Unfortunately, the route she'd taken had been identified by Japanese security services as that typically taken by white collar drug dealers. She was arrested, put in prison, and severely interrogated for three days. Her profile didn't help her case – she was travelling under business cover. The twenty thousand dollars in her handbag also didn't help. But, she stuck to her story and was released. When she got back to the FIA headquarters in Buenos Aires, she pinned the analyst up against a wall by his throat and said to him, "You idiot. You're paid to know about drug routes. You nearly got me killed." She was sacked for the assault. That's when Casero stepped in. He met her at her apartment and said, "I have a job for you, if you can prove yourself to me. But, I don't believe you've ever killed anyone. Do you have a problem learning how to kill?" She'd pulled out a gun and placed it against Casero's head. Casero could have easily stopped her from doing so, but he didn't. He was testing her. She'd said, "When you have nothing, pulling a trigger is the least of your problems." Casero told her to report to him the next morning. She'd passed selection and subsequently executed fourteen men and women on behalf of Special Projects.

Now, Major Casero stood in front of Rojo, Fontonia, and Sosa. They watched him, silent. He said, "A new job. I'll be with you in the field. So, we're a four person deployment. We work alone and with different angles. But we must stay in contact with each other. We need to find someone and neutralise that person." He tossed brown files at the operatives. "Rojo: you're a shipping insurance guy, seeking evidence on a series of drownings. You want to pay the insurance money. You are a good guy. Fontonia: you are an investigative journalist. You are looking for evidence to support a rumour that Argentina is making provocative military gestures against Great Britain. You are tough but fair. Sosa: you are in the early stages of pregnancy from a one night stand with a man who died at sea. You want to track his friends and family. You are emotional and scared."

The unit didn't flinch.

Sosa asked, "And you?"

"I am a British intelligence officer, sent from London without the knowledge of the UK military bases in the target location."

"Meaning The Falklands," said Rojo.

"Correct. I will be investigating a situation that will enable the British government to go to war against Argentina. It will be a discrete role. The islanders will help me."

Fontonia said, "You're playing with fire."

"*We're* playing with fire. It is ever thus in the unit." Casero sat at the table and prodded one finger on each file. "Choose your passports with care. You can't be British because I've already taken that nationality. But you can be Australian, New Zealanders, or white Africans. You must not be Americans or Canadians. And the three of you must be different nationalities. There must be no crossover. We work different angles."

"What's happened," asked Rojo.

"We had a vessel monitoring the Falklands. A stupid idea, as far as I'm concerned. A few nights ago, the vessel contacted HQ and said they were under heavy fire from a local fishing boat. Our boat tried to return to Rio Grande but it sunk on route due to damage to its hull. We have recovered the boat and its dead crew. It is clear that our spy ship killed the four men who attacked them, then dumped their bodies in the sea. We know this because of the penultimate transmission we received from our sailors." Casero withdrew a slip of paper and read its contents out loud. "Four hostiles in the sea. Shot dead. We're returning to homeland now. Heavily damaged. British military weapons found on the vessel. Gunshot wounds to our crew. Stand by. Message ends." Casero put the slip of paper back in his pocket.

Sosa asked, "What do you want us to do? Take on the British army out of retaliation?!"

"No." Casero looked serious. "Our spy ship reacted valiantly to the attack. Some people in our nation think it's a victory. I disagree. It's not yet an act of war but it might be due to one other factor."

"Meaning," asked Fontonia.

Casero replied, "It's public information that four Islanders died in a drowning incident that night. It's a cover up. I know for certain that the British don't want the islanders riled by the knowledge that the men were shot by Argentinians. I also know that the British are searching for reasons to justify an assault against us. The dead men's details are in your files. They are Eddie Wilson, Rob Taylor, Billy Green, and Mike Jackson. Only Green wasn't a native islander, though he assimilated into the community. I want you to memorise everything in the files, then burn the papers."

Rojo flicked through his file. "We have no mission. Three Argentinian men and one Argentinian woman die at sea, close to our coastline, due to gunshot wounds, a deficient boat, drowning, or a combination of all of those factors. Four islanders are killed by our guys one mile out from the Falklands. Our people were simply defending themselves."

Casero shook his head. "We were in British waters. The islanders were drunk. We were professionals. We didn't defend ourselves; we expertly murdered them before limping towards home."

Fontonia said, "There's something you haven't told us."

Casero eyed them all. They were such bright people. So ruthless. And even though he only thought of his unit's members as loners, he still felt a duty of care over them. They were his family. He'd assembled them. He'd stripped everything they held dear away from them. He'd recreated them. "I'm coming on this mission with you because it is of vital importance. Yes, there is something I haven't told you. It's not in your files. On the night the islander's trawler attacked our ship, it is clear that four islanders were killed by our people. But before it sunk, our vessel sent its last transmission. It said, *"There was a fifth man on the islanders' boat. He escaped back to the islands on an emergency raft. We couldn't pursue. He is a witness to what happened.* The message ended there. We estimate our boat got flooded and sank minutes after. The signals man must have been terrified. We don't know the identity of the fifth man. He is the key witness. His testimony will bring war. We must do everything we can to stop that from happening."

Sosa nodded. "We find the fifth man and shut his mouth by putting two nine millimetre bullets in the back of his skull."

CHAPTER 7

Ben Sign cooked bacon, scrambled eggs, beans and toast. Knutsen was outside, doing an early morning run. When Knutsen entered the cottage he was breathless. It was impossible to tell whether his saturated T-shirt was soaked with sweat or snow or both.

"Smells good," said Knutsen. "I need a quick shower."

Ten minutes later they ate in the lounge, both men wearing their hardy outdoor gear. Sign had also prepared a pot of tea. He said, "This is rustic fare but it was all I could muster. Plus, we are in a rustic place so needs must. How far did you run?"

"Six miles, along the coastline."

"In future conserve your energy and be conscious that a twisted ankle will not serve us well. Plus, remember that people may come to kill us. I need you alive and upright."

Knutsen laughed. "This coming from the man who once trekked eighty miles across a desert to rescue a Syrian child while being pursued by rebels."

"It was eighty three miles and I was younger then." The forty nine year old shoved bacon into his mouth. "I've done worse journeys. On all occasions, I was lucky. Minimise risk, Mr. Knutsen. We may have plenty of opportunity to expand our lungs and hearts while on active duty. Pointless jogging in the snow is not advisable."

Knutsen ignored the comment. "Active duty today?"

"We must talk to Sally. She runs a pub in Stanley. She is young, quite pretty, and loyal to other islanders. She won't fall for your charms."

"The thought hadn't occurred to me." Knutsen frowned. "How are you feeling, being here?"

Sign stared at him. "Because my wife was Argentinian? And because she was killed in El Salvador?" He looked out of the window. In a distant voice, he said, "I think about her every day. I can smell her hair on the sea breeze. I feel her homeland. I imagine her growing up there – childhood escapades, family barbeques, college, early romances, and friendships. Then there is the reality of what I experienced. I met her in Buenos Aires when I was in MI6 and she was an NGO worker. My goodness me, she was a stunner. Extremely bright. Full of laughter. I'd never met anyone like her. We got engaged. I met her family. The women were lovely. My fiancée's brothers said they'd slit my throat if I did anything wrong to their sister. They were happy days. We married. She was murdered in Central America. And that is that. I'm still and always will be mourning. But, to answer your question, she is not truly here. She is buried near West Square." He looked at Knutsen and said in a firm voice, "It does not sadden me to be in a location close to my wife's birthplace. You and I know that the demons of loss always remain. The tactic is to keep the demons in a locked cage." His expression and tone of voice changed. "Now, sir – we must change the conversation."

Knutsen didn't speak for a minute. Instead he thought about Sign. He'd never met anyone like him. And having worked with him for six months he still couldn't pinpoint his character. Sign was brilliant, charming, temperamental, unconventional, powerful, lonely, and loyal to the bone to those who invested their trust in him. Right now, the only person Sign trusted was Knutsen. Still, every day Knutsen was learning more things about Sign that put off-kilter his previous preconceptions of the man.

"You'd have made a superb chief of MI6," said Knutsen.

"Different topic!"

"You should get married again."

"That would mean you'd have to move out of West Square and live with your criminal pals in some god-awful part of London."

"You could give up detective work and do consultancy to the prime minister. I hear there's good money in that."

"No fun. Plus, where would you rather be with me? The corridors of Westminster or hunting down a lead near the Antarctic?"

Knutsen smiled. "You really know your own mind."

"No I don't. Slice my brain open when I'm dead and somehow tell me what you see." Sign polished off the rest of his breakfast. "We should head down to Stanley. The pub opens early to serve breakfast diners. Sally will be on shift."

Forty five minutes later they were in the pub. The tiny pub was empty. Only Sally was there, washing glasses and attending to other duties behind the bar. Sign and Knutsen approached the bar.

Sign said, "Pretty lady – we wish to speak to an employee of this establishment. Her name is Sally. I presume you are Sally."

Sally eyed them with suspicion. "Who are you?"

"My name is Ben Sign. This is Mr. Tom Knutsen. We are from London. And we are at your service. We are private investigators and we wish to further establish the circumstances surrounding how Eddie Wilson, Rob Taylor, Billy Green, and Mike Jackson drowned. I'm led to believe they were drinking in your fine establishment on the night they died."

Her suspicion didn't ebb. "Who's employed you to investigate their deaths?"

A clever question, thought Sign. "We represent a British law firm. For now, our client wishes to remain anonymous. That will change when they release their report. Essentially our client is looking for evidence that the fishing rights of Falkland Islanders are being violated by Latin American countries. Moreover, our client wishes to prove that offshore drilling rights for oil or gas must remain in the hands of islanders. In the case of Wilson and his friends, our client wishes to establish whether their deaths were as a result of trying to gain justifiable dominance over fishing grounds that were being illegally used by non-Falklands vessels. Perhaps that's how the accident happened. If so, we can use their deaths to build a case that bolsters and enforces the protection of your waters. Probably, that will ensure that a Royal Navy frigate is permanently stationed here."

Sally placed down the glass she was cleaning. "How do you get paid? How does the law firm get paid?"

"We are on a retainer with the law firm. Our client gets paid upon results by the British government. If the Falklands loses a penny because of Argentina, the British will take action. We represent you."

Sally's expression softened. "Do you have a badge or something? Anything that proves who you say you are?"

Sign shook his head. "We're private investigators, not the New York Police Department. You must make a decision. Do you trust our credentials? Or do you think I'm spinning you a lie?"

Sally poured three cups of coffee and nodded at one of the two tables in the pub. "Sit there." She brought the coffee and placed it in front of the men. "Breakfast service has been shit this morning because of the weather. Deliveries haven't come through; people are staying at home; and I'm the only sucker who's come out in the snow to serve no one breakfast. You're my first customers. Your coffee's black because there was no milk run this morning. Drink it or leave it. I don't care."

"Marvellous." Sign cupped his hands around his mug. "Coffee should always be black, softened with a little cold water to prevent burning. The taste is infinitely superior to coffee polluted with cows' milk." He sipped his coffee, showing no indication that its scorching heat was burning his lips and that the liquid tasted foul. "Would you be so kind as to tell us what happened that night?"

Sally told them what she knew.

Knutsen asked, "How drunk were they?"

Sally shrugged. "I've worked this place for six years. You pick up on things. I've seen people get drunk on just two pints if they're in a bad mood. I've seen people neck a bottle of whiskey and walk out without any symptoms, because they're in a good mood. But on that night," she hesitated. "On that night, Wilson and his mates were in an awful mood but just kept drinking. It was man stuff. Adrenalin I guess. They wanted a fight. They were drinking to give them courage and anger. You know how it is when men drink like that. Their sentences get shorter. They become more certain. Then they take action."

Knutsen nodded. "What did they take action against?"

Sally wafted her hand in the air. "A load of silliness. We've had an Argie ship watching us for a few months. It never bothered us. We thought it was a joke. But male pride's a funny old thing, isn't it. Wilson, Taylor, Green, and Jackson got it in to their dumb heads to sail out and do something about the Argie boat. God knows what they were going to do. I bet even they didn't know what to do. Four pissed blokes, a boat with an engine, end of."

Sign looked away, faking agitation. "But, they fell off their boat and drowned. That's a serious matter."

"Who's to say they weren't pushed off?"

Sign looked at Sally. It was imperative that she didn't know the truth – that they were shot by the Argentinians. "We take violation of sovereign waters very seriously. The Argentinian vessel you referenced may have caused your friends to change course and inadvertently get caught up in a rip tide. Who's to blame? The Argentine vessel? Four drunk islanders? My client will err towards the former option. Wilson was an expert skipper. Yes, he was inebriated and the climate that night was atrocious, but five percent of his faculties would have been compos mentis."

"He'd have known what he was doing, a bit anyway," Knutsen said in plainer language.

Sign asked, "Who else was in the bar that night?"

Sally grew suspicious again. "Why do you want to know?"

"I'm merely trying to paint a picture of the scene in here before the men went to their boat."

She looked away, conflicted. After a twenty seconds she said, "Carl and Nick. They're sheep farmers. Carl works his farm six miles from here; Nick's place is eight miles away."

Sign nodded. "I presume they know Wilson, Green, Taylor, and Jackson?"

"Of course. Everyone around here knows each other."

"Were they friends?"

"They weren't enemies. Now and again they helped each other out with work. But I wouldn't say they were friends. Just acquaintances, I guess."

Sign paused. He was about to nudge his questions to a new level. "Is it possible that Nick or Carl joined Wilson and his friends on the boat that night?"

The question confused Sally. "Everyone on that boat died. And Nick and Carl are still very much alive." She laughed. "Carl's seventy years old and suffers from arthritis. He wouldn't have been able to walk onto the boat, let alone stand on the damn thing. Nick's younger but gets seasick just by looking at water. Neither of them would go anywhere near a boat. Plus, they stayed here 'til closing time. I saw them drive off towards home. Speak to them if you like. I'll give you their addresses. But, they'll tell you exactly what I've said." Her expression turned serious. "You promise me you're asking these questions for the benefit of our islands?"

Sign replied with the truth. "I can assure you I am." He was about to ask another question.

But Knutsen interjected. "Did they ever come in here with a fifth friend?"

Sally frowned, deep in thought. "No. I don't remember that ever happening. It was either the four of them, or two or three of them. They seemed to have got their tracks aligned, as us publicans like to say. Just the four of them. They didn't need another drinking partner. I can tell when men have long ago decided who they want to drink with. They stick with it. No deviations. No new friends. On a Sunday here we do a roast. Alongside the trimmings, we serve roast chicken, beef, gammon, and turkey. Wilson always has beef; Taylor, chicken; Green turkey; Jackson gammon. They've been doing that every week for years. It says something about their characters. They know what they like and dislike. And when they find something they like it becomes etched in their brains. Foods, friendships, routines, clothes they wear, you name it. They knew their own minds."

"They were loyal to their tastes," said Sign.

"Yes." Sally had a tear running down her face. "They were such loyal customers. More than that, they were good men. Helped me out. Helped others out. No fighting. They swore like troopers, but never at anyone. Now and again they got drunk and drove home way over the limit, but they'd drive carefully, sleep it off and be up and at 'em for work at four AM. They were hard men but you'd want them by your side if shit hit the fan." She wiped away her tear. "Excuse my language. I'm just saying they are missed."

Sign withdrew a pristine white handkerchief and handed it to her. "My dear – Mr. Knutsen and I have been around death all of our lives. It never gets easier to deal with the consequences of loss. If anything it gets harder."

She took his handkerchief, dabbed her face, and handed it back to him, her mascara smudged below her eyes. "You knew I'd cry. Your handkerchief was washed and ironed this morning."

"Nonsense. I carry a handkerchief at all times. I'm prone to hay fever. I sneeze when the pollen count is off the scale."

"In winter? In the Falklands?" Sally laughed, though was still emotional.

"Alright. Maybe I carry the handkerchief because Mr. Knutsen is accident prone. He's always falling over and grazing his knees. I have to dab the blood off him."

The comment cheered Sally up. "Your friend doesn't look accident prone." She breathed deeply.

Sign leaned forward and said in a sympathetic tone, "My dear – is there anyone you know who might have accompanied the men on that fatal night? A fifth man. We believe he might have survived. We'd dearly like to speak to him. He's not in trouble. On the contrary, his evidence might prove invaluable to further our case."

Sally took a swig of her coffee. "I just don't know. Wilson and Green divided their days at sea and in my bar. Wilson had the hots for me. Maybe that's why he kept coming here. Green isn't an islander but you wouldn't be able to tell that. He's got a kid on the island though he never saw her. Taylor worked the land and had the stamina of a huskie. Ditto lighthouse keeper and part-time fireman Jackson. Like I said, they were hard men. They slotted together because they saw themselves in each other. Least ways, that's my take. I can't imagine they had room in their minds for a fifth member of their gang. They were too close knit."

Sign asked, "What about suppliers? Someone who gave Wilson and Green their fishing nets; a man who supplied meal for Taylor's sheep; anyone who sorted the electrics in Jackson's lighthouse; or variants therein; anything that springs to mind?"

"Someone who was useful to the men," said Knutsen.

Sally upended a beer map and withdrew a pen from behind her ear. "Good luck. In the Falklands, everyone not only knows everyone, we also make sure we're all taken care of. But, I don't know who Wilson and his friends used to support their businesses. It might be someone near here on the east island. But it could also be someone on the west island. If so, be careful visiting that place. It's mostly uninhabited. You might die if you go there – no petrol, no food, no water, just penguins." She wrote on the white underside of the beer mat. "This is Carl and Nick's addresses. You can say that I sent you. They won't mind if you do that. They *will* mind if you turn up saying you're busybodies from London." She handed the mat to Sign. "Be careful. We love and trust the British. We also hate them nearly as much as we hate Argentina." She stared at Sign with piercing eyes. "Does that make sense?"

"It does indeed." Sign stood and extended his hand. "We are here to help."

Sally shook his hand and glanced at the bar. "Breakfast was a waste of time. I'm on a split shift. My dad's doing the midday roster. I'm back on this evening. When I'm between shifts, I'll have a spliff and a couple of hours sleep."

"A spliff?"

Knutsen explained. "A cannabis cigarette."

Sally looked tired. "Don't judge me for that."

Sign was utterly sincere when he said, "I never judge hard working honest souls. Mr. Knutsen! We must leave this young lady to her duties. Thankyou Sally. Let's hope the weather abates and allows you more custom later today."

She shook her head. "Don't hold your breath. This weather's not going anywhere soon." She smiled. "Take my advice – you can tell Carl and Nick that I gave you their addresses but don't say you're PIs from London. They'll clam up. Just so we reading from the same page, come up with another story."

Sign replied, "We're scientists, based in South Georgia. We've been tasked to investigate the deaths and whether they're related to aggressive intrusion of fishing rights and whether such intrusions are causing Falkland Island sailors to take unnecessary risks with their boats."

"Why didn't you spin me that lie?"

"Because we trust you and want you to know the truth. I judge you to be the eyes and ears of Stanley. Probably you don't have your finger on the pulse on matters further west on the islands. That doesn't matter. But if anything else does occur to you please let us know." He handed her a slip of paper. "We can be contacted via RAF Mount Pleasant. The number on the paper is not widely known."

Outside the pub and while standing next to their jeep, Knutsen said to Sign, "I don't think she was lying or holding back."

"I agree. But, we bounced her today and she was fatigued and emotional. Sometimes, what's important is not just what we remember, but what we forget."

"True. And she's a dope smoker – she'll forget quite a few things."

"Give her time. The important thing is that if anything does occur to her about a fifth man, I know she'll call us."

Knutsen wasn't convinced. "She might get wasted off shift and forget things in her private life. But in the pub she'll be on point. She has to be. She knows everything that goes on in the bar. She hasn't forgotten anything about Wilson and his mates."

"I fear you may be right, sir. And that takes us back to the starting line. We must visit Carl and Nick."

Knutsen drove six miles west out of Stanley. Though the four wheel drive was designed for treacherous conditions, Knutsen still had to drive slowly and with skill to avoid careering off the road. The windscreen wipers were on full and the pathetic heater was on maximum. Steam was coming out of the men's mouths. The land around them was becoming increasingly rugged, visible only between small breaks in the snowfall.

Sign had a military map on his lap. For the most part, GPS was useless in a Falklands winter. "Turn right here. Follow the track. Carl's place is four hundred and fifty yards at the end."

At the end of the track was a house and barn. Knutsen stopped the jeep outside the house and said, "I hope he's not miles away, tending to his sheep on the mountains."

"I doubt that's the case. I would imagine his sheep are in the barn. Even sheep feel a chill."

They approached the house. Sign knocked on the door.

A woman opened the door. "Yes?"

Sign gave her a variation of the line he'd given Sally and concluded, "We want to help the islands and Mr. Wilson, Taylor, Green, and Jackson." He also embellished and elaborated, "Our client's based in London but we're from South Georgia."

The island nine hundred and sixty miles east of the Falklands.

She looked dubious. "No one lives there. No one *can* live there."

"We do. We're from the British Antarctic Survey's base on Bird Island. We're scientists. Our client reached out to us because we have mutual interests and because we were closer to the source of the problem – namely the deaths of four Falkland islanders. Is your husband at home?"

"He's on site. You'll find him there." She nodded at the barn and withdrew into the house, closing the door behind her.

Sign and Knutsen entered the barn. As Sign had predicted, the place was full of sheep, eating grass, some of them baaing and bleating, all of them contained in pens. There were seventy of them, with blue dye markings on them identifying they belonged to Carl's farm. Sign and Knutsen walked down the central aisle, pens either side of them. Alongside the cacophony of noise, the stench of cooped up wildlife was palpable. There was no sight of Carl.

Sign spun around three sixty degrees. "There will be a private place here. One that Carl doesn't want these sheep to know about."

Knutsen jogged back down the aisle, looked up, saw nothing of interest, turned around, and pointed at the other end of the aisle. "Outside. I'm guessing an annex."

"Yes."

Both men exited the barn. Knutsen was right. There was a small outhouse, attached to the barn. They entered. An elderly man was inside, his back against them. A tethered lamb was in front of him. The man held a pneumatic pistol against the lambs head and pulled the trigger. A six inch metal spike exited the pistol and penetrated the lamb's brain, before retracting into the gun. The lamb's death was instant. The man used ropes attached to the ceiling and a motorised winch to raise the lamb. It was now dangling mid-height in the room.

"Carl?"

The man turned. "Who's asking?"

Sign gave him the same story he'd given Carl's wife. "We can wait for you in our car if now's an inconvenient time?"

Carl shrugged. "You can talk here, so long as you're not squeamish." He picked up a razor sharp knife, slit open the lamb's belly, placed his hand inside the creature, and yanked out its innards, all of which went into a bucket. He lifted the bucket and put it to one side. "Nothing goes to waste. I'll mince the guts and organs up. It'll feed my dogs for a few days. You want to know about Wilson and his friends? There's nothing I can tell you that Sally hasn't already told you. Damn fools were drunk that night and got in their boat. I heard they fell overboard, a mile out at sea. Must have been a swell or something." He started using the knife to remove the lamb's coat, slicing portions underneath the wool, ripping parts, then repeating the process. He winced and held his wrist. "Bloody arthritis. There were times when I could do this job in minutes. Now it takes me an hour."

Knutsen said, "Let me do it for you. I'm handy with a knife."

Carl shrugged. "Can't say I couldn't do with the help." He handed Knutsen the knife. "But it won't be just a case of skinning the lamb. You'll have to butcher it as well. Follow my exact instructions. Don't mess it up. The meat will be exported for a pretty price but I only get paid it the joints are perfect." He sat on a stool and used a cloth to wipe blood off his hands.

Forty five minutes later the job was done. The joints of lamb were laid out on a large wooden chopping board.

"Not bad for a beginner," said Carl. "These will sell. Here," he tossed Knutsen a leg, "put that in a roasting pan. It's for your troubles."

"Thank you, sir," replied Knutsen.

"Call me Carl." The elderly farmer rubbed his ankles. "My son's taking over the farm. He's in Scotland at the moment, finishing off his PhD. But next week he'll be done and will be returning home with his wife and kids. Mable and I have enough rooms. He's a good lad. He knows about farming. His PhD was in ethical farming, or something like that. I don't care. What I do care about is that he's got the muscle I once had." He stood and placed each cut of meat on trays, which he wrapped in cling film and labelled. "Four men died in an accident. The Argie boat that's been spying on us might have made them change course and make a mistake. But, I don't know. I know nothing about the sea. As far as I'm aware, the Argies have buggered off. They might have been nowhere near the boat that night."

Sign said, "We're trying to solve the deaths. Is it possible that Wilson and his friends had a fifth man with them that night?"

Carl looked nonplussed. "It's possible I suppose. But, I don't know who."

"Maybe a man who had access to guns. There were weapons on board Wilson's boat."

Carl looked stern as he said, "Help me bring the trays of meat into the house. I'll show you something."

After the meat was placed into the kitchen chest freezer, Carl guided them to his home's shed. "You talk of guns. We all have guns. Look at this." He opened a steel cabinet. Inside were three shotguns and a bolt action hunting rifle. "The shotguns are for bird game, when in season. The rifle's only used in bad situations – a lamb's got stuck up a mountain, I can't get to him, he can't get down, he's injured and in agony, that kind of thing. The kindest thing is to end his misery." He shut the cabinet. "Everyone around here has guns, for the same reason."

Sign asked, "Do you have weapons from the Falklands War? Trophies?"

Carl shook his head and genuinely looked upset by the question. "After the war we worked with the army to clear as much shit from the islands as we could. It was only the landmines that proved a bugger. None of the islanders were trophy hunters. We wanted our islands clean again. Why do you ask?"

"Because Wilson, Taylor, Green, and Jackson sailed out to confront the Argentinian spy ship, armed with five British Browning handguns and two SLR assault rifles. The weapons were almost certainly picked off the battlefields during or after the war. We are not talking about two shotguns and a hunting rifle. We're talking about military-grade devices that are designed to kill humans."

Carl looked puzzled. "I don't know anyone who'd store stuff like that. We're honest folk. We look after our animals. We feed them; shelter them at this time of year. We cull them when it's time. We shoot geese or whatever when it's that time of year to put something on the table for Christmas. But we *don't* keep military weapons. Least ways, not to my knowledge."

"Someone did. And I think that person is now very scared. He supplied his weapons to Wilson and his friends. He went out on the boat. They had an accident. Wilson, Taylor, Green, and Jackson drowned. The fifth man panicked and rowed ashore. He's in hiding because he supplied the guns and is worried he might get in trouble. The truth is, he's not in trouble. He's a witness. If there was a swell, as you suggest, or a large wave, or similar, and Wilson had to bank his vessel hard left or right to avoid the Argentinian ship, we need to know. Our client is a law firm. They'd say it was manslaughter by an illegal invasion of sovereign waters. But we need evidence. The fifth man can give us that." Sign stared at Carl.

Carl sighed. "I'd like to help. I really would. Did Sally give you Nick's address?"

Sign nodded.

"He's a lot younger than me. He's more likely to know the type of man that would store military weapons."

Five minutes later Knutsen and Sign were in their vehicle, driving west. Knutsen asked, "Do you think Carl's right – we're looking for a younger man? It would make sense. Older men wouldn't hoard military weapons unless..."

"He'd served in the war and wanted mementos. We must ask Richards to check his records to see if any veterans settled here after '82."

Knutsen thought it through. "The average age of British soldiers who fought in the war back then must have been at least twenty five. The government didn't want to send rookies to recapture the islands. That would make most of them in their mid-sixties now."

"Let's keep options open. The fifth man could be a trophy hunter. He could be a veteran. He could be the son of a veteran. He could be an islander or a foreigner. One thing's for sure – we're no nearer to identifying him. But I wonder..." Sign's voice trailed.

"What?"

"It's just an idea. I wonder about his profile. It is possible he's a loner. That would mean he doesn't live in Stanley. And that means our search is considerably narrowed down."

"A loner?"

Sign said, "Show me your weapon."

Knutsen placed his pistol in Sign's hand.

Sign checked its workings. "You cleaned and oiled it last night. You care about this weapon, but not because you love it; rather, because you don't want it to fail you. It is a tool that must be effective in extreme circumstances." He handed the gun back to Knutsen. "The weapons found on Wilson's boat were, according to Colonel Richards, in immaculate condition. Their owner made sure of that. But, why were the guns so cared for if he was just a trophy hunter? No. He wanted military grade weapons to be in their prime in case he needed to use them. I doubt he's a Falklands War veteran; or the son of one. I think he's an islander. And I think he has few friends and is a survivalist."

Knutsen stopped the jeep, tucked his handgun into his belt, and looked at Sign. "You're making huge assumptions."

Sign chuckled. "No. I'm tickling the possibilities of the truth. The fifth man was not like Wilson, Taylor, Green, and Jackson. He wasn't the kind of man to prop up a bar every night with his pals, while bantering about this woman and that and who he wanted to fight. He's thoughtful. He's a loner. Most likely he's perpetually paranoid. That would explain why he ran from the crime scene and has gone to ground. He's the type of man who thinks everyone is out to get him. But, he will have a connection to Wilson and the others."

"Maybe they had something on him." Knutsen started driving. "It's possible they blackmailed him to give them his guns and join them on the ship."

"No. That doesn't wash. Remember – loner, survivalist, paranoid, immaculate military weapons. He gave them his guns and went with them that night because he wanted to take the fight to the enemy. Alas, the poor fellow was not up to the task when hellfire unleashed. But his heart was in the right place. You must remember that the islanders live in constant fear that their land will be invaded and rebranded Islas Malvinas. Sometimes the islanders get to breaking point. The fifth man could never be blackmailed by Wilson or anyone else. Figuratively, he had his back to the wall with a gun in his hand. I think Wilson or one of the others went to him that night and explained the situation. The fifth man finally saw a means to hit back at his paranoia about Argentina. He supplied his troops with good war guns and he went to battle. It was a battle too far. Fight or flight. The fifth man chose flight." Sign smiled. "But, I concede that everything I've just said may be utter balderdash."

"It makes perfect sense. The fifth man was scared. And when it came to it he was a coward. Men like that treasure guns. He's a good guy who just wants to be left alone."

"Correct. Give me five minutes with him and I'd talk to him about a different way of life. It would work. He'd finally be happy." Sign looked at his map. "Seven hundred yards, take a left, slight incline."

They stopped outside a house that looked similar to Carl's place; ditto there was a nearby barn and a garage. Knutsen knocked on the door. No answer. They tried the barn and the garage. Both were locked. Knutsen tried the house again, but still there was no answer.

Sign withdrew a pair of binoculars from his jacket and scoured the hills around the farmstead. "There. On the escarpment. I'd say about five hundred yards away. It will be Nick. It looks like he's making repairs to some kind of shed on the hill. It must be where he stores food for his cattle. We'll meet him there. Watch your footing."

"Baby heads," stated Knutsen.

"Yes. Baby heads. Also bogs and the possibility of unexploded landmines."

They trudged uphill. Snowfall remained heavy and due to the amount of snow on the ground it was impossible to see any dangers under foot. Twice Knutsen lost his footing and Sign had to grab his jacket to prevent him going face down onto the grounds. They were breathing heavily as they neared the shed.

The man looked at them, looked right, and ran, shouting, "You fucking bastard!"

Knutsen whipped out his gun.

Sign placed his hand over the muzzle. "Calm, my friend. All is not what it seems. Look what he's running to."

Nick stopped and picked up a sheep. He walked back to the shed and put it inside. Sign and Knutsen approached him. Sign asked, "Nick?"

Nick was leaning against the shed, exhausted. "Yeah. That's what my friends call me. Who are you?"

Sign delivered their cover story, the reason they were visiting the islands and added, "We've spoken to Sally and Carl this morning. They both advised us to speak to you."

Nick was still sucking in air. He slapped the shed. "I got all of my sheep into the barn, except this fucker. Couldn't find her. Bastard. But she ain't going anywhere now until the snow melts." He stood upright, his breathing now normal. "I'm not having this conversation out here. We'll freeze our tits off. I'll be making a brew in the house. Join me if you want. Don't if you don't want."

Sign and Knutsen turned with the intention of walking back to the house.

But Nick said, "Not on foot. Too dodgy. You can hitch a ride with me. They followed him to the other side of the shed. Parked there was a large quad bike with a plinth on the back. He pointed at the plinth. "Sit there. I'll just be a minute." He entered the shed and re-emerged carrying the sheep. "You're going to have to earn your brew by helping me get this fucker down to the barn." He placed the sheep on Sign and Knutsen's lap. "Grip her hard, stroke her face, and don't take any shit from her. She's strong and can be a right cunt." He carefully drove them into the valley, placed the sheep into the barn containing the rest of his flock, and drove them to his house. When they were all inside, Nick put on the kettle and removed his oilskin jacket. "Sit in the lounge." He made a fire, returned to the kitchen, then brought out three mugs of tea on a tray containing a jug of milk and a bowl of sugar cubes. "The milk's goat's milk. Blokes like you will either like it or hate it."

"I'll take my tea black," said Knutsen.

"Goat's milk! Wonderful!" said Sign as he added a dash to his tea. Sign was partially lactose intolerant. Goat's milk was the last thing on earth he'd want to consume.

Nick sat down and gulped his tea. "So, your scientists playing cops, right?"

Knutsen laughed. "We're not playing cops. The police and coastal services know how Wilson, Taylor, Green, and Jackson died. They drowned. It was an accident. But, we're experts in all matters maritime. In particular, we specialise in the Antarctic and its surrounding waters. Our client – the law firm my colleague mentioned – engaged us because it wants to draw upon our expertise to see if there was anything that helped facilitate the accident – an unusual rip tide, a freak wave, a swell, other potential factors."

"Or whether it was just four pissed blokes who shouldn't have been out at that time of night in that weather." Nick drained the rest of his tea and held his hands near the fire. "They were on a mission to get really drunk that night. I'd lay money that they took beer with them on the boat, maybe spirits too. I don't know much about our coastline but I do know it can get shitty at this time of year. If those idiots were out on deck, swigging their beers, all it would have taken is for a wave to tip them over the side of Wilson's tin-pot piece of junk. And then they'd have stood no chance. A mile out, I've heard. An Olympic swimmer wouldn't have been able to make it to shore. He'd have died from the cold. Wilson and his drunken pals, probably dressed in cold weather gear, wouldn't have got more than a few yards. And they would be hypothermic. No chance they'd have been able to get back on the boat. I've seen Wilson's trawler. There's no ladders or ropes on the hull. If the boat tips you into the water, you're fucked."

Sign said, "Your hypothesis sounds completely laudable. We wonder, however, whether there were extraneous factors that may have prompted the accident. *Human* factors that caused Wilson to go against his instincts and change course, thereby putting the boat at risk of the sea and the weather."

Nick smiled. "You mean like another boat blocking its way or driving right at it?" Nick looked serious. "We've had an Argie boat patrolling our waters these last few months. It's gone now. Last time it was spotted was on the night of the drownings. Maybe it was involved, maybe its disappearance was a coincidence, or maybe it wasn't involved but witnessed the drownings and its crew freaked out and left. Who knows?"

Sign asked, "Did you know the deceased well?"

Nick shrugged and said nonchalantly, "I saw them a lot in the pub, but never drank with them. Rob Taylor helped me a few times with repairs on my farm. But he wasn't a mate. I paid him for his work. Mike Jackson helped put out a fire on my land after four dumb-witted squaddies stopped on a march and lit a calor gas to make a brew. They set the heath on fire. But Jackson was just doing his job as a fireman. Aside from that, I had little dealings with them. Jackson was a part-time fireman. His main job was operating the lighthouse. Wilson and Green were fisherman. Lighthouses and fishing are of no interest to me apart from what catches are brought in. On a Friday I like to buy a nice piece of cod from the store in Stanley. We were blokes who drank in the same boozer. Nothing more to it than that."

"Carl said the same. And yet you are friends with Carl and drink with him." Sign leaned forward. "I wonder what differentiates Carl from Wilson and his friends."

Nick looked nonplussed as he said, "Carl's my dad. My brother's going to help run his farm. The old man's getting a bit creaky."

"Of course he's your father. I knew that the moment I saw you. It's very kind of you to share a pint or two with your dad after a hard day's work. He will be most appreciative. But, mapping the family connections of the Falklands is not why we're here. We have a lead. There was a fifth man on board Wilson's vessel that night. He escaped. We'd dearly like to talk to the chap. He's a witness."

Nick frowned. "A fifth man? Are you sure?"

"The British military are cooperating with our investigation. They had thermal imagery of Wilson's vessel before the snow blizzard cut out all visuals of the boat."

"Maybe the man also drowned."

"It's possible, although Wilson's vessel's escape dingy was found two miles on shore from Stanley. And it was dragged over the beach and hidden in bracken. It would have been impossible for the sea, regardless of conditions, to have positioned the dingy in such a way. Do you have any idea who the fifth man may be?"

"Was it you?" asked Knutsen.

Sign immediately said, "Forgive my friend's direct approach. We are merely here to ask for any insight you may have."

Nick looked angry, but Sign's interjection softened his demeanour. "I don't do sea. I fucking hate the stuff. You can put me on a plane or a tractor or a bus, but never put me on a boat. You'd see the contents of my guts if you did." He stared at the fire. "A fifth man? That would be unusual. Eddie, Rob, Billy, and Mike kept themselves to themselves. They were close knit. Didn't need anyone else."

"What about a man who could supply guns – *military* guns. You know they went out that night to confront the Argentinian vessel. They got help from the fifth man. I think he gave them weapons that he'd stored since the war."

Nick looked genuinely confused. "Military guns? I mean, it's possible, but everyone I know has no need for that stuff. Most of us in the sticks have a shotgun or two. But that's about it. We're farmers. I was too young at the time to remember this but my dad told me that it took an age to get rid of all the shit that was left here after the war. What I do remember is that years later we were still finding shit – landmines, machine gun belts of bullets, grenades, guns, ration packs, army ruck sacks, artillery shells, you name it. The army helped us whenever we found something. It wanted the islands as clean as we did. They were worried about accidents to their men, islanders, and to our cattle. Do you reckon it might be a serving squaddie who went with them on the boat? Maybe he gave them the guns?"

"No. The handguns on board Wilson's vessel were Browning 9mm. They are still used in the British army but are being phased out. And I know for certain that there are no Brownings in the military base on the islands. The assault rifle on the boat was an SLR. That gun has long ago been decommissioned. It is highly improbable that a serving soldier would have access to these weapons. The person we're looking for is an islander." Sign looked around. "Do you live here alone?"

"Yes. I had a girlfriend who moved in for a month. But she was from Stanley. She told me she felt too isolated out here. She moved out last year. So, it's just me and my bloody sheep."

Knutsen laughed.

Sign said, "It's possible we're looking for someone who lives on his own in a place like this; maybe further west; possibly even on the west island. If anything occurs to you, would you be so kind as to give us a call?" He handed Nick a slip of paper containing the Mount Pleasant phone number. "We're not here to cause any problems. On the contrary and as we told your father, we're here to help."

Nick took the paper and placed it in a pocket. "Nothing springs to mind. But I can put the word out."

"I'd be eternally grateful if you didn't. The fifth man is obviously scared. We need him to feel safe. Word might get to him. Then, he might run."

Nick nodded. "If he gives you evidence that the Argie boat was somehow involved that night, what will you do with the evidence?"

"It will be escalated up the food chain – the commander of the military base, the governor of the islands, the British chief of defence staff, foreign secretary, and ultimately the British prime minister. They will decide what to do. Rest assured, if an Argentinian vessel was in any way involved in the death of four British citizens – whether by accident or by a provocative manoeuvre –action will be taken."

Nick stood. "I've got to feed my sheep. You might be on a wild goose chase. I still think this might be four pissed blokes falling off the side of their boat after a wave hit them, or something."

Sign replied, "You may be right, sir. Or you may be wrong. Please do call us if you think of anything that could bring this case to a close."

Outside, Sign and Knutsen watched Nick go into the barn.

Knutsen was frustrated as he said, "We're getting nowhere!"

"Keep calm, dear chap. Turn your thinking on its head. Every time we come up against a roadblock, it enables us to further narrow our search."

Knutsen replied with sarcasm. "How very *glass half full* of you." He got into the jeep. When Sign was sitting in the passenger seat, Knutsen said, "Look. Maybe Nick's right; that this is a wild goose chase. It's possible that Green supplied the guns. He's an ex-soldier. He could have had access to military weapons."

"No. He was a Royal Engineer commando, stationed here between 2009 and 2011. For the same reasons I articulated to Nick, Green was too young to have access to Falklands War British guns."

"Maybe he found them on one of his patrols. Kept them as souvenirs."

"Highly improbable. And you're forgetting about the fifth man. He was there on that night for a reason."

"Maybe there is no fifth man!" Knutsen started the engine.

Sign placed his hand on Knutsen's forearm. "Hold your nerve and hang tight onto your faculties. There is no doubt there was a fifth man – the drone footage Richards showed us; the dingy on the beach; guns on board Wilson's vessel that honest fishermen, farmers, and lighthouse keepers would have no means to ordinarily access. We are painting a picture of the fifth man. And like the slow darkroom exposure of a photograph, we are gradually getting a clearer image of our petrified witness."

Knutsen gunned the engine and drove. "Where to?"

"It's getting late. It's not recommended to be out on the roads after dark. Let's head back to the Bluff Cove cottage."

An hour later they arrived at the cottage. Knutsen stoked the log burner and bathed and changed clothes. Sign made a casserole, put it in the oven, parboiled some potatoes and beans, and set the potatoes aside for roasting thirty minutes prior to eating, and the beans aside for a three minute flash in a pan with a little water and butter when needed. When Knutsen was out of the bathroom, Sign too washed himself and changed out of his sodden clothes. Both men loaded their snow-caked garments into the washing machine. Later, the clothes would dry on a rack in front of the log burner.

After eating and cleaning dishes, Sign and Knutsen sat in armchairs in front of the fire. Both had a brandy. Lamps were on, but no overhead lights because they were too fierce. Sign and Knutsen liked the ambience of subtle lighting. The cottage was warm, despite high winds and snow battering the exterior of the property. It was now dark. If either man had stepped outside, they wouldn't be able to see anything but black. The glorious stars frequently visible in the southern hemisphere were shielded tonight by the snow clouds.

Sign opened the log burner and placed a piece of wood inside. He looked at Knutsen. "Sir, you got a little riled today."

"Riled?"

"Well, you nearly shot a man who was trying to rescue a sheep. And later you thought our investigation might be a waste of time. It doesn't take a rocket scientist to spot your current state of mind."

Knutsen bowed his head. "This island stuff is not something I'm used to. And the bloody snow – I used to love the stuff. But here it's ridiculous. No matter what we wear it's fucking freezing. And the people here all claim they know each other, but when push comes to shove it seems they don't. I'm a fish out of water."

"Mr. Knutsen. You were once the most highly decorated undercover police officer in the Metropolitan Police. You infiltrated highly volatile places that others couldn't."

"That was London and parts of Europe. Not places like this."

Sign had to gee Knutsen up. "You've been cold before, yes?"

"Many times – on London streets playacting a homeless man, chasing a criminal in a sewer in winter, doing all night surveillance on roof tops, so many other experiences."

"And you've dealt with the complexities of the human condition – whether criminal or otherwise. I'd hazard a guess that when you infiltrated the gangs in London, sometimes people were not as they seemed. You'd meet diabolical men. But you were also confronted with compassion and uncertainty. Some of the gang men were good. You didn't want to arrest them or shoot them."

"Yes."

Sign leaned forward and tapped his glass against Knutsen's glass. "Mr. Knutsen, men like you and I are not fish out of water. Instead, we're fish who deliberately swim in the wrong waters. Imagine the Falklands as Great Britain in winter. It has an epicentre – in this case Stanley – and it has countryside on its borders – in this case the hills and mountains of the east and west islands. The people here don't know us and are suspicious. You experienced suspicion when infiltrating the criminal underworld in London. We are unravelling a complicated knot. It takes patience. And you've had an exemplary career requiring patience. I heard from your previous commissioner that you had to bide your time for fourteen undercover months to simply get the mobile phone number of a major criminal." Sign sipped his brandy while keeping his eyes on Knutsen. "Never underestimate yourself again. You know this kind of territory. You know this type of people. Remember who you are. And remember what you've achieved in dreadful environments."

Knutsen looked up and smiled. "I guess it's because I can't get it out of my head that the Falklands are the other side of the world."

"Then, do a mind trick on yourself. Imagine they're the Scottish Highlands. Stanley is Inverness. Everything west is mountainous bandit country."

Knutsen laughed. "Yeah. When you put it that way it works." He sipped his drink. "I'm not like you. I worked a patch. I didn't travel the world undercover."

"Stick with me and you may well do. You are eminently well equipped to do so." Sign had achieved what he needed. "Now, Mr. Knutsen, tomorrow we must visit the homes of Wilson, Taylor, Green, and Jackson. At some point we will also need to speak to their families. But tonight we are housebound. I note there's a stack of DVDs next to the television. I wonder if we might watch The Imitation Game. It is historically flawed but nevertheless is a fine drama with near-perfect characterisation."

Knutsen looked at the stack. "I'd prefer Goodfellas."

"Heaven forbid. What about When Harry Met Sally?"

"Are you serious?"

"Of course not. I have my eye on The English Patient."

"Nah. Too maudlin." Knutsen now felt fully relaxed. "I tell you what, why don't we just sit here and swap war stories."

Sign smiled. "That would take us one or two steps back in the past. I believe a man should always step forward. The solution to this evening's entertainment, on such a dreadfully inclement night, is I believe to play a board game. There is a tiny selection on the mantelpiece. Would you prefer Monopoly, Scrabble, or Trivial Pursuit?"

"You'll beat me in Trivial Pursuit and Scrabble. And I know you – you'll cheat in Monopoly." Knutsen drained the rest of his drink. "Monopoly it is. But no way am I letting your conniving ass be banker."

CHAPTER 8

Major Casero arrived in Mount Pleasant via a direct flight from Santiago, Chile. If any official at the airport asked him why a 'British' man had flown to the islands from South America, he'd say he'd been on British government business in Panama. Then he'd keep his mouth shut. But, he wasn't challenged at the airport. Rojo was already on the islands, having taken the earlier flight from Santiago. Fontonia and Sosa were due to arrive in an hour, having flown up to Heathrow, and taken a coach and taxi to Brize Norton, before boarding a flight back down south. It would have been an exhausting journey, but the women were used to such hardships.

As Casero exited the airport he checked his watch. He had time to book in to the Southernwind hotel in Stanley, shower, and get changed. He picked up his hire car and drove into the tiny capital. Rojo was staying in a bed and breakfast, one mile outside of Stanley. Fontonia and Sosa would be staying in cottages. It would have been easy for the team to covertly infiltrate the islands via boats or scuba gear, once they'd been offloaded by a fake fishing vessel or a military submarine. But they needed to look the part, if ever challenged on the islands by police or the army. Possession of air tickets was vital. So too possession of fake passports that matched the Anglo-Saxon names on the air tickets. Thankfully, Casero, Rojo, Fontonia, and Sosa could bluff the rest in their sleep.

Casero was a British government official who was on top secret business.

Rojo was a white South African insurance official.

Fontonia was a Kiwi investigative journalist.

Sosa was a pregnant Australian who divided her time between Melbourne and the South Pole. She was to pose as an engineer who'd visited the Falklands and had a fling with one of the drowned men.

All of them were allegedly here to work out what happened on that tragic night.

In truth, their agenda was the same – find the fifth man and kill him.

After Casero had checked into his hotel and washed and changed, he lay on his bed and slept for two hours. The rendezvous was not until 1000hrs. He had time to re-charge his batteries. At 0900hrs, he exited the hotel and drove northwest. The ground was still thick with snow, but thankfully the air was clear. He spotted three vehicles adjacent to the bleak coast, stopped by them, and got out. The occupants of the other vehicles also got out – Rojo, Fontonia, Sosa.

Casero walked up to them. In perfect English, he asked, "Any problems?"

They shook their heads.

"The cache?"

Sosa replied, also with pitch-perfect English. "We've dug it up, got what we needed, and re-sealed the cache."

The cache was one of many planted by Argentina in the remote parts of the Falklands. All of them contained items of use to special operatives. The one Sosa dug up was no different. She placed her small rucksack on the bonnet of her car and withdrew items. "Four cell phones and chargers."

"Use the word 'mobile'" snapped Casero. "We are not Americans."

Sosa was unperturbed. "Four Sig Sauer handguns with extra magazines. Maps. Ten thousand British pounds each. Thermal binoculars. Bullet proof vests. And these," she picked up one of four identical items, each the size of a packet of cigarettes. "Cameras. They have a far greater range than mobile phone cameras, and images can be uploaded onto our phones and shared." She leaned against her car. "The vests are merely damage limitation. If you get shot in the upper body with anything as powerful as these," she lifted one of the handguns, "you'll most likely end up with a cracked sternum or broken ribs. The vests are too thin to fully protect us from military or police weapons. But, they give us a chance to escape or take down the enemy."

Casero asked, "Have the phones been programmed?"

Sosa nodded. "There are five contacts in each phone. Four of them are identified by letters. Casero is 'A'. Rojo is 'B'. Fontonia is 'C'. I'm 'D'." She'd put different coloured stickers on each phone in order to remember which phone belonged to whom. She handed the phones out. "The fifth contact is our way to get out of here. It's listed as 'Travel Agent'."

The team collected every other item.

Casero was pleased. Everything was on track. "Work the angles. And remember – other people might be looking for the fifth man. If you establish who those people are, identify them, take photos of them, share the images with the rest of us, follow them, and neutralise them once they've led us to the target. Hopefully it won't come to that. Let's hope we can find the fifth man before anyone else does."

Fontonia said, "Maybe the fifth man has given himself up and is under heavy protection in Mount Pleasant or has been taken off the islands by the Brits to another secure location."

Casero checked the workings of his handgun. "I very much doubt that. At best what happened when our ship was attacked would prompt a major diplomatic incident between Britain and Argentina. At worst we'd now be at war. The fact that nothing's happened means the fifth man's gone to ground." He placed his pistol in a pocket. "We find the fifth man. We kill him and anyone around him. Whoever makes the kills summons the rest of the team. We dispose of bodies. We exit via the trawler, codename 'Travel Agent'.

The trawler was an Argentine boat that belonged to FIA. It was anchored thirty miles off the islands. It would come to shore once the assassination was done. Casero, Rojo, Fontonia, and Sosa would swim a few hundred yards to the boat and get on board. The swim would be agony, but they could do it. Then, they'd go back to Argentina.

Casero looked at his team. "Let's hope the next time we see each other is when we're mopping up and getting out of here." He stowed his equipment in his car and drove back to Stanley.

Over the next four hours, Sign and Knutsen searched the homes of Taylor, Green, and Jackson. There was no need to force entry into the properties – Colonel Richards had given them keys. They found nothing of interest.

The last property to investigate belonged to Wilson. His home was a small house near the Stanley quay. They entered. It was clear there was no woman's touch in the place. The tiny kitchen's sink was crammed with dirty dishes. On the adjacent surface were empty foil ready-meal containers and pint glasses. Half-drunk bottles of cider and ale were on the floor. There was one upstairs bedroom. The bed's duvet was twisted and looked like it hadn't been washed in an age. The room smelled of fish and musk. The bathroom toilet was dirty. The sink contained whiskers from Wilson's shaving. By the taps were one toothbrush and toothpaste, a razor, and shaving foam; nothing else. The adjacent shower only contained one bottle of shower gel. The downstairs lounge had a sofa, a TV positioned on top of a chest of drawers, lobster pots hanging from meat hooks attached to the wall, rolled up maps of the Falklands' coastline, an overflowing ashtray, a rack that had dank-smelling cloths on them, and a mantelpiece that had a framed photo of four men huddled together, arms on shoulders, smiling, on board Wilson's boat.

Sign picked up the photo. "Wilson, Taylor, Green, and Jackson." He turned the picture around. There was a label on the back. Handwritten on the label was 'Feb 2017. Beers and fishing day'." Sign opened the frame and withdrew the photo. There was no inscription of any kind on the front or back.

Knutsen was rummaging through the chest of drawers. "Bills. More bills! Phone charger leads. A bottle of aerosol deodorant. Passport in Wilson's name. Bank statements. Loose coins. Cream for cracked heels. First aid kit. Packet of condoms – unopened. Tea towels. Nothing else."

Sign said, "Take the bills and the bank statements." He looked at the photo. "I wonder who took this shot." He carefully rolled the photo up and placed it in his fleece pocket. Leaning against the wall in the corner of the room was a shotgun. Sign examined the weapon. "This hasn't been fired for a long time." He put the shotgun back against the wall. "There's nothing more we can do here."

Knutsen placed Wilson's paperwork in his backpack. "If only we had the murdered men's mobile phones. We'd be able to find the fifth man in seconds."

Sign shared his frustration. "Navy divers searched the seabed underneath Wilson's boat. It was a futile task. Tides and currents could have taken the mobile phones anywhere, *if* they were thrown overboard after Wilson and his men were killed. There are two other possibilities: the Argentinians took the phones back to their country; or the fifth man took them because he didn't want the police to know he'd been roped into the mad escapade that night."

"The police analyse the phones. They identify the man who supplied the men with military weapons."

"Yes, but would he have had time to get their phones, with the spy boat so close? His priority was to escape." Sign moved to the centre of the room, staring at nothing while deep in thought. "It remains a hypothesis. And by definition, a hypothesis is an idea that can only be proved or disproved by evidence. We need more than evidence. We need fact. My hypothesis is that the fifth man is a loner and a survivalist. He is an islander; not an ex-military foreigner. He is fit. I posit that he may be in his thirties or forties, no younger, though folk around here are hardy so it could be he's in his fifties or sixties. I will tag another label to my imaginary profile of our quarry: he knows seamanship. Getting an emergency craft off deck and into the sea while under gunfire, boarding the vessel, and rowing it to shore, is no mean feat."

"So, he's a fisherman." Knutsen wanted to leave the house. There was no heating on. It was at least minus ten degrees.

"*Maybe* he's a fisherman. Certainly he knows the sea." He nodded his head, his voice quieter as he said, "What bothers me are the missing phones. If the Argentinians have them why haven't they done something about the fifth man?"

"Killed him. In which case the police would be aware that there's been another murder of an islander."

"Precisely. It would have been impossible for the spy ship not to have spotted the fifth man on Wilson's vessel. And it would have been impossible for the spy ship crew not to have seen him escape. But they had work to do. They had to cleanse Wilson's boat, dump the bodies into the sea, and get back to Argentina. They couldn't risk chasing the fifth man to shore." Sign frowned. "Why isn't the fifth man dead? It's because he hasn't been identified. If the Argentinians knew who he was he'd be shot by them in a nanosecond, so to speak. They absolutely *must* cover their tracks about what they did that night. The consequences for them if they didn't would be awful. The mobile phones may have been tossed overboard by the Argentinians, or they may - by some miracle - have been grabbed by the fifth man while bullets were raining down on him. Most likely they were taken by the Argentinians." Sign looked at Knutsen. "Maybe the evidence never made it to Argentina. Maybe the boat was damaged in the gun fight. The spy ship sunk somewhere between the Falklands and Buenos Aires. Argentina doesn't have the phones. The fifth man doesn't have the phones. They are forever lost." He looked grave as he said, "But Argentina will want the fifth man as much as we want him."

"Maybe they don't know about the fifth man."

Sign shook his head. "With the technology on their boat, the Argentinian spies wouldn't have missed a thing. They'd have seen the fifth man rowing to shore." He ran fingers through his hair. "This is so terribly annoying and dangerous."

Knutsen was puzzled. "Dangerous."

Sign snapped, "Idiot Richards and his idiot boss, the chief of defence staff, are gunning for a fight with Argentina. In turn, Argentina will pull out the stops to prevent that from happening. We and the fifth man are in the middle."

Knutsen walked to the front door. "There's an Argentinian special forces assassination squad here now, isn't there?"

Sign walked past him and out of the house. "Yes there is."

That evening Sign prepared a beef bourgeon and placed it in the oven, while Knutsen analysed Wilson's bank statements and bills. Sign walked out of the cottage and looked at Bluff Cove. He knew the penguins would be there, huddled together. He imagined they be feeling miserable as they tried to sleep. But he couldn't see them or anything else beyond the cottage. It was dark and the moon and stars were hidden by cloud cover; and there was no artificial light for miles around his temporary accommodation. Snow was falling fast, but Sign didn't notice the weather. All he could think of was that somewhere out there was the fifth man. He imagined the man was lonely and frightened. The fifth man couldn't trust anyone, least of all the police and the British military. Sign was convinced he'd not only supplied guns to Wilson and his friends, he'd also engaged the Argentinians. Post combat trauma was likely. Sign knew all about that.

He shivered in the cold, bleak weather. But he stayed for a few more minutes, collecting his thoughts. He wondered if what he and Knutsen were doing had moral purpose. There was a case to be made to let the fifth man stay off the radar in order to avoid a British assault on Argentina. Sign didn't want war. He'd seen too much death in his career to revel at the prospect of witnessing more death, thanks to his actions. But, if his hunch was correct that there was an Argentinian death squad on the islands the fifth man was a dead man walking unless he and Knutsen could get to him first. Sign was adept at looking at the big picture, protecting the national interest of Great Britain. But, so often in the front line field of special operations in came down to protecting those around you – your foreign agents, colleagues, civilians who'd helped you. Sign didn't know the fifth man, but he did feel a connection to his plight. On that basis, Sign and Knutsen's job in hand had integrity and honour. What Sign didn't yet know is what he'd do when he found the fifth man. Hand him over to Richards? Or debrief the man and tell him how he could go into permanent hiding? The latter option would involve him having to lie to Richards and his boss. Still, Sign had never been averse to lying to people in power.

He re-entered the cottage. The smell of the casserole pervaded the lounge and kitchen. Knutsen was sitting in front of the log burner, clutching Wilson's papers.

Sign sat opposite him. "What do you make of the documents?"

Knutsen sighed. "For the most part there's nothing that leaps out from the invoices and bank statements. It's all standard stuff – debit card transactions for the grocery store in Stanley, purchase of petrol, vehicle repairs, rent and utilities, bank transfers to suppliers – all of them fishing related, cash withdrawals, itemised sales of fish, tax returns, purchase of clothes, and on and on. In other words, regular stuff that a single guy would do with his cash and fishing income."

"The cash withdrawals – what was the pattern of behaviour in terms of typical amounts withdrawn?"

Knutsen smiled. "Twenty pounds here, thirty pounds there. But you've spotted the one thing that has perplexed me. On the day before his death he withdrew five hundred pounds. At six PM on the evening of his death he withdrew a further five hundred pounds. I'm guessing five hundred pounds per day is his maximum withdrawal limit permitted by his bank."

"Yes. But, he needed a thousand pounds in cash and he needed it urgently. The money won't have been for a knees-up in Sally's bar on the night of his murder. The amount is too exact and way beyond what four men could spend in one night in a modest coastal pub."

"Maybe he had medical bills to pay."

"With cash? No."

"Purchase of illegal narcotics? Sally said she smoked cannabis between shifts. Maybe there's an underground cottage industry on the islands. Or Wilson and his mates were smuggling in drugs and needed to pay their suppliers."

Sign waved a hand dismissively. "One thousand pounds wouldn't cover the costs of a covert return trip in Wilson's boat to South America to buy drugs. And with a population of approximately three thousand, the islands simply don't have enough people who ingest narcotics to demand such a trade. If, on the other hand, a small number of islanders are growing cannabis locally, one thousand pounds strikes me as a significant amount of money to buy – as, I believe, you cops and criminals call it – weed. Am I correct?"

Knutsen shrugged. "It's possible to spend that amount of money for personal use. Cannabis takes a while to grow and harvest. When it's cropped, it can take months for the next batch to be ready. Maybe Wilson was bulk buying to see him through the winter and spring."

"From what we know about Wilson, he doesn't strike me as a druggy. Drink was his tipple of choice. And he had no traces of narcotics in his system when the post-mortem was conducted. And his lifestyle – hardworking, hard drinking, up at four AM to strike the fishing grounds. No. His profile doesn't match that of a drug user."

Knutsen laughed. "You don't know much about drug users."

"Maybe not. But, there is one thing notable about the transactions. They were urgent."

"Five hundred pounds one day. Five hundred pounds the next."

"And both within a forty eight hour period that culminated in his death. The coincidence is too great. This is not about drugs. But I do suspect it is to do with something else illegal."

Knutsen put the papers to one side.

Sign was deep in thought. "We have no facts. All we can rely on is our imagination. Let's suppose that Wilson got it in to his head that he wanted to confront the spy ship. To do that he needed guns. There was a man on the islands who could supply the guns. But he wasn't Wilson's friend. He was the fifth man. And the fifth man wasn't going to part with his guns and assist him unless there was a business transaction to be had. The man demanded one thousand pounds, payable on the night he delivered the guns and joined Wilson, Taylor, Green, and Jackson on the trawler."

"It holds together, but it is only a hunch."

"I prefer the word *theory*." Sign stared at the fire. In a quiet voice he said, "My experience in life has not been a cold-hard-facts-police-procedural approach towards the problems I confronted. The issues I faced overseas were far more nuanced. And, I worked alone in hostile territories. I had no team of analysts and cops to support my work. I had to make my own judgements. Very often that meant that I had to deal with the realms of the possible. And the starting point for that approach rested in my head." He looked at Knutsen. "My instincts are telling me that the one thousand pounds was a cash-for-guns transaction."

"If that's true, why did the fifth man join them on the boat that night? Why didn't he just give Wilson the guns and tell him to return them when the job was done? Or, maybe the guns were sold to Wilson and didn't need to be returned. Either way, I don't understand why he risked his neck that night by joining a bunch of drunken blokes who were not his mates."

"When we find the fifth man, we will pose that question to him. For now, there are many possibilities. What would you say is the strongest reason for him being there during the battle?"

"It could be he didn't trust Wilson. Maybe he was only going to be paid after the job. So, he tagged along to keep an eye on his guns and Wilson. But, I think the strongest possibility rests on a more simple and immediate imperative – the fifth man wanted a fight with the Argentinian spy boat."

"Bravo, Mr. Knutsen. Simplicity is usually the route to the truth. Almost certainly you are right. Testosterone-fuelled aggression came in to play, requiring the fifth man to join the combatants. His anger against Argentina would have been simmering within the fifth man for years but not bubbling over. Until now. The spy boat was a tipping point."

"He lost the plot."

"Yes." Sign stood when the oven alarm pinged, telling him their dinner was ready. He seemed distracted when he said, "However…"

"What?"

"Oh, it's probably nothing."

"There's something you're not telling me," said Knutsen in a firm voice.

"I have a theory I've been carrying in my head ever since we first met Colonel Richards in London. It may amount to nothing or something." Sign held up his hand before Knutsen could ask more questions. He smiled. "We must eat, dear chap. There is nothing more that can be achieved this evening."

"What are our tasks tomorrow?"

Sign folded his arms. "This is indeed a difficult case. Sally, Carl, and Nick have not proven instructive. Nor should they be. They were simply witnesses to Wilson and his friends' behaviour in the bar. But, it is nevertheless regrettable that they have no inkling as to who may have joined the men on that fateful night"

"Could we ask the police to tell the islanders that any person involved in the escapade will not be prosecuted? Maybe the fifth man would then come forward."

"Were it so simple. Richards wouldn't allow that to happen. He wants secrecy. In conjunction with the Ministry of Defence in London he's preparing not only for the protection of the islands but also to use the archipelagos to be used as a launch pad for hostilities."

"How do you know this?"

"Logic and my analysis of Richards. But, Richards is also hampered by his impotency in this situation. He can't go public on anything. We're here because he can't use the police and military investigators. If he does, the cat will be out of the bag. As it is, Sally thinks you and I are merely meddling private investigators from England; Carl and Nick think we're scientists from South Georgia; and Richards has agreed to our cover as high-ranking army officers visiting the islands for an unspecified task." Sign kept talking as he went into the adjacent kitchen and served up dinner. To accompany the beef bourgeon he'd prepared double-fried chips, diced cabbage mixed with crispy lardons and chillies, and slithers of boiled carrots. "Tomorrow we must meet Richards." He returned with two plates of the food and cutlery. "As usual, we eat on our laps, in front of the fire."

Knutsen asked, "Why Richards?"

"Oh, just to see if there's something he's not telling me."

Knutsen ate a mouthful of the casserole. As usual Sign's food was delicious. Knutsen wondered how Sign conjured up such world class cuisine, even in locations where local produce was basic and limited. "You must have some other ideas as to what we can do. Use that brilliant brain of yours." The latter comment was said with sarcasm.

Sign breathed in deeply. "It is for you to decide whether I'm brilliant or stupid. But I can tell you categorically that I'm not a magician. I can't conjure something substantial out of something insubstantial. I'm running out of options to source the fifth man."

Knutsen replied, "If this was a police operation, faced with the same problems in a murder investigation, we'd do door-to-door. Maybe that's what we should do – simply knock on every door on the islands until we get answers."

Sign ate his food. "It would be relatively easier in the western areas of the islands, where the population is spread out. Not so easy in Stanley. The population of the Falklands is just over three thousand, on top of which are military personnel. But, restricting our search to islanders would mean we'd have to ascertain how many houses we'd have to knock on and how many interviews we'd have to conduct. Let's make an assumption that the average household on the islands contains three people. It won't be accurate because some houses will contain four or more people and others will only contain one. But the mean of those variables gives us approximately a headcount of three per property. So, we'd have one thousand houses to visit, spread across the islands, in the bleakest winter the Falklands has known for years. We could possibly do a maximum of ten households per day in Stanley. With its population of two thousand plus, divided by three, further divided by ten, it would take us sixty six days to cover Stanley. Then there's the remaining one thousand people spread across the islands. We'd be lucky to interview more than two or three in a day." He was silent while finishing his food, before placing his empty dinner plate to one side. "Door-to-door would take us a minimum of three months. More likely six."

Knutsen placed his empty plate on top of Sign's plate. "It's still worth a thought." He smiled. "After all, we're not going anywhere for now. All planes out of here are grounded. We're trapped."

"We don't have the luxury of time."

Knutsen placed another log in the fire. "Maybe the fifth man has left the islands on a plane."

Sign shook his head. "Since the night of the murders there have only been four flights that have landed on the islands. Two were from Brize Norton. You, me, and Richards were on one of them. There have also been two flights from Santiago. The planes have left but were not allowed to carry passengers due to the severity of the weather. Since those flights, all incoming and outgoing flights have been cancelled until the weather clears. There is the option that the fifth man is a sailor and took his boat to Argentina, but…"

"He'd be sailing to the last place on Earth he'd want to be."

"Yes. The fifth man is on the islands. Now, no one can come in; no one can get out. We are on Alcatraz until flights are resumed."

Knutsen rubbed his face. "We should check the flight manifests of the incoming planes from Santiago and Brize Norton. If, as you suspect, there's a four person assassination unit looking for the fifth man, they'd have been on one of those flights."

"I will be requesting that data from Richards tomorrow." Sign stared at the burning logs. "We have different agendas but I sympathise with the Argentinians. They are in the same mire as us. How do they find the fifth man?"

"They'll know Wilson, Taylor, Green, and Jackson's names. The drunken idiots would have been carrying their ID on them. When the Argentinians boarded Wilson's boat, they'll have searched them before chucking the bodies overboard. No wallets or any other forms of ID were found on their bodies. That means the assassination unit has the same starting point as we have – the identity of the dead men. Nothing more, nothing less."

"Correct. So what do they do?" Sign bowed his head and was silent for a minute. "The Argentinian unit will be on the islands under alias. The operatives will have been chosen for their looks and their command of language. They'll be posing as British, South Africans, New Zealanders, or Australians. Maybe the unit will take one nationality apiece."

"Why not United States nationality?"

"They'd stand out too much if the posed as north Americans. There are no legitimate US citizens working on the islands. Nor does the States have a reason to deploy workers here. The Falklands is a thoroughly British protectorate with solely British interests in trade and security."

Knutsen said, "Put bluntly, the States and its businesses can't be bothered with the islands."

"You could put it that way. I'd put it in more polite terms. The United States simply cannot see any business opportunities here. It knows that Britain would squeeze them out. Thus, an American on the archipelago would stand out like a sore thumb. However, there is a track record of South Africans, Kiwis, and Australians working here in a variety of temporary roles – engineers, traders, lawyers, insurance experts, vets, geologists, builders, et cetera." Sign listed his head. "When I see the flight manifests, I'm eighty percent certain I'll be able to identify the assassination squad. The question is: what do we do with that information?"

"If we have their fake names, we could take them to the governor of the Falklands and advise him to expel them."

Sign shook his head. "On what basis? That they may or may not be assassins? If they were legitimate Australians or whatever, we could risk opening up a can of worms. We need to keep this investigation discrete. That's why Richards brought us in. The governor knows about the murders. I very much doubt he knows about the fifth man. He will most certainly not have deduced there is a strong probability that Argentina has sent covert operatives onto his islands. Even Richards won't have thought that far ahead."

"Will the Argentinian unit be operating together?"

"No. Not until the last minute. For now they'll be in investigation mode. That means they'll be in a divide-and-conquer drill – each of them pursuing their own leads, minimal contact with each other unless something urgent arises, lodging at separate properties. Their drill will change when they identify the fifth man. That's when they'll come together in order to eliminate him and escape the islands."

Knutsen drummed his fingers. In a forthright voice he said, "If we come onto their radar, they'll come for us; probably torture us to find out what we know."

"If they attempt that, you kill them." Sign's eyes were twinkling as he smiled and added, "I gave you a gun for a reason. And remember – outside of Stanley, everything is bandit country. Bad things can happen west of the capital and not be discovered for weeks, months, or ever. If they come for us, gun them down. You and I will deal with the bodies."

"Richards has authorised this?"

"Not in so many words. He gave me the gun you're carrying in order for us to protect ourselves. But, the word *protect* is open to interpretation. That said, I'd prefer an outcome wherein anything extreme we do does not come to the attention of the authorities – Richards included."

Knutsen laughed. "This will be a first – me taking on a highly trained hit squad."

"You are up to the task." Sign placed his hand on Knutsen's shoulder. "You will not be alone. I will be there to help." He stood and said in a serious tone of voice, "Mr. Knutsen, we are swimming in murky and dangerous waters. Instead of swimming for shore, we must venture further away from safety."

"Only you could come up such a melodramatic statement." Knutsen's expression became serious. "That said, I get the point." He looked out of the window. There was nothing but black out there. To himself, quietly he said, "I didn't expect to die in a place like this."

CHAPTER 9

The following morning Casero woke up in his hotel, showered, shaved with a triple blade razor, and dressed into a two hundred pound white shirt, one thousand two hundred pound Saville Row charcoal suit, immaculate leather black shoes, and a silk tie befitting of British government mandarins and generals. Before arriving in the Falklands, he'd ensured his hair was clipped in the style of English army officers – not long, but not too short; rather that of a man who was posing as a gentleman in important service. He applied dabs of Harvey Nichols aftershave to his throat, placed his fake passport into his pocket, grabbed his wallet and car keys, donned an expensive heavy woollen overcoat, and stood in front of a full-length mirror. He smiled. He looked every inch the persona he wished to convey.

He left the hotel and drove across Stanley. The house he was seeking was almost the last property on the outskirts of the capital; overlooking the sea, modest in size, a small garden in front. He stopped his hire car outside the home's fence, got out, and rang the front door bell.

A woman in her sixties opened the door. "Yes?"

Casero spoke with impeccable English, with an accent that suggested he'd been schooled in Eton or Harrow before receiving further education in Oxford or Cambridge. "Mrs. Wilson. My name is Peter Sillitoe. I am a representative of Her Majesty's government. I have flown to the islands from London with the express intention of speaking to you about your son's tragic death. May I come in?"

The woman looked confused. "What's there to talk about? My son drowned with his friends." Her bottom lip trembled. "I had to identify his body. The police interviewed me. Then the army. I had to bury him. What more can I do?"

"My sincerest condolences, Mrs. Wilson. This won't take long, I can assure you. I'm not here to cause you further anguish. Nor do I wish to besmirch your good son's name. I represent a government department that wishes to ascertain whether your son's accident was in any way prompted by the presence of a nearby Argentinian ship. Do you know what I'm referring to?"

Wilson's mother nodded. "We all know about that boat. It's gone now. Hasn't been seen since Eddie died." She looked back down her hallway, seeming uncertain. "Alright. Come in." She led Casero into her lounge. "Would you like tea?"

"That's very kind but I had a cuppa just before coming here." He sat on one of the chairs.

She looked suspicious as she sat near him. "Which British government department do you work for?"

Casero looked away. "It's delicate." He reengaged eye contact with her. "Let's just say I deal with problems that are of interest to our prime minister."

"You're a spook then?"

He smiled. "Were it so easy to be candid." His expression turned serious. "I don't represent the military bases here. Nor do I represent the governor of the islands. In fact, they don't know I'm here. I am an emissary and guardian of London's gates. If you talk to me you are talking to power."

"How can you prove you are who you say you are?"

Casero waved a hand dismissively. "I can't. There are numbers you could call in London. They're freely available on the Internet. Alas, it is government policy not to respond to any enquiries pertaining to members of staff. You must trust me, or not. All I can say is that I'm here to help."

Mrs. Wilson picked up a framed photo from the adjacent coffee table. She stared at the picture. "My boys." She wiped a tear away. "My son. Bob Taylor. Billy Green. Mike Jackson. They were so close in life. Together in death." She placed the photo back on the table. "They were good lads. They didn't deserve this."

Casero looked at the picture, memorising their faces. "What did the police tell you about the incident?"

"You should have all the facts!"

"I do but sometimes facts overwhelm nuances. I'd dearly like to know your take on matters." He placed his fingertips together and was silent as he waited for her response.

She breathed deeply. "I don't know anything more than you know. That bloody Argie spy ship has been nipping at the islands' ankles for a couple of months. It annoyed everyone here, though didn't cause us any harm. But it was like, you know, an insult to us. Eddie in particular hated it being in his fishing waters. I could see he was getting more and more angry with it being here."

"How often did you see Eddie?"

"At least once a week. My husband passed away two years ago. Eddie came here to check on me and do work around the house if needed."

"So, you were gifted with a good barometer for his temperature?"

"What?"

"You could tell his mood."

"Yes, yes." She wrung her hands. "But, he was a quiet lad and didn't give much away in words. I could tell, though, from his eyes and the odd comment he made. He wasn't happy with the Argie ship. He blamed the British military for doing nothing about it. After his death, the police and military didn't tell me anything about why he was out on his boat that night. He fishes when he has to but for the most part he had a routine – night fishing, day fishing, twelve hours rest in between. One day off a week if he can get it. And he was getting drunk in Sally's pub in Stanley on the night of his death. As you know, Rob, Billy, and Mike were with him. Eddie never drinks before sailing. It makes no sense for him to have suddenly decided to do a night fish. Anyway, Rob and Mike aren't fisherman. I can't see why they'd have been on the boat with him, hauling in nets."

"And that is why I've been sent to see you. The police and military are in no doubt that this was a tragic accident. I agree with their conclusion. I'm sure it would give you greater peace if there was a better reason for your son's death than simply a drunken slip into the water. Did the coroner tell you about weather conditions that night?"

She nodded. "She told me that the navy said the weather was atrocious that night; that there were swells and fast tides. They should never have gone out that night."

Casero chose his next words carefully. "Do you think the Argentinian ship was in any way responsible for the accident? Maybe it crossed your son's path and caused him to make an emergency manoeuvre. Or something similar."

Floods of tears were coursing down Mrs. Wilson's face. "I don't think so. Eddie knew these waters. My guess is he and his friends went out there on some drunken rampage, got close to the spy ship, went on deck with beers, and started hurling insults at the Argies. They got hit by a wave or whatever. That's when they went overboard."

"I regret to say that we agree with your analysis. As you say, The Argentinian boat has gone. We know that." Casero chose his next words carefully. "It is a shame that there were no witnesses to the incident. The Argentinians on their ship may have seen what happened but they are of no use to us. We've made a formal request to the Argentinian government for assistance. Predictably they denied having a spy boat in the islands' waters. I wonder though." Casero faked a look that suggested a thought had just occurred to him. "Would it be possible someone else was on Eddie's boat when the tragedy occurred? Maybe that person also drowned but his body was washed out to sea. Or maybe he survived but is either too embarrassed or traumatised to come forward to local authorities."

Mrs. Wilson looked perplexed. "Another man? None of you lot have asked me that question before. I don't think so. Can't see how that could happen. Eddie had three friends. That's all he needed."

"Did he ever mention anyone else to you – an islander whom he had dealings with?"

She looked exasperated. "Everyone here has dealings with other islanders. We're a small community. We rely on each other."

"In particular, I wonder if there was anyone that Eddie knew who would be keen to join his crew in order to taunt the Argentinian boat. It would probably be a male; someone who hated the spy ship; maybe a drinker, maybe not."

"You're talking about every man on these islands. But, no. Eddie never mentioned to me anyone who might be the type to join him, Rob, Billy, and Mike. Why do you think there might have been someone else on the boat?"

Casero shrugged. "I don't. It's just wishful thinking on my part. I have to pursue every line of enquiry. I fear that when the weather abates I must fly back to London and advise my masters that there is nothing to report." He stood. "Once again, I'm so sorry for your loss. And I'm sorry to have intruded on your grief. Thank you for your time Mrs. Wilson."

When he was in his car, Casero called Fontonia. "I have a lead - Sally who runs a pub in Stanley. The men were heavily drinking in the bar on the night of the incident. See if she knows anything about a fifth man."

Sign was wearing a suit as he attended the headquarters of RAF Mount Pleasant. After getting through security checks, he was ushered to a room where he sat and waited.

A young RAF woman opened the adjacent door and said to Sign, "The colonel will see you now." She left the door open and exited the room.

Sign entered Colonel Richards' office. It was large and contained an oak desk at the far end of the room, behind it were windows overlooking the runway, chairs facing the desk, and wall-mounted pictures of previous military commanders of the base.

Richards was sitting at his desk, rifling through paperwork. "Mr. Sign. What do you have for me?"

Sign sat on one of the seats. "I'm not here to report progress. Instead, I'm information gathering. I'd like the flight manifests of every plane that landed here after the death of Wilson and his friends."

Richards frowned. "What use would they be to you? You should be concerned about who's left the islands after the incident, not who's come in."

Sign lied. "I'm wondering if someone came in to help the fifth man. Maybe a relative or friend. No one has been able to leave the islands since the gun battle. Thus, if a relative or friend of our mysterious witness came here, then that person is still here. He or she won't be able to leave until the RAF permits flights to recommence normal duties. I'm particularly interested in passengers who may have a connection to the islands. That means most likely the person was on one of the two Brize Norton flights that left England after Wilson, Taylor, Green, and Jackson were murdered. But – belt and braces – I'd also like to check the manifests of the two Santiago flights that arrived before lockdown was imposed."

Richards was unconcerned with the request. "As you wish. I can't see the point, but I suppose you have to check all angles." He made an internal phone call. "Flight manifests for the four planes that arrived before we suspended passenger flights." He hung up and looked at Sign. "Have you made *any* progress?"

Sign smiled. "None whatsoever. Knutsen and I have interviewed some locals but so far we've not ascertained any new data."

"I paid you to get quick results!"

Sign held the Royal Marines commander's gaze. "*You* didn't pay me. The Ministry of Defence paid me. The MOD reports to the minister of defence who in turn reports to the prime minister. Shall I call the PM and tell her that we have a problem? She'll do what I tell her to do. She'll ignore you and the chief of defence staff. You'd be on the next flight out of here, enjoying early retirement and beekeeping in Surrey, or such place."

Richards' face reddened. "You have no right to talk to me like..."

"Yes I do, Richards." Sign maintained his calm persona and tone of voice. "Know your place. You brought me in to solve this riddle. But, I am not your employee. Until this case is closed you are *my* employee." Sign crossed his legs and clasped his hands. "If I find the fifth man what are your plans?"

"That's classified!"

"Not from me. You've already told me that you're planning war. Your islands would be the launch pad for a strike on Argentina. It would be a nice feather in your cap before you retire. The chief of defence will no doubt promote you to brigadier before you leave government service. That will be a nice hike in your pension. You have a vested interest in the death of Argentinians."

Richards sighed. "If you get a testimony from the fifth man, one that clearly identifies the Argentinian ship as the perpetrators of murder, we will punish Argentina. There will be air strikes on their military bases, naval bombardments of ships and docks, and air strikes on communications systems. Then, we will back off because the point will have been made. It will be a sledgehammer to crack a nut. The end game is, for once and for all, to get Argentina to forget the phrase *Islas Malvinas*. We maintain our security and strike capability in this part of the southern hemisphere. The Argentinians fuck off for good."

"It is ever thus that countries like Britain want to carve up the world according to their perceived needs." Sign was nonchalant as he said, "You pretend that you want to protect a few sheep and their owners, wherein the truth is you want a military platform. To you the Falklands is in essence a massive, static, aircraft carrier."

"And I have no problems with that. It's my job."

"Indeed it is." Sign decided to change tack. "My job is different. Knutsen and I will continue our investigation until we solve this problem. The task in hand is difficult. We just need to find an access agent."

"Meaning?"

"Someone who knows who the fifth man might be. That person can then facilitate a meeting with the fifth man. Depending on circumstances, that introduction will either be done with or without the access agent's knowledge that Knutsen and I will be there to pounce on our target."

Richards sighed. "I can't be bothered to ask you what that spy stuff means. But I can be bothered to tell you that we need fast results. What are your next steps?"

"Knutsen and I will continue interviewing locals. But in tandem the flight manifests may speed up matters. I presume there is still no sight of the spy ship, or any other Argentinian presence in our waters?"

"Correct."

"So, the islands are safe."

"For now."

Sign nodded. "Good. Are you still deploying army routine foot patrols on the islands?"

"Of course. A bit of snow doesn't stop our security protocols."

"Cancel all patrols. Restrict your men and women to your bases. And tell the police not to do routine patrols; rather to only respond to emergency situations."

"What?! That would be absurd! It would serve no purpose."

Sign said, "It would produce an aura of calm. The fifth man will continue to lay low if he thinks he's being watched by authorities. I want him to think that the weather has gotten the better of your men and that they are putting their feet up in their barracks. Ditto the police. I want them to be brewing tea and coffee in their station and playing cards to kill time."

"I have no jurisdiction over the police! The governor of the Falklands is the only person who could issue such an order to his law enforcement officers"

"Technically you have no jurisdiction over the governor. In practice you do. Tell him to stand his officers down from all but the most critical incidents. Lie to him. Say to him that there is a team of investigators on the islands searching for a wanted man who's fled from England to the islands. Tell him that a lack of police presence will allow us to do our job. Do not name me or Knutsen. Conclude that this is only a temporary situation until the man is captured."

Richards was incredulous. "You're telling me – the military commander of the Falklands – and the governor – the highest ranking politician on the islands – to not do our jobs over the coming few days or weeks?!"

"Yes." Sign elaborated. "The weather is atrocious. It would not seem odd if locals saw the suspension of routine military and police patrols. But, the locals are hardy folk. They'd think you're weak and would laugh at your inability to continue normal business while they carry on with work regardless of conditions. If my assessment is correct that the fifth man is a local, he too will think it's a joke that an eight man unit of British soldiers thought it was too treacherous to venture out of Stanley, that your helicopters won't take off, that police are worried about getting their cars stuck in snow drifts. The fifth man needs to make a living, doing whatever it is he does. Zero sight of military personnel and cops with the power to arrest will induce complacency in him. In other words, he will come out of hiding."

Richards couldn't believe he was hearing this. "I could be court martialled for issuing such an order and for lying to the governor."

"I will make a call to the powers that be to ensure you are not chastised. On the contrary, I will say that you came up with this ingenious plan whilst cognisant that there is currently no threat to the Falklands. In Whitehall, you will be lauded as brave and smart. It will be another feather in your cap."

Richards looked confused. "I… Of course I have authority to do this. But, to all intents and purposes you're making the islands a lawless territory."

"Only for a brief period. Once we get the fifth man, we bring him in, normal duties resume, and you can have your war. And if you want your war, you have no alternatives. The fifth man is key. Without him you have nothing other than speculation. No fifth man, no war." Sign was silent as he stared at Richards.

Richards bowed his head for twenty seconds. He looked up and said in a quiet voice, "You really are a piece of work. I'll do it. Just make sure you make that call to Whitehall. The flight manifests are with my secretary in the adjacent room. Unless there's any further business to discuss, I bid you good day!"

Mrs. Wilson was outside her house, using a shovel to shift snow from her driveway. The task was backbreaking, compounded by the arthritis in her wrists and fingers. She was making little progress. But the job had to be done. She had a two wheel drive vehicle in her garage that, with the flick of a dashboard switch, could be transformed into four wheel drive. Alas, the switch no longer worked. Snow was a major problem. The roads in Stanley were regularly cleared. But that was of no use to her unless she could get her vehicle out of the driveway. She winced as she persisted with the task. She knew it was fruitless. There was at least a ton of snow to clear and more of it was pouring from the sky. If only Eddie was here. He'd have gotten the job done in a jiffy.

Knutsen stopped his vehicle on the road by her house. He got out and approached the woman who was oblivious to his presence. "Mrs. Wilson?"

She stood up and turned toward him, wincing as she rubbed her back. "Yes. Who are you and what do you want? I'm busy."

"I can see that. My name is Tom Knutsen. I'm a scientist, working with the British Antarctic Survey in South Georgia. I specialise in the southern hemisphere oceans."

"What's that got to do with me?"

"I've been sent here to see why your son and his three friends fell off their boat on the night they died. If it was a human error, then the matter is out of my field of expertise. If, however, it was down to a natural phenomenon such as a swell or a tidal wave, then I'd be interested to ascertain why we were unable to predict such changes in sea behaviour."

Mrs. Wilson was angry. "Do you think I have a clue what the sea was doing when my Eddie died?! Fishing's been in my family for generations. But I've never been on a boat. I've got other things to worry about. You're speaking to the wrong person."

"I do apologise. I wonder if you have a theory about Eddie's death."

She walked up to him. "My husband – Eddie's dad – is dead. The sea got him. He died in bed in this house; but he might as well have been swallowed up by the waters out there. A lifetime of working the nets will do that to a body. He died a smashed up man. Eddie knew what he was getting into when he took over the business. He knew the risks. Fancy scientists like you don't know what a hard day's work is. The sea's a cruel mistress, my grandfather used to say. He was right about that." She continued shovelling snow, her teeth gritted as she struggled with pain.

Knutsen placed a hand on the shovel. "Let me help you. In return, I could do with a cup of tea."

She was hesitant. Then she handed Knutsen the shovel and entered her house.

It took Knutsen thirty minutes to clear the driveway.

Mrs. Wilson came out with a mug of tea. "Thank you." She handed the mug to Knutsen and sighed as she looked upwards. "Another night of this snow means that what you've done will have been pointless."

Knutsen drank the hot brew while breathing fast. "You could grit and salt your driveway. Or you could park your car on the road."

Mrs. Wilson stood next to him and looked at the nearby road. "Grit and salt don't do anything when the weather's this bad. Only snowploughs can keep the roads clear. Yes. I'll park my car on the road. I wish my husband and Eddie were here."

Knutsen looked at her.

She didn't look at him. Instead, she looked at the sea. "Why are so many people interested in my son's death?"

"I didn't know they were."

"Police; army; this government bloke this morning; you. My son drowned because…"

"The sea is a cruel mistress." Knutsen slammed the shovel into the bank of snow adjacent to the driveway. "Out of interest, who was the government man who came to visit you this morning? I thought I was the only one investigating the sea conditions on the night of your son's accident."

Mrs. Wilson shivered. "He wasn't a scientist; I can tell you that. I don't quite know what he wanted. London government type. He was more interested in the Argie spy ship. I reckon he was a British spook."

Knutsen faked a relaxed demeanour. "Oh, that makes sense. I know London was worried that the Argentinian ship might have sailed in front of your son's trawler on the night of the accident. I don't think that's what happened. But before I leave the islands I need to file my report to the British Antarctic Survey. If British Intelligence is investigating the Argentinian ship, a copy of my report will need to be submitted to them. He was probably using a fake name but did the man who visited you this morning give you any form of identification? I may know him."

She frowned. "Why would he give me a fake name?"

"Standard practise. Don't worry. It just means he wants to be anonymous. And he's obviously trying to do the right thing by you."

This line seemed to placate Mrs. Wilson. "He told me his name is Peter Sillitoe."

"That name doesn't ring a bell. Then again, lots of people come and go through the islands. That said, I'm staying in the officer's quarters in RAF Mount Pleasant. Maybe he's staying there as well. What does he look like?"

She shrugged. "Mid to late thirties, I'd say. About your height. Well dressed. Well spoken. Brown hair cut like, you know, army officers have it cut – not like squaddies. Clean shaven."

Knutsen smiled. "That sounds like most people in the officers' quarters. Did he give you his mobile number?"

"No."

"That's a shame. If he comes back could you ask him for his number? I'd like to swap notes with him on this case."

Mrs. Wilson nodded.

Knutsen gave her a slip of paper containing his mobile number. "If anything occurs to you please don't hesitate to call me." He walked down the driveway. "And don't forget to put your car on the road."

As he was driving back to his cottage, he called Sign. "Are you still with Richards?"

"No."

Knutsen told him who he'd just visited. "Does the name Peter Sillitoe mean anything to you? He's allegedly British Intelligence. I presume MI6. He visited Wilson's mother this morning."

"No, but if he were MI6 he'd be using an alias."

"Did you get the flight manifests?"

"Yes, but if you're expecting me to find the name Sillitoe in there you'll be mistaken. He'll have travelled in here under one alias and he'll be operating on the ground with another alias. Meet me at the cottage. We've work to do."

An hour later Knutsen arrived at the Bluff Cove cottage. Light was fading. The temperature was minus fifteen degrees Celsius. As he entered the warm interior of the house, Knutsen could smell the rich aroma of food. The log burner was lit. Sign was sitting next to the fire, wearing his suit trousers and shirt, no tie. He was analysing the flight manifests.

"What's on the menu tonight?" asked Knutsen.

Sign didn't look up. "Chicken pan-fried in butter, with herbs, salt and pepper, and a sprinkle of paprika. I've made a red wine sauce, with sweated onions and seasoning, that's been simmering and reducing for the last hour. Thirty minutes prior to plating up, I'll also be cooking spicy sautéed potatoes and vegetables."

Knutsen sat opposite him. "Is there anything interesting in the flight manifests?"

Sign nodded. "In the two Brize Norton flights to the islands, the majority of passengers were military personnel. I've spent the afternoon on the phone to Richards' secretary. She's confirmed their identities. Over and above that, fifteen passengers are islanders. All of them booked their return flights to England months in advance. They're of no use to me. That leaves five passengers who made bookings at short notice – you, me, and Richards, on the first flight, and two women on the second flight."

"The women?"

"A New Zealander called Helen Lock. When she arrived at Mount Pleasant she told immigration that she was a freelance journalist. The other woman is an Australian engineer called Michelle Chandler. She works in Melbourne and the South Pole. Apparently she's here to look up old friends."

"Did they sit together on the flight?"

"No." Sign glanced at the second of the two folders. "The Santiago flights are also illuminating. Once again, many of the passengers are British military personnel, returning to the islands after rest and recuperation. But on the first flight there were eighteen civilians. Twelve of them are islanders; flight bookings were made well in advance of the murders. Of the remaining six, two of them were Chilean holiday makers in their seventies; here to take photos of the star constellations."

"They picked the wrong time of year for that."

"They picked the right time of year to see the most beautiful images of stars. No one predicted the weather would be this bad. Nevertheless we can discount them, due to their age."

"And the remaining four?"

"A Chilean clothes manufacturer who's been trading with the islands for over a decade; a Peruvian timber merchant who's here to sign off on a bill of sale – he has one arm after a logging accident in 2005; a French author who is here to conduct a series of interviews with the governor in order to produce a biography of the man – the interviews were set up eight months ago. None of these people are of interest to me. But, the fourth person is of interest. His passport says he's South African. He's never been to the islands before. He told immigration that he was an insurance expert specialising in shipping. He's here to investigate an insurance claim. His name is Max Bosch. He stands out."

"The other Santiago flight?"

"A similar ratio of profiles. There's only one person of interest. A British diplomat. Name: Henry Parker. I've never heard of him, but that means nothing. If he's Foreign & Commonwealth Office, or another department, there are tens of thousands of people I've never met or heard of. Diplomats are so spread out across the world that for the most part their paths never cross. If, however, he's MI6 and using diplomatic cover, his name will be false. I'd have no way of confirming he's British Intelligence unless I saw his face. He gave immigration no justification for why he was here."

"That must be Sillitoe."

Sign placed the manifests down and sighed. "Sillitoe; Parker – what difference does it matter what he calls himself? Tomorrow he'll use a different name. And that is the issue. If, as I suspect, Lock, Chandler, Bosch, and Parker/Sillitoe are the four person Argentinian assassination unit, while they're on the islands they'll be using whatever names suit them, depending on who they're talking to. It is unlikely that we'll get to them through their names. Their tradecraft will be too good. I expected as much. But my work today has not been a waste of time. On the contrary, it has been instructive. I wanted to see if four people came in to the archipelagos at short notice, bearing passports of nationalities that wouldn't stand out in the islands. Two men and two women did precisely that. Of course, I can't be certain that they are an Argentinian team. But, if I was deploying four killers into the Falklands, I'd make sure my operatives had similar covers. And I'd have to cross my fingers and wish for luck, because the only thing going against the team is they had to deploy at short notice."

"If there is a team on the ground, maybe they came in by other means – boats, submarines, small planes, that kind of thing."

"They wouldn't risk that. If they got stopped and questioned by military or police patrols, they'd want to prove they entered the islands by legitimate means. If they couldn't prove how they got here, this whole situation would be blown wide open. Argentina and Britain don't want what happened on the night of the murders to be made public. One or more Argentinian spies caught on the islands would be information that would eventually get out and would spread like wildfire – not just here, but across the world." Sign smiled. "It is, however, unfortunate they couldn't predict that I'd be here."

"What do you mean?"

"Today I told Richards to cancel all routine army and law enforcement patrols across the islands. To all intents and purposes, you and I are currently the only law in the Falklands. If the Argentine squad had predicted that, they wouldn't have had to enter the islands via planes and fake passports."

Knutsen frowned. "Why did you do that?"

"To make the fifth man feel safe. The last thing he needs is to get twitchy every time a patrol passes near his property. He's been in hiding. I want that to stop."

"But, you could be putting a death sentence on him! If we don't get to him first, the Argentinians will kill him!"

"If we do nothing, the assassination unit will inevitably get to him. We have to take a risk." Sign stood. "I shall get changed into my scruffs before dinner." He paused at the base of the stairs, turned around, and looked at Knutsen. "If only this investigation could have been handed over to the local police. They'd have canvassed the entire islands, appealing for witnesses who could help them with their murder enquiries. Specifically, the police would spread the word that they suspect there was a fifth man with the group and that he should not fear coming forward and telling them what he knows. Alas, matters are significantly more complicated. The islanders knew about the Argentinian spy ship. Some of them knew that Wilson and his friends went out that night to confront the boat. So far the islanders have bought the line that the men drowned due to a drunken accident. To tell them the truth would cause widespread outrage on the islands. But in doing so it would push the fifth man further underground. He's scared for his own skin. So, this is not a police matter; it is an issue of national security. Thus, you and I must be unconventional. And that means we have to play with fire. I have no choice other than to fuel the fire with risk."

At ten thirty that evening, Fontonia entered the pub in Stanley where Sally worked. She was wearing waterproof trousers over her jeans, hiking boots, ski gloves, a woollen hat, and a jacket of the type used by Arctic and Antarctic explorers. There were seven customers in the tiny establishment. Two of them were sitting at a table, playing cards; another three were playing darts; the remaining two were standing by a window, chatting and quaffing their ales. No one was sitting in one of the four barstools that Wilson, Taylor, Green, and Jackson always used when drinking here. Music was playing in the background, but it was quiet. The whole ambience in the room was subdued.

Fontonia sat on a barstool, removed her gloves, and addressed the young woman working behind the bar. "Can I have a double whiskey. Nothing expensive. I just need something to warm me up."

Sally smiled and poured Fontonia her drink.

After paying, Fontonia sipped the spirit and faked a shiver. "God, that's better. I'm not used to this climate."

Sally asked, "Have you arrived in the Falklands recently?"

Fontonia smiled. "You can tell from my accent that I'm not from the islands? Well, you're right. Yeah, I got here a few days ago for a job interview at the military base." She swigged her drink. "Logistics manager. They want someone who can help run the base. I doubt I'll get the job. The guy who interviewed me seemed like a right knob."

Sally laughed. "Where are you from?"

Fontonia drained her drink. "Grew up in Tasmania. But I moved around a lot with work – England, the States, Germany, Hong Kong. Recently I've been living and working in Bermuda. Met a guy there. He moved in with me. A month ago I found out he'd been cheating on me. I kicked him out and applied for the job down here." She slid her glass towards Sally. "I need a change of scenery. But, if this is what your winters are like, I'm not sure I chose wisely."

Sally empathised. Her last boyfriend had cheated on her. "Do you want another drink?"

"One more. After that, I have to hit the road and the sack. I've got a second interview tomorrow morning with knob-face." She downed her drink, stood, and shook hands with Sally. "Thanks for the drinks. My name's Debbie. Wish me luck for tomorrow."

"Good luck and it was nice to meet you. My name's Sally."

Fontonia left the pub and entered her nearby car. She watched the pub. Over the course of the next thirty minutes, the customers she'd seen in there left the establishment in dribs and drabs and drove away from the building. At eleven thirty, Sally exited the bar, locked up, and drove south through the small capital.

Fontonia followed her, while keeping her distance. It wasn't a difficult job. Snow was still falling, but it was lighter compared to earlier in the day; thus visibility wasn't too bad, despite it being night. There were no other drivers on the coastal road. All Fontonia needed to do was follow Sally's vehicle's taillights.

Sally stopped her vehicle outside her house. The property was a small wooden building with a slate roof. It was facing the sea. There was another vehicle parked outside. Who did the second vehicle belong to? Fontonia thought fast. Husband? Unlikely because of Sally's age and due to the fact she wasn't wearing rings when she'd seen her in the bar. Then again, she could have removed her engagement and wedding rings in order not to get them scratched and dirty when working. Boyfriend? A possibility, though islanders don't like gossip. Two unmarried people cohabiting together could be deemed inappropriate by Falklanders. There was a possibility she was wrong. She didn't discount the option. A strong, youthful boyfriend could pose a problem. The third option was that Sally was cohabiting with a family relative. This seemed a more likely scenario. Unless Sally had inherited money from deceased parents, she wouldn't be able to afford to run the pub. Somebody else was the owner of the pub. Most likely it was her mother or father. It was impossible to guess which gender lived in Sally's house. But, Fontonia was sure about one thing – only one other person lived in the house. It was too small to contain three people. She decided that the most probable scenario was that one of Sally's parents had died and that the other was the owner of the pub. She or he was in the house. That was for sure. Lights were on inside the property before Sally got home. It wouldn't have been due to Sally taking security precautions before her evening shift. Burglary didn't exist on the islands.

Sally entered her home.

Fontonia waited a few minutes.

She got out of her vehicle, approached the front door and turned the handle. It was locked. She looked left and right. Some of the houses on the street had internal lights on. She wasn't worried about CCTV – it didn't exist on the islands, outside of RAF Mount Pleasant. Nor was she overly worried about prying neighbours. It was too dark for her to be visible. Nevertheless, she decided to minimise risk and not force entry into the front of the house. She walked to the back of the property. The windows were double glazed. They could be smashed with repeated swings of a sledgehammer. But Fontonia wanted her entry into the house to be a surprise. She tried the rear door. It too was locked. But this time she wasn't worried about being randomly spotted by a neighbour. The back yard was in complete darkness. She withdrew from her pocket a leather pouch, unfolded the pouch, and ran her fingers over the small tools that were aligned inside the bag. She didn't need light. She'd memorised the exact location of every item in the container. Fontonia was adept at picking locks. It was a difficult task for two reasons: First, one had to identify what kind of lock was in situ; second, one had to crack the damn thing. Sometimes the process required using three or four tiny instruments to gently nudge the different internal lock's levers out of place; other times it a more brutish approach of using a specialist drill to bore out the lock and render it useless; on occasions one had to use a different kind of drill to dig a hole around the lock and then remove it; and worse-case scenario one had to use a lever to force the door until the lock broke free from the door frame. On this occasion, Fontonia was fortunate. The lock was a simple design and was easily picked. And it was done silently. That was good. She entered the house.

She could hear music in the lounge. Sally was in there, smoking a cigarette while watching a YouTube video of a rock band. She was on the sofa and had her back to Fontonia. The Argentinian assassin ignored her and walked up the stairs.

There was a bathroom and two bedrooms upstairs. The bathroom was in darkness; so too one of the bedrooms. But the other bedroom had a dim glow of light emitting into the hallway from the room. She could hear keyboard tapping. She got prone and crawled to the edge of the door. Very slowly, she peered around the doorframe. A man was in the room. He was hunched over a laptop that was on a bedside table. He wasn't facing the door. Even if he was it would have been unlikely he'd have seen her. The hallway was dark; and people don't tend to look at the first six inches of the base of an entrance. Making no sound, she stood and moved fast.

She ran into the room, grabbed the man's jaw and head, and twisted his head until his neck snapped. Almost certainly he was dead. But to be sure of death, She grabbed a pillow from the adjacent bed and held it firm over his mouth for three minutes. She tossed the pillow back onto the bed.

The man was in his late fifties or early sixties. Most likely he was Sally's father, Fontonia decided.

She walked downstairs. Loud music was still playing from the TV. Despite the noise, she moved carefully as she approached the sofa where Sally was sitting. Fontonia's breathing was calm. Her pulse rate was a mere sixty beats per minute. It had to be that way. Heightened emotion or fear were enemies of the job in hand. This was purely business, she always told herself. Emotion only came into play when she was back in Buenos Aires and dating a guy or watching a sad movie.

She grabbed Sally by the chin, hauled her backwards over the sofa, slammed her to the floor, stamped on her face and chest, and punched two fingers into her eyes. Sally was screaming and immobile. Fontonia put one of her ski gloves into Sally's mouth. Now all that could be heard were muted gasps of desperation and pain. In any case, the neighbours wouldn't have heard the brief screams. The music was too loud.

Fontonia grabbed a wooden chair, lifted Sally on to it, and expertly tied her hands and legs to the piece of furniture. She removed the glove and said, "I don't like screaming. Nor should you."

Sally was in shock. Her body felt like it had been hit by a bus. Her vision was blurry, eyes throbbing. She blinked rapidly while breathing fast. Every breath was excruciating. Her face was as bloody and swollen as a boxer's face after doing twelve rounds with a superior fighter. Her head was pounding and her mind was confused.

Fontonia turned down the music and sat on the rim of the sofa, facing Sally. "Remember me?"

Sally blinked faster. Her vision was blurred. "I... I remember your voice. Woman from the bar."

"Woman from the bar." Fontonia laughed. Her voice was cold when she said, "Not everything is what it seems."

"Please! Please! Why?"

"I'm just here to chat. You have something I want – information."

"Don't hurt me again. I've done nothing wrong!" Sally's vision was returning to normal, though her eyes were still in awful pain. "Who are you? What do you want from me?" She twisted her head and looked at the base of the stairs. "Dad! Dad! Help!"

Fontonia smiled. "Your father is unconscious. I did that to him. And I'll do the same to you unless you cooperate with me."

"You hurt my Dad?" Sally whimpered. "No, no, no, no!"

Fontonia picked up Sally's half smoked cigarette and took a drag on the tobacco. "So, this is how it works. I ask you a question. You answer."

Sally was still sobbing, even though her tears stung like Hell as they coursed down her bruised face and intermingled with blood. "Let me go. I don't know anything about anything."

Fontonia stubbed the cigarette out. "A few days ago four men died while sailing a trawler. They were washed up on a beach near Stanley. You know those men."

"Debbie... Debbie, I..."

Fontonia snapped, "My real name's not Debbie. Come on Sally! Work out a lie when one slams you in the face! Stay focused! If you do, I'll leave you alone. You knew the men, yes?"

Sally's head slumped.

"Head up! Look at me!"

Sally lifted her head. In doing so, pain shot down her spine. "I knew the men. They used to drink in my pub." She was shaking with uncontrollable emotion.

Fontonia lit a fresh cigarette from Sally's packet and placed the cigarette in her mouth. "A couple of puffs might calm your nerves."

Sally inhaled smoke, coughed, and spat the cigarette onto the carpet.

Fontonia used the soul of her boot to extinguish the cigarette. "We must be careful. We don't want there to be an accident."

Sally was moaning. "Who are you?" she repeated.

Fontonia's tone of voice remained calm and icy as she replied, "Who I am is of no relevance to you. And who you are is of no relevance to me. All that matters is what you know about the four dead men."

Sally shook her head while continuing to shake. "What's there to say? Eddie Wilson was a fisherman. Billy Green also worked on Wilson's boat. Rob Taylor was a farmer. Mike Jackson divided his time between being a lighthouse keeper and a fireman." Defiance entered her demeanour. "Are you telling me the truth about my Dad? If you are I'll make sure you rot in hell. The police and the military here know me and my Dad well. You'll never get off this island. They'll put you in prison for life. Or they'll shoot you on sight."

"Let them try. Maybe I didn't hurt your father. Maybe I just tied him up and gagged him. Either way, one thing's for sure – he can't help you now. Tell me more about the men."

Sally breathed deeply. Though she was still in shock, she tried to summon strength in order to get out of this situation. Anything she said about Wilson and his friends couldn't hurt them. They were dead. Compliance with the woman in front of her was her only option. Survival was all that mattered now. "They used to come to my pub. They used to sit at the bar. They didn't talk much. They'd usually stay until closing time. Then they'd go home."

"Who else drank with them?"

"No one."

Fontonia slapped her hard on the face. "Who else?!"

Sally was wincing as she repeated, "No one. There'd be others in the pub, but the men would never mix with them. Wilson, Taylor, Green, and Jackson only ever drank together."

"Before they died, they were in your pub. What did they say?"

Sally stared at her.

"What did they say?!"

Sally wished she could rub her eyes. "There's been an Argentinian ship watching the islands for a couple of months. We all knew about it. Wilson and his mates got drunk that night. They said they were going to drive Wilson's boat out to the ship and once and for all get rid of it. I told them not to do something so stupid. They left. That's the last time I saw them. And that's all I know!"

Fontonia withdrew a hunting knife and tossed its hilt back and forth between her hands. "On the night they died, there was a fifth man on the boat. Who is he?"

Sally stared at the razor sharp blade, her eyes wide with fear. "I don't know!"

"Yes you do," said Fontonia in a slow and deliberate voice.

"I'm telling you the truth! You're not the first person to ask me this."

Fontonia held the knife in one hand. "Who else has approached you on this matter?"

Sally kept her eyes on the knife. "Two detectives from London. At least, that's who they told me they were. Do they work for you?"

"Give me their names and I'll let you know."

"Ben Sign and Tom Knutsen. They said they were staying at Mount Pleasant."

"Ah yes. They're colleagues, though are working through this matter from different angles. I hope you cooperated with them."

"I told them what I told you; that I know nothing about a fifth man! Who do you all work for? Military? Intelligence? Police?"

"Something like that." Fontonia said, "Tell me about someone Wilson or his friends might know who has access to guns."

"What?"

"It's relevant to our investigation."

Fresh tears were streaming down Sally's face. "Lots of people on the islands have guns. Hunting rifles. Shotguns. That kind of thing. They have to register them with the police. It's all tightly controlled."

Fontonia smiled. "Shotguns and small calibre hunting rifles would be no match for a ship. I'm wondering if there's a man on the islands who has access to military-grade weapons. You may know that person."

Sally's head slumped again. "Don't know. I don't know."

"Yes, you do. You just need something to jolt your memory." Fontonia walked up to Sally and placed the tip of the knife against her stomach. "If I put this knife into your gut – and, trust me, I'm very willing to do so – I will ensure that I miss your vital organs. I will have done you a kindness. It would be possible that you could survive the wound. But, there would be a downside. The knife will have penetrated your stomach lining. You'd have massive internal bleeding. And if the knife was pulled out without an expert medical team present, you'd bleed out within twenty minutes. Or die from shock. RAF Mount Pleasant has a superb unit of combat paramedics with access to helicopters. They're on permanent standby. If I called the base, the unit would be here in minutes. They'd treat you here and evacuate you to the base. They have surgeons on the military compound. They'd treat you as if you were an injured war combatant. You wouldn't get better medical care anywhere else in the world. I'd make that call, providing you cooperate with me." Fontonia angled her head. "Do you want me to put the knife in you and take your chances? You decide. Who on the island has access to military grade weapons?"

Sally was petrified.

Fontonia stared at her.

Sally sucked in air. "Terry…"

"Yes?"

"Terry Maloney."

"Where does he live and why does he have the weapons?"

Sally gritted her teeth and closed her eyes. "He's got a farm and shooting range in Goose Green west of here, halfway across the east island." She tried to move her hands but they were bound too tight. "He's an islander but is contracted to the army. He lets them use his range for target practice."

"That's good Sally." Fontonia crouched in front of her. "Do you think Maloney might have been the fifth man on the boat?"

"I… I don't know."

"Have you met him?"

Sally shook her head. "My Dad told me about him. My Dad and some other men once went up to the range to deliver sandbags and help make repairs to the shooting range. It was a cash in hand job. That's the only contact my Dad had with Maloney. Seems like he keeps himself to himself. He's never been in our pub."

Fontonia sliced the knife through three inches of Sally's jumper, ensuring that she avoided Sally's skin.

Sally rocked back.

Fontonia grabbed the chair to avoid Sally crashing onto her back. She sat back down on the edge of the sofa. I think you're telling me the truth." She faked a look of sympathy. And she lied. "Your father will be okay. You must understand that people like me are investigating a matter that affects Western security. I'm not from Tasmania. I work for the Australian government. And in turn we're cooperating with other nations. Sign works for the Brits. His angle is obviously to protect the islands. Knutsen works for the Norwegian government. His angle is to ensure Argentina doesn't inadvertently discover that Norway has a top secret listening post in the Antarctic. And my employers' interest is to ensure that Australian mining rights in the Falklands' waters are not jeopardised by covert or overt military action. To get to the truth of what happened that night, all of us need to take desperate measures." She sighed. "If you want peace and stability on the islands, it's best that you don't breathe a word of our conversation this evening. Tell your father the same. If you say anything, it would go bad for everyone you know who lives here."

"Why are you telling me all this?!"

"Because I want you to know that a few aches and pains in your body have not been for nothing. On the contrary, you've done a service to the Falklands. I'm going to cut you free and leave. You'll never see me again." Fontonia moved behind her.

Relief overwhelmed Sally.

Fontonia withdrew a standard-sized hammer from the inside of her jacket and repeatedly smashed it against Sally's forehead and the crown of her skull. She did the same against her stomach, the base of her spine, the parts of her abdomen where her kidneys and liver were located, and against her chest. It was impossible to tell whether Sally died from shock, a heart attack, brain damage, or organ failure.

But, she was most certainly dead.

And there was not a drop of blood on the chair or floor. The only blood present was soaked into Sally's clothes. She secreted the hammer in her jacket and searched the lounge, hallway, and kitchen. She found what she was looking for: the keys to the old Land Rover that Sally drove. Her father's vehicle was too modern and therefore of no use. She went upstairs and lifted the dead man onto her shoulder. It would have been easier to have dragged him downstairs, but that would have meant that a strip of the fibres in the room and stairs carpet would possibly be facing the same direction. A clever forensics analyst would be able to tell that a heavy object had been dragged in one direction. So, she carried him downstairs and gently laid him next to Sally. She went outside, entered the Land Rover, and reversed it up the driveway adjacent to the house. This location wasn't overlooked by neighbours. Plus, it was pitch black. She re-entered the house via the rear kitchen door, left the door wide open, picked up Sally's Dad, and laid him down on the jeep's back passenger seat. Back in the house, she untied the ropes around Sally, put the ropes in a pocket, and carried Sally to the jeep. She dropped her on top of her father. She re-entered the house and moved the chair Sally had been sitting in, placing it back into the spot it had been when Fontonia had first entered the property. Using a separate key on the car key fob, she locked the back kitchen door once she was outside. She got into the Land Rover, started the engine and drove northwest out of Stanley.

Twenty minutes' later she was in an area that was completely uninhabited and rugged. The sea was to her right. Wind was buffeting the jeep; snow was falling fast; the sound of waves smacking the shore were just about audible. She slowed the vehicle in order to find a spot off the road that would suit her purposes. It only took her a couple of minutes to find that place – a flat strip of land that was fifty yards wide and led to a cliff, beyond which was a forty yard drop onto rocks and seawater. She reversed up the coastal road, stopped, engaged the gears in first, gunned the accelerator, lifted her foot off the clutch, and droves as fast as she could, going through the gears as she did so. She yanked the steering wheel right and went off the road. She stopped and turned off the engine. The vehicle was pointing at the deadly drop. She got out and hauled Sally into the front passenger seat and her father into the driver's seat. No seatbelts were applied. The jeep had no airbags.

She leaned into the driving area while keeping her feet outside. She placed the man's foot onto the clutch, his other foot onto the accelerator, and turned on the engine. She pressed Sally's Dad's leg to rev the accelerator. Then, she put the jeep into fourth gear. This was important for two reasons: fourth gear would indicate the Land Rover was travelling at speed; it would also mean an extremely slow start when the clutch was lifted. She pulled the dad's leg off the clutch, slammed the door, and watched the four wheel drive vehicle amble at slow speed toward the edge. It went over. Even within the din of the weather, Fontonia could hear the crash on the rocks below the precipice.

And that was everything that needed to be done.

If cops could be bothered to analyse the road, they'd see that the jeep was travelling at high speed before it careered off the road.

All injuries sustained by Sally and her father would be attributed to the crash.

Fontonia's footprints in the snow would be obliterated by more snow, in minutes.

Sally's home was secure and normal – no blood, no sign of violence whatsoever.

The accident would be due to a tragic driving miscalculation within treacherous weather.

The only question the cops would be asking themselves is why Sally and her father were out at this hour and where were they going. That didn't matter. The cops would never get answers to that question.

She walked ten miles back down the coastal road. It was hard going, but she'd done far worse in her training and subsequent deployments. She reached her car, near Sally's home, drove it to her cottage, and called Casero. "Terry Maloney. He lives near Goose Green. He's got a gun range and access to military weapons. That should be our next stop. But, we also have a problem. There are two blood hounds down here, trying to find our target. I think they're British. Their names are Ben Sign and Tom Knutsen. What are your instructions?"

CHAPTER 10

The following morning, Knutsen gathered up logs from the wood shed outside the cottage. He carried as much as he could into the house. Sign was cooking bacon for their breakfast. Knutsen placed some wood into the log burner and got a fire started. He felt low and knew that Sign felt the same way. They were getting nowhere with the investigation. No leads. No breakthroughs. Nothing. He sat next to the fire and held his head in his hands.

"Cheer up, old fella." Sign handed him a bacon bap. "A hearty breakfast will put a smile back on our faces."

Knutsen ate in silence while Sign did his best to lighten the mood.

As he ate, Sign said, "People say I was the most successful MI6 officer of my generation. It's certainly a flattering observation. And it's fair to say that I've had a number of significant successes. But, for every great success, there can be ten other operations that end in failure." He smiled. "My goodness me, I've had some stonking failures. We all have. I've been caught in rough places by rough men and had to escape or blag my way out of the situation. I've run agents that turned out to be double agents, working for the other side. I've targeted individuals who I thought had access to secrets I needed, paid them money, until I found out they were fraudsters." His smile faded. "And on more than one occasion I've had loyal foreign agents simply disappear. They were my friends. I tried to track them, day and night. But they were gone. Vanished in Russia, the Middle East, Asia, places like that. Of course, deep down I knew what had happened to them. Snatched; interrogated; executed; bodies dumped in the sea, or similar. But I didn't give up looking for them until I finally accepted the inevitable." His smile returned. "Ask any intelligence officer, cop, fireman, doctor, or soldier, and they'll all tell you the same thing – no matter how expert we are there will always be matters that fall through the cracks. A foreign spy successfully persuades an MI6 officer that he wants to defect to Britain, wherein the truth is he wants to steal our crown jewels. A specialist police unit spends months observing a drugs warehouse, based on information from a snitch; armed officers raid the warehouse; it's empty; the snitch had tipped off the drug gang. A highly experienced team of firefighters try to rescue a mother and daughter from a blaze in their home; but they're too late. A senior doctor gives CPR to a man who's collapsed on the street; the man vomits in her mouth and turns green; he was dead before she could get to him. A sergeant and his eight-man commando unit come under heavy fire in Afghanistan; they're trained to deal with this; they fight bravely; but ultimately they have to beat the retreat or die. Failure. It permeates the sharp end of life."

"Win some; lose some." Knutsen finished his bap. "You're saying we should chalk this up as an inevitable failure?"

Sign leaned forward, his expression earnest. "I never accept failure. Nor do you. I know all about your incredible police record as an undercover operative. Men like you and I never walk away until the job is done."

"That doesn't mean we succeed."

"Then, sir, we die trying."

Knutsen nodded. "We need a lucky break in the case. We've already agreed that we can't tear the islands apart, knocking on the door of every Tom, Dick, and Harry who lives here. We have to try to remain under the radar. Right now we have to be reactive, not proactive."

Sign leaned back. "We are being proactive. Remember, we believe there is a four person Argentinian assassination unit on the ground. Possibly it's comprised of two men and two women, based on our analysis of the flight rosters. I've ensured that all routine police and military patrols west of Stanley are temporarily suspended, save for emergency situations. That frees up the assassination unit to cause mischief. We're giving them enough rope to hang themselves. And in the process, they'll lead us to the fifth man. As far as I can see that's anything but being *reactive*."

"How will they lead us to our target?"

"They'll do so because they'll deploy brutish tactics. They'll give us a paper trail."

"What do you mean?" Knutsen went wide eyed. "You mean they'll torture or kill people and we wait to see where it leads?! Jesus Christ, Ben!"

"I don't want that to happen. I just want them to make a mistake."

There was a loud knock on the door. Knutsen answered.

Colonel Richards was there, accompanied by a police constable. Richards said, "I need you and Sign to come with me. Right now!"

"What's happened?"

"The barmaid in the pub the men drank in on the night of their... drowning." Richards had to choose his words carefully because a cop was present.

"Sally?"

"Yes. Sally. We can't be exact on timings, but sometime around midnight she and her father drove on the northern coastal road out of Stanley. They lost control of their vehicle and veered off a cliff. They're dead."

Sign was now standing alongside Knutsen and had heard everything Richards said. He placed his hand on Knutsen's shoulder. "We'd best get our boots and jackets on."

Forty five minutes later they were on the area of rough land where Sally's vehicle and come off the road. In front of them was the cliff. On the beach below was the mangled wreck of Sally's Land Rover. A police officer was down there, searching through the vehicle. The cop who'd attended Sign and Knutsen's cottage with Richards wandered off while saying he was going to find the path down to the beach so that he could assist his colleague.

Now that they were alone, Richards could speak freely to Sign and Knutsen. "This looks like an accident. In all probability it was. But, I hate coincidences. Four men who frequented Sally's pub died. Then Sally dies. What was she doing up here?"

"What's north of here?" asked Knutsen.

"Nothing to speak of. It's uninhabited. The only reason the coastal road extends beyond this point is to help farmers access their sheep and to help my men set up camp to do their foot patrols. There's no reason why Sally and her father would be up here at such a late hour."

Sign asked, "Who was driving?"

"Her father. He owns the pub in Stanley. He has no debilitating health conditions and, like all islanders, he knows how to drive in snow." Richards pointed at the road. "The constabulary has done an accident assessment. The jeep was driving normally on the road; speed in the region of fifty miles per hour. For some reason it lost control, came off the road, drove over the patch of land we're standing on, and went over the cliff. Seatbelts weren't on. There are no airbags in the vehicle. Sally and her father died on impact. Their bodies are at the hospital. Sally's father had a broken neck and broken limbs, as well as lacerations to his torso. Sally also had many lacerations, but she died from massive blows to the head. The lacerations would have come from the shattered windscreen and shards of metal from the doorframes. The blows to the head and neck would have come from the dashboard." Richards walked right up to Sign. "I know you interviewed Sally. Did you spook her? Maybe she didn't tell you the whole truth." He pointed north. "Maybe the fifth man is out there somewhere and she was going to see him. Possibly she was trying to warn him that you two were snooping."

Sign nodded. "You could be right. Were there provisions in the car? Food? Blankets? Clothes? Anything that might assist a man on the run?"

"There was the usual cold weather emergency provisions that islanders carry in their vehicles at this time of year – a tent, spare fuel, sleeping bags, water, tyre chains, torches, oil, tinned rations, a flare gun, et cetera."

"Most of which could be useful to a man who is in hiding. Were one or both of them carrying mobile phones?"

"No."

"That's odd. People driving in these conditions tend to carry phones in case of emergency." Sign peered over the edge of the cliff. "I presume you found the phones at their house."

"They didn't use mobile phones. We've checked. Sally's father had a radio transmitter that linked him to the police. But on the night of the crash he wasn't carrying it."

Sign nodded. "The accident investigation is in good hands. There's nothing we can do here."

Richards grabbed Sign by his collar. "What you can do is tread more carefully! This accident smacks of distraction. Sally and her father took their eye off the ball while driving. You made them scared. And desperate to help the fifth man."

Sign disagreed but didn't say so. "I'd take your hand off me if I were you."

Richards smiled. "Why?"

"Because Mr. Knutsen is pointing his gun at your head. And trust me – he'll have no qualms about pulling the trigger."

Richards slowly turned. Knutsen was behind him, the muzzle of his handgun inches from Richards' skull. Richards released Sign. "Maybe I should never have got you two involved in this!"

"Only you can decide. But, it's too late now. We've been commissioned by the British Ministry of Defence and we'll see this project through to fruition." Sign crossed his arms. "What gear was the jeep in when it crashed?"

"Fourth gear." Richards was impatient. "It shows they were driving at speed."

"Yes." Sign held out his hand. "I'd like the keys to Sally's home, and her address."

"It's already been searched! There's nothing in there that gives any clues as to the whereabouts of the fifth man."

"I'm sure you're right. But there's never any harm in having a fresh pair of eyes and all that. Colonel – the keys and address! And be quick about it! I'll return the keys to your base once we're done."

"I'll come with you."

"There'll be no need. Drop us back at our cottage. We'll drive to Sally's house ourselves."

Knutsen's gun was still pointing at Richards' head.

Sign nodded at his colleague.

Knutsen lowered his weapon.

Richards sighed. He gave Sign the keys and the address. "Look – there are accidents on the islands. It comes with the territory. But, right now it's a sensitive time. The islanders have lost four of their sons. Now they've lost one of their daughters. In the space of a week. I'm here to not only protect the islands from an Argentinian invasion; I'm also here to keep the peace. Tread lightly." He turned to Knutsen. "And if you ever pull a gun on me again I'll walk through you and make sure you disappear. Do you understand me, soldier?"

Knutsen held his ground and smiled. "Let's hope it doesn't come to that, *sir*."

"Good." Richards' anger receded. "There's someone you should talk to. His name's Terry Maloney. He lives near Goose Green. Call my secretary and she'll give you the exact address. He runs a gun range. Sometimes we let our soldiers do target practice on the range."

Knutsen asked, "Does he have military weapons? Specifically SLRs and Brownings?"

Richards shook his head. "Islanders are not permitted to have military weapons of any sort. Maloney's no exception. But, he is a gun enthusiast. If someone is illegally in possession of trophies from the war, maybe he knows who that person is."

"Maybe Maloney is the fifth man." Knutsen placed his gun under his belt.

"Impossible. Maloney has one hand after he had to have the other amputated a few years ago. He was firing one of my men's assault rifles on the range, under supervision. He got carried away and momentarily ignored instructions. The rifle discharged and mashed his hand. There's no way he could have rowed to shore from Wilson's boat. Plus, he's seventy years old. He doesn't strike me as someone willing or able to get on a boat at midnight with four drunken sailors."

Sign made no attempt to hide his irritation. "Why didn't you tell us about Maloney before?"

"Because I didn't know about him until 0400hrs this morning. Turns out my troop commanders knew about him and secretly used his range. They knew I'd never allowed that breach of protocol. But I overheard two of my sergeants talking about him and moaning that they couldn't wait to get back on patrol and fire off some rounds on Maloney's range. I spoke to the sergeants and they confessed that they'd been out to Goose Green regularly. I told them they could face disciplinary charges for not only using the range, but also for falsifying records of ammunition taken out on patrol and ammunition accounted for when they return. We're supposed to know the number of every single military bullet in our base. Any discrepancies have to be investigated. Alas, I'm a busy man. I defer that responsibility to my troop commanders."

Sign was deep in thought. "Don't discipline your sergeants. Just give them a stern telling off. We don't want Maloney to be at the forefront of their minds."

When they were back at the Bluff Cove cottage and Richards was gone, Sign said to Knutsen, "Don't worry about Richards. He's juggling balls. I don't blame him for being tense. Come on, let's go."

They drove to Sally's house. Once inside, Knutsen said, "I'll start searching the place."

"Not yet," said Sign. "Follow me." He went upstairs and looked at Sally's bedroom. He entered her father's room and looked around. The bed hadn't been slept in. He looked at the adjacent computer desk. The laptop looked like it was switched off. He moved the computers mouse. The screen lit up and required a password to activate the desktop. The laptop hadn't been shut down; it had gone into sleep mode due to hours of inactivity. He examined the chair in front of the desk, rocking it back and forth. The wood creaked with each movement; its legs were a fraction loose. He got prone on the floor and examined the carpet. He got to his feet and walked downstairs. Knutsen followed him into the lounge. The small smart TV was on standby mode. Sign picked up the controller and pressed the enter button. The TV activated and showed the YouTube home page, with subcategories. He spun around and looked at the chair where Sally had been murdered. He sat on it, intertwined his fingers and closed his eyes. Knutsen knew him well enough to leave him in peace when he became like this. Knutsen began an expert search of the house, opening drawers and cabinets in the kitchen, bathroom, and bedrooms, looking under beds and behind pictures, lifting furniture, examining paperwork in the father's desk, and doing many other things. He was looking for any clue as to why Sally and her father would have driven away from their home at such a late hour. He found nothing of interest. Ignoring Sign, he searched the lounge. Once again, he saw nothing unusual.

He said to Sign, "This has been a waste of time."

Sign opened his eyes. "Not exactly. We must leave. We need to visit Terry Maloney. But first we must drop Sally's house keys off at RAF Mount Pleasant. We don't want to infuriate Richards further by not adhering to our word to him."

Javier Rojo pulled his car up outside Terry Maloney's cottage. Surrounding the property was a rolling landscape. In spring and summer, heather, waterlogged gullies, and rocks would have been visible in the rugged countryside. Now, as far as the eye could see, a blanket of snow covered everything. Maloney's place was two miles west of Stanley. It was a location where a man could find peace and solitude.

Rojo was wearing winter gear and boots. He trudged through snow but didn't knock on the door. Instead, he walked around the property, and stopped. Facing away from the property, he placed his hands in his pockets and hunched to make it look as if he was cold. In truth, he didn't feel the chill. He'd operated in far worse climates and was adept at training his mind to zone out from any discomforts afflicting his body. He stared at the gun range. It was one hundred yards away from the house. He walked to the range. Like everything else around here, it was covered with snow. But, based on his knowledge of ranges, and the shapes and other indicators, he could visualise how it looked when clear of snow. There were sandbags at the end of the fifty yard range, low metal fences either side of the four-lane alley, more sandbags at firing stations, a waist-height metal box for spent cartridges, a separate unit for fire extinguishers and other emergency equipment, and two flags – halfway down the range, outside of the fences, that were operated by underground cables attached to switches on a post near the firing stations. A flick of one switch would activate a red flag – visible to shooters and telling them to lower their weapons, activate the safety catches on their guns, and under no circumstances shoot at anything on the range. The other switch would activate a black flag, meaning it was safe to commence target practice. On the range itself were posts that were grounded in troughs that allowed them to be moved to different sections and be fixed in place. Targets would be attached to them when Maloney or others used the range.

"Can I help you?" a man shouted. He was standing outside of the house, but made no attempt to walk over to Rojo.

Rojo turned, and walked over to the man. He smiled and said in a South African accent, "I was just admiring your shooting range. I bet you're looking forward to the snow melting so you can get the range active again."

The man looked suspicious. "How can I help you? Not many people come out here."

Rojo held out his hand. "Max Bosch. I've recently arrived on the islands."

The suspicion remained on the man's face as he shook Rojo's hand. "Terry Maloney. I own this place and pretty much everything you can see beyond it. How did you know about my range? It's barely visible in this weather."

Rojo shrugged nonchalantly. "Last night I had a drink with some locals in Stanley. They got talking and mentioned your range. I don't have any business today so I thought I'd take a drive out and do some sightseeing. I was intrigued by your range so thought I'd take a look." He smiled wider. "When I'm back home in Durban I like to spend a few hours on my nearest shooting range. It helps me destress after long flights."

"Are you police? Army?"

Rojo's smile remained. "Nothing as glamourous as that. I work for an insurance company. Can I come in? You'd be a lifesaver if you had coffee." He stamped his feet on the ground. "We don't get winters like this in SA."

Maloney laughed, his suspicious expression no longer evident. "Sure. But, if I were you I'd head straight back to Stanley after you've finished your drink. They've forecast more heavy snow in an hour or two. You don't want to get stuck on the Stanley road. Come in. I'll put the kettle on."

In the lounge was an open fire. Maloney placed two logs on the flames and used bellows to blow air into the fire. Once he was satisfied it was roaring nicely, he said, "Bloody heating in this place is faulty. Sometimes it works; other times it doesn't. If he can get here, I've got a man coming out this afternoon to take a look at the gas tank and heating unit. Keep your coat on and take a seat by the fire. How do you take your coffee?"

"No sugar. Milk if you've got it; no milk if you haven't." Rojo sat by the fire.

When he returned with two mugs of coffee in his one hand, Maloney also sat near the fire. His breath steamed as he spoke. "What guns do you use on your range in South Africa?"

Rojo beamed. "We get access to all sorts of crazy stuff. Assault rifles. Pistols. Machine guns. Crossbows. It's fun. I must admit I don't know the make and models of the weapons. The instructors just hand them to us, tell us how to use them, and we shoot at the targets."

Maloney smiled. "That does sound like fun."

"What do you use on your range?"

Maloney held up his left arm. "No hand, no shooting. Those days are behind me. Ah, it's mostly military patrols that use the range. When they're coming through here I let them camp on my land. They get bored. I let them fire off a few rounds. They like it, and it reminds me of the times when I could fire a weapon." He drank his coffee. "What's an insurance guy doing down here?"

Rojo pretended to look bored. "Just completing paperwork for a claim. I specialise in shipping. There was a vessel here that had an accident. The skipper's insurance with us. I guess he took out the insurance by shopping online for the best deal. He chose us. Doesn't matter that we're headquartered in South Africa. Most things are done on the Internet these days. But, there was an accident. When that happens we still need to do things the old fashioned way. My company flew me over to take photos of the boat, speak to the police and coastguard, get them to sign some forms, and then I fly back. It's all just a formality."

"Which boat?"

"A fishing vessel. Four islanders died while sailing it at night."

"Yeah, I know about that. Wilson, Taylor, Green, and Jackson. They drowned, I heard. Weather must have got 'em."

"That's my assessment. I have to visit their next of kin. I hate that part of my job – you know, meeting people when they're grieving. The only upside is I'll be there to get them to complete various documents so they get our insurance pay out. Then I get on the next plane out of here, whenever that will be."

"It'll be no more than a few days. The RAF bods at Mount Pleasant are good at keeping their runway clear of snow, even at this time of year. The only reason planes are grounded is because of high winds. The snow will last for another month or so. But, the winds will die soon." Maloney stood. "You'd better hit the road. This isn't a day for sightseeing."

Rojo swallowed the rest of his coffee. "You're right. But, before I go there is something you might be able to help me with."

Sign and Knutsen drove out of RAF Mount Pleasant, on route to Maloney's place, fifty eight miles west of Stanley. Knutsen was driving and had the windscreen wipers on full.

Knutsen said, "When I dropped Sally's keys off with Richards' secretary, I was told we shouldn't stray too far from Stanley today. Apparently the weather's going to take a turn for the worse."

Sign said nothing.

Knutsen carried on driving for another fifteen minutes, before saying, "You're very quiet."

Sign looked at him. "I'm thinking."

"Oh, I'm sorry I..."

"No, it's alright. I have been dwelling on matters pertaining to this morning." Sign rubbed his face and inhaled deeply. "I have a strong intellect. But, so do lots of people. What has always made me different from most other clever souls is my ability to read people and situations. It stood me in good stead within MI6 and it should stand me in good stead in this case. However, knowing *how* something happened is one thing. Knowing *why* something happened can often be a different challenge altogether. Colonel Richards lied to us this morning. I could tell. His story about overhearing his two sergeants talk about Maloney is, frankly, cock and bull. The question plaguing me is why he'd lie. Why did he know about Maloney and not say anything to us in London or when we first arrived here? The British guns on Wilson's trawler are integral to the case. They will lead us to the fifth man because he supplied the weapons. I'm convinced of that. Maloney has a shooting range that is laid out and equipped to accommodate military guns. It sounds highly improbable that Maloney is our man, but it's likely he may have an inkling as to who on the islands has access to weapons that were used in the Falklands War. It is also likely that the fifth man used his weapons on Maloney's range. So, why would Richards decide to withhold that information until this morning?"

Knutsen's mind raced. "There are a number of scenarios. He didn't think it was relevant, until this morning when the penny dropped that it could be a useful lead. Or, he didn't want it leaked to his bosses in London that he breaks rules by letting his men use Maloney's range. Similarly, he may be bunging Maloney a few quid for use of the range; in doing so he's misappropriating government funds. Or, maybe he doesn't want us to find the fifth man. This has all been a charade."

"Then why tell us about Maloney? And there's one thing I'm absolutely certain about – Richards wants to find the fifth man. He wants war. Nothing is going to take equal or higher priority over that imperative." Sign stared out of the window. "But your other points are salient. In my experience, ninety percent of the time people lie to cover their own backsides. Ten percent of the time they may lie for other reasons that are nothing to do with saving their skins; even then they may be lying to protect someone they care about." He nodded. "Roberts knew he was breaking operational procedures by letting his men use Maloney's range. And a stringent audit of his budget would show that a few hundred pounds here and there were taken out of petty cash and could not be accounted for. But that was okay until Wilson and his friends died. Richards was officially in the wrong, though one has to be sympathetic to the colonel. In a place like this it's hard for him to keep his men motivated, particularly when he's sending them on God-awful and boring treks across the islands. Keeping moral up is key. Richards had to use a stick to get his men off the base. But he also dangled a carrot – a chance for his boys to let rip with their guns on Maloney's range, in an environment that was wholly less sterile than the shooting range in Mount Pleasant. He didn't tell us about Maloney for two reasons: first, he hoped we'd have found the fifth man by now; second, he was embarrassed. The trigger point for him telling us about the rifle range was Sally's death. He suspects she was driving to see the fifth man. Richards doesn't want any more islanders to die on his watch. That's why he told us."

Knutsen smiled. "You have your answer. So, you think Sally was going to see the fifth man – either to warn him off, or supply him, or both?"

"No. I think she and her father were murdered."

Knutsen glanced at him. "Driven off the road?"

"I very much doubt that. You and I have both done offensive and defensive driving courses. The stretch of land between the road and cliff is approximately fifty yards long. And a Land Rover is a heavy vehicle. If someone driving another vehicle smashed into Sally's jeep, it may possibly have caused the Rover to go off road. But there was ample time for Sally's father to stop the vehicle before the plunge. I don't think the murders took place in the countryside where their bodies were found. I think they were killed in Sally's house."

Knutsen frowned. "There's no evidence of any struggle in the house. I've worked murder scenes when I was a cop. There are always signs that something bad had happened."

"Not when highly trained spies are involved. The father's computer was still on, though it had gone to sleep. It's not a weak assumption to make that he would have shut it down before driving. Sally's TV was on standby. She was watching music videos. And we know it was her because, given his age, it is far less likely that her father was watching young rock bands on the television. So, Sally was in the lounge; Sally's father was in his room. That, I believe, is the correct deduction. The father's chair was rickety. Maybe it had been that way for a while. Or maybe something put a strain on it on the night of his death."

"All of that makes sense, but there's no evidence of foul play."

"Correct, Mr. Knutsen. Therefore, now we must explore my imagination based on my experience of these types of matters. What would I have done if I was their killer? We must ascertain the *how* before addressing the *why*." Sign pictured himself approaching Sally's house. "Sally was facing the front of the house. If I force entry through the front door, Sally will see me in the hallway. She will scream. Her father will rush downstairs and realise why Sally is so perturbed. I then have two problems to deal with at once. Probably I could deal with that but it doesn't serve my purpose because I want quality time with Sally alone. If she's witnessed me seriously assaulting her father, she will be too traumatised to help me. So, I enter the house through the rear kitchen. Sally is oblivious to my presence. I'm silent as I take each step, though I'm assisted by two factors: the volume of Sally's music and the fact that if there's anyone upstairs and they hear a creak on the stairs they'll assume Sally's going to the bathroom. I glance in Sally's bedroom. It's in darkness. I move to the next bedroom. A man is sat at his desk, his back to me. He's on his laptop. The man's of no use to me. I grab his head and jaw, rock him back in his chair so that he's off balance, and twist his head as if I'm removing a corkscrew. I put the man's chair upright and leave the corpse there. I return downstairs, approach Sally from behind, and inflict significant injuries on her. But I don't use weapons and I'm careful not to draw blood. I tie her to a chair and talk to her. I will tell her that her father's unconscious but he'll be fine. I question her about Wilson, the fifth man, and the guns." Sign paused. "This is where we get into the realms of the unknown. We therefore need to further stretch our imaginations to conjure up what Sally might have said to her assailant."

"It's probable she said nothing of value to her interrogator. She told us she knew nothing."

"But, we weren't putting the thumb screws on her. That said, I don't think she knew who the fifth man is. She was genuinely upset by the deaths of Wilson, Taylor, Green, and Jackson. If there was anyone out there who could help us ascertain what really happened on the boat that night, I believe she'd want us to talk to that man. And if she didn't trust us, she'd call the police and give them the identity of the witness. She didn't know there was a fifth man on the boat until we told her. Or, so she says. But if she was lying to us, I believe she'd still call the authorities after we visited her and would have given them a name – most likely the call would have been anonymous. That call wasn't made. Sally carried on with her life, as normal. She wasn't withholding a secret. No. We can rule out the possibility that she supplied the name of the fifth man."

"I still think there's a strong probability she had nothing to say."

"You could be right." Sign frowned. "But pain's a funny old thing. It can jog memories, or bring to the fore matters that may now be significant. The assailant would have threatened her with further pain, maybe even death." He looked at Knutsen. "She'd have mentioned our names. Possibly she'd have asked her captor whether we were working with him or her. The assassin would have said yes. That means we're now targets. But, it's also possible that she remembered something else – maybe someone she'd met, or maybe the name of someone mentioned to her by her father or a friend." He breathed in deeply. "It is possible that name was Maloney. If so, we must tread carefully at Maloney's house."

"What happened next?"

"Sally was bludgeoned to death. Her injuries to her head would be consistent with a dramatic fall over a cliff, in a vehicle that had no air bags. The assassin carried the father downstairs and placed him on the back seat of the Land Rover. The assassin cut Sally free and also placed her in the back of the car. He re-entered the car and made sure the house looked normal. Then he left the house, locked the door, and drove the vehicle out of Stanley."

"Why didn't he turn off the TV and shutdown the father's computer? Surely, an assassin of this calibre would have better tradecraft?"

"He or she has perfect tradecraft. The Argentinians know about the fifth man. They're sure we know about the fifth man. The TV and laptop were left on in order to make it appear that Sally and her father left the house in a hurry. Any British official in the know about the fifth man would wrongly assume that the two publicans were urgently visiting him in the dead of night. But that lead is now dead to British investigators, because Sally and her father are dead. So, the assassin drove them a few miles up the coastal road, chose a spot to go off-road and send the vehicle over the cliff, accelerated hard on the road, swerved onto rough ground and stopped. He placed Sally in the front passenger seat, and her father into the driver's seat. The father's feet were placed on the clutch and accelerator. The assassin leaned in and engaged the gears into fourth. Land Rovers have sufficient grip and power to drive off in fourth. Fourth gear was important – it would indicate the father was driving at speed when the crash happened; it would also mean that – from a standstill - the vehicle would amble at one or two miles an hour until it was able to pick up speed. That meant the assassin could easily duck out of the vehicle after she removed the father's foot from the accelerator. The assassin watched the vehicle drop over the cliff, then walked to her car, most likely near Sally's house, called her colleagues to tell them what she knew, and vanished."

Knutsen nodded. "Do you think the assassin's left the islands?"

"No. I remain convinced that we're dealing with a team of four. They'll stay here until the job is done – executing the fifth man. Then they'll extract via covert means."

"If there's a possibility they're on to Maloney, I need to be prepared." He withdrew his handgun and gave it to Sign. "I cleaned it last night, but a lot's happened since then. Plus we've been out in this damn weather. Can you check it for me?"

Sign removed the magazine, expertly stripped down the gun, checked its working parts, reassembled the weapon, and placed the magazine back into its compartment. He handed the gun to Knutsen. "It's in perfect working order."

An hour later they were approaching Maloney's remote cottage.

Sign put his hand on Knutsen's arms. "Stop the car. Now!"

Knutsen could see why Sign had issued the instruction. Seventy yards away was Maloney's house. Parked outside the front was a pick-up truck. Next to it was a jeep.

Sign said, "On foot from here. We enter through the front door, with force if necessary."

They walked towards the house, their boots crunching in the snow and making depressions of up to six inches. It was hard going, and they had to keep their arms partially extended by their sides to maintain balance and avoid toppling over. The front door and its immediate surroundings were covered by a canopy. There was scant snow here. Any that had found its way onto the porch was regularly shovelled off the decking by Maloney. Knutsen stood on one side of the door, his back against the exterior wall. Sign did the same on the other side of the door. Sign nodded at Knutsen and held up three fingers, then two then one. Sign turned the door handle. It was unlocked. He pushed the door open. Knutsen swung into the entrance his gun at eye level. Sign put his hand on Knutsen's shoulder in order to guide him if the former cop got disorientated. It was the classic way that that small teams of special operatives worked when storming a building.

It all happened so fast.

Maloney was on the kitchen floor.

A man was standing over him, pointing a pistol at his head.

Maloney's face was bloody.

The man spun around to face Knutsen and Sign.

Knutsen shouted, "Drop your gun!"

The man looked startled.

Maloney kicked his stomach, causing the man to reel back by a foot, and lose his aim on Maloney's head.

While still off balance, the man shot Maloney in the chest, and turned to run out of the rear door.

Knutsen shot him in the leg.

But the man, kept moving, limping through the snow, a blood trail behind him.

Knutsen ran.

The man was heading towards the gun range. It was a futile escape. Beyond the range were mountains and nothing else. He'd either bleed or die from the weather conditions and terrain before he made much more than a mile on foot.

Sign rushed to Maloney and examined the wound. It was catastrophic. Maloney was still alive but would not be able to survive the injury.

Knutsen slowed to walking pace.

His quarry turned and raised his gun.

Knutsen threw himself to the ground, a fraction before two bullets were fired at the spot where he'd been standing. He kept his breathing calm, while maintain his pistol's aim on the man. He shouted over the noise of the wind, "Stop! It's no use."

The man staggered onto the range, turned, and fired more shots. The bullets were only just wide of their mark, penetrating the snow inches away from Knutsen's prone body.

Knutsen got to his feet.

Sign held the back of Maloney's head. "We're British army investigators. Who did this to you?"

Blood was pouring out of Maloney's mouth. His eyes were wide; his teeth gritted.

"Who did this to you?!" Sign repeated.

Maloney coughed and arched his back, his face screwed up from the pain. "He said…said…"

"Yes?!"

"Name… Max Bosch. Insurance. South African."

Urgently, Sign asked, "Did he ask you about someone on the islands who has access to old British Military guns? Did he ask you about a fifth man on Wilson's boat on the night Wilson and his friends died?"

Maloney nodded.

"What did you tell him?!

"Man comes here… my range…uses his guns."

"Name?!"

"Peter… Peter Hunt. Lives… lives on west island. That's all I told him." Maloney was struggling to breathe. "Then you arrived."

"Was Hunt on Wilson's boat on the night Wilson died?"

"Don't… don't know."

"Did he test his weapons on your range close to the date Wilson died?"

"Day… day before. Get me help. Please!"

Help was of no use. Maloney only had seconds to live. "Help is on its way. When did Hunt use the range before that day?"

"Two… maybe three months ago." Maloney went limp. He was dead.

Sign rested his head on the floor. In Latin, he muttered, "Mortui vivos docent."

The dead teach the living.

Sign ran out of the house.

The assassin was halfway down the shooting range, wildly shooting off rounds as he tried to make further distance from the cottage. Knutsen was at walking pace, following him, his gun at eye level.

The killer dragged his useless leg a few more yards, collapsed onto the snow, forced himself around to face Knutsen and aimed his gun in Knutsen's direction. He fired twice, but the bullets were nowhere near Knutsen.

Sign was running as fast as he could in the heavy snow. He had to get to Knutsen. His colleague's Glock 37 .45 calibre handgun would have punched a massive hole in the man's leg. Chances of survival were slim. But, like an injured and cornered tiger, the man was still capable of inflicting death on anyone who came near him.

Right now, the man wasn't going anywhere. He was three quarters of the way down the range. He knew there was no way out of this mess. There was splashes of blood all along the path he'd taken from the house.

But, he was ex-special forces.

He was Rojo.

He was a highly trained assassin.

He wasn't going down without a fight.

He had two more bullets left in his gun. It took all of his strength and willpower to raise his weapon. His hands were shaking due to adrenalin and shock. He tried to muster every semblance of control. He pointed the gun at Knutsen and fired.

Knutsen yelped and fell to the ground, just as Sign reached him. The bullet had grazed Knutsen's right arm. It was agonizing. Knutsen was breathing fast while lying on his back. He stared at Sign, who was crouched over him, a look of utter concern evident on Sign's face. Knutsen asked, "Do we need him alive or dead?"

Sign didn't answer.

"Alive or dead?! I can't use my right arm. And… and I'm shit at shooting with my left arm."

Sign looked down the range.

Rojo was trying to lift his gun. One bullet was left in the chamber.

"We can't allow him to make a mobile call to his colleagues. He has the information he needs. We must shut him down. He won't talk in prison. He'll never betray his associates."

"Then shut him down!" Knutsen thrust the gun into Sign's hand. "Shut him down!"

Sign moved away from Knutsen. He hadn't fired a weapon in years. He'd turned his back on delivering death by his hand. But, having Knutsen's pistol in his hand brought everything back. Maybe it was muscle memory. More likely it was training and decades of using a weapon in the most extreme circumstances.

Rojo fired his last shot. It grazed Sign's jacket but didn't touch flesh.

Sign walked fast down the range, firing two shots into Rojo's chest. He stood over the dead man and put another bullet into his brain. He sighed and crouched. He'd knew that later he'd feel emotion about how the day had unfolded, but now was not the time to dwell on such matters. He searched Rojo and found nothing – no ID, phone, wallet, receipts, maps, or anything else that might prove useful. He walked back to Knutsen. "How are you, dear chap?"

"Stings a lot, but that's about it. Pull me up." He extended his good arm.

Sign got him to his feet. "We'll get you sorted. Let's get in the house." When inside, Sign used Maloney's landline to call RAF Mount Pleasant. "My name is General Ben Sign. I need to speak to Colonel Richards urgently." When Richards was on the line, Sign said, "I need you to come to the house belonging to the man you mentioned to me this morning. Bring three trusted men who are privy to the knowledge about the fifth man. Also bring two body bags, bleach, a mop, bin bags, and shovels. Two of your men must not be squeamish and must understand how to leave a house pristine after a killing. The third needs to be medically trained to deal with a minor gunshot wound. He must bring supplies." The colonel tried to reply, but Sign snapped, "Just do it now!"

It took Richards and his three soldiers two hours to arrive at the scene. They'd made excellent time, given Richards would have had to assemble his men and their kit before making a drive that ordinarily would take at least an hour and a half, usually more in this weather.

Richards entered the house with his soldiers. "What are we looking at?"

Sign pulled him to one side, out of earshot of Richards' men. He had to partially tell the colonel the truth, and partially lie. "The man on the floor is Maloney. He needs to be disposed of. The site around the killing needs to be sanitised. I can tell you how to do that, if you like."

"I know how to do it!"

"There's another dead man on the shooting range. He killed Maloney. Knutsen and I had to shoot him. He also needs removing and disposing of somewhere. No one must know about this. The snow contains blood. It needs rotavating. That's what the shovels are for. More snow's coming, I know, but we need to cover the blood in case someone comes here in the next hour or so. No one must know what happened here."

"And what *did* happen here?"

Sign gave him a version of the truth, adding, "The man in the firing range was trying to kill us. He could be the fifth man, or a friend of his. He came here to shut Maloney up. But, I can't yet tell you for certain that I'm right. I need to continue my investigation to be sure."

Under no circumstances could he tell Richards that there was an Argentinian assassination squad on the ground. If he did so, Richards would be compelled to spring into action. Sign's under-the-radar investigation would have zero chance of progressing.

Richards nodded. "Okay. We'll dispose of the bodies and clean up the place. I'll make sure my three men don't talk. We'll patch up Knutsen. You're going to need to check the jeep outside."

"I'm not hopeful. Most likely it was bought with cash. It's untraceable. There'll be no car insurance, no road tax, nothing that links the car to its owner."

"DNA?"

Sign shrugged. "If you want to DNA test every islander, good luck with that. They might think something's a little off. It will set tongues wagging."

Richards stamped the ground. "Damn it." He composed himself. "You're right. This needs to be covered up." He glanced at Knutsen, who was being patched up by Richards' medic. "We'll sort this mess out. As soon as Knutsen's been attended to, I want you both to get out of here. Head back to your cottage. Lie low for the night. I'll try to find out the identity of the dead man on the range, though I'm not hopeful." He looked at the ground. "If he's the fifth man, you've killed the only hope we had of proving that Argentina committed an act of aggression on British nationals. There will be no UK retaliation. The Argentinian spy ship will have got off scot-free."

Sign said, "Come with me." Outside the cottage, Sign said, "There is a possibility that the dead man isn't the fifth man. In fact, I can't see why the fifth man would come here and kill Maloney. The fifth man is scared and in hiding. He might be worried that men like us might put two and two together and link him to Maloney. That's one thing. Shooting a man in cold blood is another matter altogether. Trust me on that."

Richards did. He'd seen a lot of death during his time in the SBS. "We'll sink the killer and Maloney in the sea. They'll never be found. That may be the end of the case. If so, you and Knutsen will be on the next flight out of here, once flights resume."

Sign couldn't let that happen. Quietly, he said, "This isn't dead in the water. There's still hope. Give me and Knutsen a few more days to find out if the fifth man's still alive. By the way, that's not a request. We'll do what we like. I'm just being polite to you."

Richards laughed. "You really are a piece of work. Okay, I'll grant you that window. But, if the killer isn't the fifth man then who is he?"

"My guess is he's a private investigator, contracted by Argentina to source the fifth man. He failed; we won. Argentina can't deploy another investigator to the islands while this weather holds and flights are cancelled. We bury this and we bury it fast."

Richards nodded.

Knutsen emerged from the house. His arm was strapped to his chest, but aside from that he looked well.

Sign said, "Mr. Knutsen. We need to examine the dead man's car. After that, it is time for us to make our excuses and leave. The colonel has this in hand. I will drive us home."

Casero called Sosa. "Our friend, Mr. R, has not called me. I've tried his mobile several times but there's no answer. Something doesn't feel right. I'll keep trying his phone over the next two hours. If he still doesn't answer, I will call you and Miss F and give you both fresh instructions."

Sign and Knutsen were back at their Bluff Cove cottage. Outside, it was getting dark. Sign insisted that Knutsen sit in front of the log burner. Sign lit the fire and went into the kitchen to prepare lamb cutlets seasoned with rosemary, mash potato, vegetables, and an onion and pepper gravy. When the dinner was cooking, he returned to the lounge, holding two glasses of brandy. He handed one out to Sign. "I know you're not a good shot with your left arm, but you can probably hold one of these." He smiled and sat opposite Knutsen.

Both men felt weary. Sign stretched out his legs. Knutsen was moving awkwardly in his seat, trying to get into a comfortable position. He said, "Sod this thing." He removed the sling, tossed it on the floor, and raised and lowered his injured arm. "Mobility's fine." He stood and walked to the dining table. On it was his Glock. He picked up the weapon with both hands, placed his left foot slightly in front of his other foot, slightly bent his knees, and aimed at a pot that was hanging from a meat hook in the kitchen. "Can you come here? I need your help."

Sign obliged.

Knutsen said, "Stand in front of the gun and place your palm against the muzzle. Give the gun two strong pushes. I want you to mimic the recoil of a .45 calibre weapon." Knutsen wanted to see if the action put his aim off. And he also wanted to know the effect it would have on his injury. Sign pressed twice. Knutsen nodded and lowered his weapon. "I'm good for head shots. My arm smarts a bit, but other than that I'm fully functioning." He placed the gun back on the table. Both men returned to their seats by the fire and sipped their drinks.

Sign asked, "How did the medic treat you?"

"He checked the wound to see if there were any bullet fragments or bits of cloth in the cut. There weren't. So, he disinfected the wound, put a local anaesthetic around it, and gave me three stitches. The stitches aren't going anywhere for a week. I asked the medic if I could exercise with my arm. He told me I could because the stitches are as strong as skin. I guess the sling was just for show – make me look like a wounded soldier." He smiled.

Sign rubbed his eyes. "I haven't killed anyone in years."

"I know." Knutsen watched his colleague. "How do you feel?"

"I feel like I had to do a job under extraordinary circumstances, but…"

"It still doesn't make it any easier. I'm sorry."

"For what?"

"For getting shot and leaving you to execute the assassin. I should have been more careful."

Sign shook his head. "You did everything right. We both know that things rarely pan out according to plan when guns are involved. That said, I truly regret that we didn't get to Maloney quicker. And I regret that I didn't advise Sally to stay somewhere safe until this matter was concluded. Their deaths are on my conscience."

Knutsen could see the anguish on Sign's face. "None of this was your fault. Sally and Maloney were murdered by Argentinian assassins."

"And I should have been one step ahead of them!" Sign slapped his hand against his thigh. "It was obvious that they'd speak to Sally, though I didn't anticipate they'd take such drastic measures. That's my fault. I didn't know that Sally was aware of Maloney and his gun range. That's also my fault." He downed his brandy in one gulp.

"You're being too hard on yourself. In any case, we can't look back. All that matters is what happens next."

Sign nodded slowly. His voice was distant as he said, "I must predict the future. And this time I must be accurate." His voice strengthened as he looked at Knutsen and said, "I don't think the remaining three assassins know about Peter Hunt. That information had only been imparted to the killer a second or two before we arrived at Maloney's house. The assassin had no phone on him. It would have been impossible to communicate Hunt's name to his colleagues. The protocol was simple and effective – the killer drives to Maloney's house; he carries no ID and mobile phone; the vehicle is either purchased or more likely rented for a week from a local farmer; it would have been a cash transaction; the assassin would call his colleagues when he was back in his accommodation. So, what happens next? His colleagues will be getting worried because they haven't heard from him. But, they'll not be overly worried for a few hours, just in case his silence is due to a misfortune – his car's broken down, something like that. But, we're dealing with professionals. There is the possibility that the killer placed his mobile into a waterproof bag and buried it a mile or so from Maloney's house, before arriving there. The assassin I shot is the man who entered this country using a fake passport in the name of Max Bosch. He's pretending to be a South African shipping insurance specialist. But wherever he was staying on the islands, he won't have used that name to secure a hotel room or holiday let. And when making the booking, he'll have switched accents to another nationality. He'll have also given the booking receptionist a different lie as to why he was here."

"We could make some enquiries. Knock on the doors of every hotel, B&B, and holiday cottage in and around Stanley. There can't be many of them."

"We could, but it will still take time. Moreover, we have three problems. First, I doubt Bosch has left anything compromising in his room, and even if he has what use will it be to us?"

"His mobile phone would be tremendously useful. It would give us access to the other three assassins. We could send them messages, pretending to be Bosch or whatever his real name is."

Sign shook his head. "I doubt they communicate via text messages. But if they do they'll have one-time codes that clarify the sender is legitimate."

"One-time codes?"

"They're unbreakable. If I send a message saying, *Let's meet at the usual RV in one hour*, I'll end that message with the word *Stradivarius* at the beginning or end of the message. The next message will have the word *Illinois*. Or random words like that. The code word can only be used once per message, and each code word is unique to the sender. The other assassins will have memorized Bosch's one-time code words before leaving Argentina. So long as he uses the correct code words, and uses them in the correct sequence, they know it's him sending the messages. And when they reply to him, he will know their respective code words. It's failsafe unless men like me can access the words. That is impossible. But, I suspect they're not using texts with one-time codes. I think they're calling each other, while being very careful about what they say on the phone. Reception on the islands is currently hit and miss. They won't risk a text message failing to be sent or received. Only a person-to-person call can guarantee that information has been relayed." Sign swirled his glass, even though there was nothing in it. "His phone is useless to us. The second problem we have is that Richards has added heavy weights to Bosch and Maloney and dumped them in the sea. We don't want to start making enquiries about a man fitting Bosch's description. It would undermine the whole point of making him vanish."

"And the third problem?"

"If we start making enquiries with multiple locals, we become visible to locals. And, if we become visible to islanders, it's only a matter of time before we become visible to the three assassins. That must be avoided at all costs."

"Because their next play is to find us and make us talk. We think Sally gave her killer our names."

"Yes."

Knutsen intertwined his fingers, ignoring the jolt of pain in his arm. "It would be *quite* hard to find us. Our cottage isn't registered in our names. Richards secured the booking. But..."

"There is Richards." Sign's eyes glistened. He liked seeing Knutsen work out what Sign had already worked out. It made him proud of his colleague. "Carry on."

"If the assassins are clever, they'll assume that Richards is somehow involved in our presence here. They might even deduce that he commissioned us to investigate the deaths of Wilson and his mates, and find the fifth man. They might think we're accommodated in Mount Pleasant. Or they might conclude that we're somewhere else, because we want to distance ourselves from the military base. Either way, the best way to get to us is through Richards."

"Correct."

"But, he's guarded by an army. The assassins know they can't get to the most senior British commander in the Falklands."

Sign wished that were true. "We must prepare for any possibility. The assassins are now desperate. And we know for a fact that they have no problem with torture. When they conclude," he looked at his watch, "any moment now that the assassin calling himself Max Bosch is missing, they will decide he's dead. They will check Maloney's house and decide that he too is missing, presumed dead. They will put two and two together and hope that Maloney told Bosch something of vital importance. But, Bosch took that information to his watery grave."

"Do you think that they'll assume you and I killed him?"

"Yes."

Knutsen was deep in thought. "Richards is an impossible target. Maybe they'll go for someone else who they think knows our whereabouts? Maybe the governor of the islands?"

"They know the governor won't be privy to this investigation. He'll be the last high ranking person to know about the fifth man and the possibility that his islands may be used as a launch pad for an assault against the Argentinian coastline. No, the assassins won't go after the governor."

"They'll go after Richards. You should warn him."

"I can't tell him about the assassins."

"Things have changed!"

Sign took Knutsen's glass, walked into the kitchen, and returned with more brandy for them both. "Change is in the eye of the beholder. It is up to Richards to deduce what we have deduced – that Sally and Maloney were murdered by an assassination squad."

"Oh come on! You can't leave Richards' fate to his own ability or otherwise to correctly deduce the threats around him. Tell him about the Argentinian operatives. Get him to summon the SBS unit in Antarctica. They'll hunt down the assassins and kill them."

"They'll be able to kill them, but they won't be able to hunt them down. They don't have our skills."

"Then, we track them down!"

Sign sipped his brandy. "You and I have a hunt on our hands, but it is not to chase assassins. Our focus is to get to Peter Hunt. We must stay rifle shot on that task. Richards can look after himself."

"But if he can't he'll lead them straight to us."

"We must take our chances."

Knutsen frowned. "There's something you're not telling me. It's not in your nature to be cavalier about someone's life. You wouldn't leave Richards hanging."

Sign placed his glass down and stared at the fire. "I've ensured that Richards is not at risk. He doesn't know this, but I've extended the lease on this cottage for a further week. And I've used my name to make the booking."

Knutsen was incredulous. "You're bringing the assassins to us!"

"Yes, and it will be all three of them. They won't take chances by just deploying one or two operatives."

"Jesus!"

Sign laughed. "Look on the bright side. The local agent I made the booking with only works nine to five. She's off work for the night. The assassins may canvas hotels and cottage lettings tonight. But if they strike lucky, it won't happen until tomorrow. We have a good night's sleep ahead of us." Sign drank the rest of his drink and stood. "Peter Hunt is our priority. I've Googled his name. Alas, there's no trace of such a man on the islands."

"That doesn't mean anything. Half of the islanders don't use Internet."

"Yes, and Hunt lives on the west island. Hardly anyone lives there. He likes to be away from the world and all its trappings. But, because he lives on such an uninhabited island, he won't be difficult to find." He looked around. "I need the car keys. Where did I put them?"

"Surely you're not thinking of driving somewhere tonight?"

"You're coming with me."

"What?"

"Don't worry. After today's events, you and I need to witness something pleasant. The journey won't take long."

Sign drove the car three hundred yards, pointed it at the sea, and stopped. Sign said, "Headlights remain on full beam. We disembark."

They got out of the car.

Sign pointed. "Can you see them?"

Knutsen could. Hundreds of penguins were huddled together on large rocks. "This is what you brought me to see?"

"Of course."

Knutsen smiled. "Before coming to the islands, I'd never seen penguins in the wild."

"And now you have. No matter how many bad things there are in the world, life goes on. Come on. Dinner's ready."

Casero called Sosa and Fontonia. He said the same thing to both operatives. "We must assume something unfortunate has happened to Mr. R. Whether Sign and Knutsen were involved cannot be determined. But we need to locate them and find out what they know about our target. Sign and Knutsen can then be disposed of. Sweep Stanley and any other place they might be staying in outside the capital. Get me their address. Report back to me. And then we'll pay them a visit."

CHAPTER 11

The following morning, Sign cooked omelettes with cheese and ham. He called upstairs. "Mr. Knutsen! Downstairs if you please. Breakfast is served." It was six AM.

Two minutes later, Knutsen emerged. He was fully dressed, though bleary eyed.

"You look like you slept in a hedge," joked Sign.

Knutsen wasn't in the mood for wise cracks. "Kept rolling in my sleep onto my injured arm. It's on the side I always sleep. For every thirty minutes I slept, I was awake for thirty minutes. I feel like shit."

Sign handed him his breakfast and made two mugs of strong coffee. As they ate in the lounge, Sign said, "Today we're going after Peter Hunt on the west island. Hopefully this will be the end of the case."

"It might be the end of our lives if the Argentinians get to us before flights are allowed to resume and Hunt can testify."

"True. So, let's enjoy our food while we can. We have a long journey ahead of us. I don't know when we'll next eat."

Thirty minutes later, Knutsen was sitting in the car, while Sign secured the cottage. He locked the back door from the inside, went into the lounge, pulled out a cabinet drawer by only two millimetres – the gap being barely perceptible to the human eye, stepped out of the cottage, and locked the front door. He got into the car's driver's seat and turned on the engine. "We must traverse the entire east island to get to the port at New Haven. That will take us several hours. The ferry crossing to Port Howard on the west island takes two hours. And when we get there we must meet a man who specialises in the conservation of elephant seals."

Knutsen shook his head and muttered, "Elephant seals? Why doesn't that surprise me?"

Sign drove the car away from Bluff Cove.

Sosa spent the morning visiting hotels and B&Bs in Stanley, plus booking agents who rented cottages in the capital or within a ten mile radius of Stanley. The seventh place she attended was a coastal house in the capital. She knocked on the door.

An elderly woman answered. "Yes?"

"Hello. I'm enquiring about your holiday let in Bluff Cove. I saw it advertised on your website."

The woman looked over her shoulder. "Lizzy. We have a customer." The woman returned her gaze on Sosa. "My daughter deals with bookings." She went inside.

Lizzy came to the door. "How can I help you?"

Sosa pretended to look distracted and emotional. "I'm looking for my uncle. His name's Ben Sign. I've been trying to call him, but his phone doesn't seem to be working. I need to reach him urgently. I have some sad family news. I wondered if he'd rented your cottage."

Lizzy frowned. "How do you know about our holiday let?"

"Your website. I…" Sosa wobbled on her feet and slammed a hand against the wall to maintain her balance.

"Are you okay?"

Sosa smiled. "I'm alright. It comes and goes. Pregnancy does weird things to the body."

Lizzy smiled sympathetically. "Is it your first?"

Sosa nodded.

"I've got two – boy and a girl. Trust me – pregnancy and childbirth is a walk in the park compared to what happens afterwards." She drummed her fingers on the hallway. "Are you a local?"

Sosa shook her head. "I arrived here a week ago. I need my uncle to go to England. We've got a funeral to arrange. It's…" Sosa started sobbing. "It's hard. I've got no husband or boyfriend. I've got to look after this," she patted her stomach, "myself. I shouldn't be down here, but we've got a very small family. No one else could make the trip. They're too old or ill. I just need to know where Ben is."

Lizzy said, "Wait here." She went further into the house and returned with a business card. "We normally don't give out the names of our guests to strangers, but under the circumstances I don't see any harm in letting you know that last night a Mr. Ben Sign secured our Bluff Cove cottage for a week." She handed the card to Sosa. "The address is on there. Please tell him that if he has to leave early, his holiday payment is non-refundable."

"I… I understand. And thank you. I've also tried emailing him, but have had no response."

Lizzy shrugged. "We get used to it at this time of year. Phones. Internet. During winter they're unreliable. When are you due?"

"Five months and two weeks."

Lizzy smiled. "Are you hoping for a boy or girl?"

"I don't mind. The bastard who got me up the duff has done a runner. Boy or girl doesn't matter, so long as they help me out when they're older." Sosa looked at the card. "Thank you. I'll drive to Bluff Cove now. Ben's always been good to my family. He'll make sure I get home safely."

Sosa turned and walked away. When she was out of sight of Lizzy she called Casero and gave him the location of Sign's holiday let.

Casero said, "We'll meet half a mile north east of the house, in one hour's time." He hung up.

Knutsen was getting bored because of the length of the journey across the east island and because Sign had to drive at less than forty miles an hour due to the weather conditions. The beads of snow striking the windscreen were playing havoc with Knutsen's eyes. God knows how Sign retained focus on the road. Knutsen said, "Let's play a game. We go through the alphabet. I choose a subject and start at A. You follow with B. Then it's my turn. You good with that?"

Sign sighed. "Yes, I'm *good with that*, to use your awkward strangulation of proper language."

"Okay. Subject is movie titles. A is Avatar."

"What's that?

"It's a sort of fantasy sci-fi blockbuster."

"Never heard of it."

Knutsen shrugged. "That shouldn't surprise me. B?"

"Buffet Froid."

"What?"

"It's a French film, made in 1979. What I like about is it's a Buñuelian depiction of the far-from-discreet crimes of the bourgeoisie."

Knutsen sighed. "This isn't going well. Look – can we just focus on films that might have shown at our local multiplex cinema?"

"I've never been to a multiplex cinema."

"Shut up! C – Captain America."

"That doesn't make sense."

Knutsen was exasperated. "Why?"

"Because grammatically it is illogical and from a technical standpoint it is false. What does *Captain America* mean? Moreover, you can have a captain who is American. But you can't have a captain of America. The rank of captain is too low. Only a president holds the entitlement to be referred to as *the president of America*. But even he or she isn't referred to as *President America*. Are you sure the film you refer to is real?"

Knutsen slammed his hand against the dashboard. "Forget this game. Let's play another. I spy with my little eye something beginning with *more fucking snow!*"

Casero stood by his car on the side of the road leading to Sign and Knutsen's cottage. He was wearing a fleece, woollen hat, gloves, waterproof trousers, and hiking boots. Fontonia and Sosa pulled up in their respective vehicles. They opened their windows. Casero called out, "Follow me." He got back into his jeep and turned off the road, driving down a farm track. After two hundred yards he stopped and turned off his engine. His colleagues did the same. He exited the car and waited for the two female assassins to join him. Like him, they were wearing Arctic gear. Casero said, "On foot from here. If you hear a vehicle, get off the road asap and take cover."

They walked back to the road and headed to the Bluff Cove cottage. Wind and snow battered their faces. They had to lean slightly forward to compensate for the gusts that were striking them. But this was easy. During their time in Special Projects they'd completed horrendously long winter treks in the Andes. And they'd had to survive in the mountains for weeks.

It took them fifteen minutes to reach the house. There were no vehicles outside and no internal lights visible. Casero silently gestured to Sosa, commanding her to cover the rear exit. She moved to the back of the cottage and waited, her sidearm held in both hands. He pointed at the front door. Fontonia tried the handle. The door was locked. It took her less than a minute to pick the lock and open the door. She stamped her feet to shake snow off of her boots and entered, her pistol held at eye level. Casero followed her. Both were silent as they swept through the house, checking every room for signs of life. When they were satisfied no one was here, Casero unlocked the rear kitchen door to allow Sosa to enter.

Casero said, "You two take the upstairs rooms. Leave no trace. I'm particularly interested in passports, other forms of ID, maps, phones, flight tickets, hire car purchase receipts, photos, and any hand-written notes. But keep an open mind. If you find anything of interest let me know. I'll search downstairs." The women were about to go upstairs. "Oh, and ladies – make sure this is an A+ search. Everything, repeat everything must be left exactly as you found it. Take photos if necessary, so you can reassemble items in the exact position you found them."

As the women set to work, Casero examined the kitchen. He searched cupboards, lifting up plates, bowls, pans, and the plastic cutlery tray to see if there was anything hidden beneath them. He looked in the bin, but didn't move anything. As far as he could tell, there was nothing unusual in there; only scraps of food, tins, and plastic disposable trays; certainly he couldn't see and pieces of paper that might contain information that was memorized before being screwed into a ball and discarded. He looked in the fridge. There was food in there, but nothing unusual. He went into the lounge. The log burner contained dying embers. But that told him nothing about when the occupants of the house were last here. Depending on the quality of the burner, the type of wood used to fuel it, the settings applied in air inflow and outflow, and the length and diameter of its chimney, a log burner could stay lit for twenty four hours or could extinguish in a fraction of that time. He opened drawers in a chest. Inside there were an instruction manual listing how to operate the house, emergency numbers for police, fire brigade, and the hospital, a few brochures on the Falklands and its attractions, and a guest book for visitors to write their feedback on their stay in the cottage. There was nothing in the cabinet that was personal to Sign or Knutsen. He closed the drawers, and searched the rest of the room, looking behind cushions on the armchairs, lifting up the chairs' padding, peering underneath the furniture, examining ornaments on the mantelpiece, and rifling through a DVD collection that was adjacent to a small TV. He found nothing.

Sosa and Fontonia came downstairs.

Fontonia said, "Upstairs has been sanitised. It's as if they were never here."

"It's the same downstairs." Casero sat in the armchair used by Sign and cursed. "We're dealing with highly trained professionals. They may be current or former special forces or specialist police. But, I think – given the tradecraft deployed here – that at least one of them has had significant intelligence experience. Shit!"

"We can handle special operatives," said Sosa.

Casero shook his head. "That's not what's bothering me. We'll have left a trace of our presence here."

Fontonia and Sosa glanced at each other, looking confused.

Fontonia said, "We searched the place exactly as you told us to. All items are inch-perfect in the same position we found them."

"Inch perfect isn't good enough!" Casero looked at the drawers. "Even a millimetre or two out of place can be enough to warn someone that an intruder has been in his house, if he knows we're coming and he's set us up for a fall." He breathed deeply. "Still – maybe it doesn't matter that they know we've been here. If anything, it might work to our advantage. They'll know they're dealing with experts. As such, they'll be under more pressure. Their ability to maintain their pristine standard of espionage etiquette will most likely falter."

"We don't have time to wait for that to happen."

Casero agreed. "We must assume that Rojo is dead and that Sign and Knutsen killed him."

Fontonia said, "Maybe the British military killed him."

Casero shook his head. "Let's work back from the problem. Sign and Knutsen were engaged by someone to investigate the murders of Wilson and his buddies. We must assume that the Brits are aware that there was a fifth man, so far unaccounted for, who was on the boat that night. They're as desperate to find him as we are. That's Sign and Knutsen's job – find the fifth man. But this is a *very* serious task that could lead to war. By extension, Sign and Knutsen are very important people. I find it implausible that Richards wouldn't know that Sign and Knutsen were on the islands. Most likely, he commissioned them to find the fifth man, or at least he was brought into the inner circle of military people who knew about the top secret deployment of the investigators. If I were Sign or Knutsen I wouldn't want Richards to interfere with my mission. I'd want to work off the radar and minimise the chances of locals finding out that their islands may soon be used as a battle launch pad. But now and again, I would need Richards' assistance. Sign and Knutsen killed Rojo; Richards cleaned up the mess. So, where does that lead us? And where have Sign and Knutsen driven to today?"

Sosa said, "It will be linked to Maloney."

"Yes." Casero looked at Fontonia. "Let's pluck out a possibility or two."

Fontonia thought it through. "Goose Green is a narrow strip of land on the east island. To its east are us and Stanley, plus a few farmers. To the west of the strip of land is not much apart from a chunk of the island, largely uninhabited. It's possible the fifth man lives there."

"Or?"

"He lives on the west island. There are no checks on the ferry between west and east islands. He could easily transport his guns."

Casero nodded. "Maloney is either dead or he's in protective custody. Either way he might have given Sign and Knutsen the identity of a man who used military grade weapons on his shooting range. If so, the investigators have gone looking for him." He stood. "We now have no leads, aside from Sign and Knutsen. Therefore, we must find them and see where they take us. But, we don't know what they look like, or what car they're driving. In this weather, only emergency services and farmers venture into the remote parts of the islands. Even farmers don't go out unless absolutely necessary; their cattle are brought into their ranches until the snow thaws. So, we have an advantage – Sign and Knutsen may stand out. I want you two to cover the western chunk of the east island, beyond Goose Green. One of you should sit tight in Goose Green – it's a bottle neck; every car passing through will be easily spotted. And one of you should take a drive west of there. I'm going to the ferry port in New Haven. I'll make enquiries there. Depending upon what emerges from those enquiries, I may travel across to Port Howard." He checked his watch. "Okay. Let's lock up the house and get moving."

Sign drove his vehicle onto the ferry. He and Knutsen were the only passengers on the boat. The ferry pilot was amazed when they'd turned up and requested tickets. He hadn't needed to ferry customers for days. But, he was a professional and had no qualms about making the crossing, even though the cost of doing so outweighed the price of the tickets.

For most of the journey Knutsen remained indoors, using his injured arm to lean against a wall and do a standing version of one-arm press-ups. The actions hurt, but were essential to get blood flowing and teach his arm to ignore pain.

Sign was on deck, the hood of his waterproof jacket covering his head, the collar of the fleece underneath rolled up so that it covered his chin. Only his mouth, eyes, and nose were exposed to the harsh elements. Snow and an icy wind lashed his face. His father had been a merchant sailor in his younger days. Until he passed away from old age, his father adored second hand book shops and antique dealers, searching for obscure books about naval history and exploits, old maps, ships' logs, souvenirs from early twentieth century explorations, and indeed anything that took his fancy because it reminded him of his own adventures at sea. Sign's father had been evacuated from London during the Second World War and had been relocated to the country. After his parents' death, he'd been placed into foster care, moving from one family to the next. That wasn't for him. He was an extremely intelligent boy, but didn't have the ability to stay on at school and go to university. He also had fire in his belly. Age fourteen, he joined the merchant navy. After six months of training, he boarded a train from Devon to Lowestoft in Suffolk. It was the longest journey he'd taken alone. All he had with him was a sack of clothes and his seafaring qualification certificate. The train journey, he'd often recount, was relentless. He was so scared that he'd fall asleep and miss the Lowestoft station. But he got there and reported to the port's merchant navy office that allocated work. In those days, one could choose which ship one wanted to be on, depending on which part of the world one wanted to go to. Sign's father had chosen to go on an old whaling boat that had been converted to carry food. It was bound for Bombay, as the capital was called back then. As he approached the boat, his sack on one shoulder, he looked at the rusty old vessel and wondered how it was possible for the boat to make the journey. But, he didn't hesitate. He approached the gangplank in order to get on board. It was then that a man emerged at the top of the gangplank – a six foot eight black man. He looked like a giant. Sign's father had never seen a black man before. The man walked past him without uttering a word. He smelled of fire. The sight of the man heightened his nerves and excitement. He was truly about to embark on an adventurous life that would take him to places and civilisations he'd only read about in books. The black man's job was to shovel coal in the ship's engine room. He, and other salty tough sailors – as foul mouthed as they were – looked out for Sign's father. They adopted him and gave him rules – he wasn't allowed to smoke, drink, or curse, until he was sixteen; when they got to shore, the older men would head to bars and chase women, but he wasn't allowed to come with them; when off-shift at sea, they could play cards and gamble with cigarettes, and he was allowed to watch but not take part; and he had to keep reading books so that he didn't become as illiterate as they were.

Sign's father travelled the world, on different ships, for the following twelve years. He went to places that, in some cases, were relatively unexplored. As a child, Sign would listen with awe to his father's accounts of giving a carton of cigarettes to natives in the Amazon so that he and a pal could borrow their dug-out canoes and paddle up piranha infested waters; doing a similar trip up the Congo; getting lost in Hong Kong and nearly missing the ship's departure time; sailing around the treacherous Cape Horn; and so many other adventures. But the one adventure that had captivated Sign the most was hearing about his father working on an icebreaker that was sent to carve a channel and free up a boat that had got stuck in the Antarctic. The icebreaker had also got temporarily stuck. His father and the rest of the crew spent three days on the ice, playing football and making snowmen to while away the time, before the ice shifted and they were able to get moving again and rescue the trapped boat.

As Sign looked south from the ferry, he felt like he was close to his father's adventure. He was holding a cardboard carton of black coffee. He raised it and said, "Dad – this is to you. Like father, like son. Without our adventures, there is no meaningful life." He drank from the carton and headed inside. "Mr. Knutsen. Port Howard is visible. We will be disembarking very shortly."

It took Casero four hours to drive to New Haven. The ferry was in port, having returned from Port Howard. Casero parked his car and entered the ticket office. He spoke with impeccable English to a bored-looking islander working behind the counter. "I wish to speak to the captain of the ferry. I'm on official business."

The islander looked nonplussed as she picked up a walkie-talkie and said, "Rob. There's someone here to see you. Don't know what it's about."

One minute later, Rob emerged from a room while eating a sandwich. His forearms were exposed and covered in black oil. He was wearing red all-in-one overalls and wellington boots. He looked at Casero. "You wanted to see me?"

Casero nodded. "Can we speak in private, in your office? I'm from London."

Rob shrugged. "Sure. Come his way." He led Casero into his office and shut the door. The room was tiny, with only a desk, two chairs, telephone, computer, overflowing ashtray, walkie-talkie, barometer, and maps of the strait between the east and west Falklands stuck to the wall. He gestured to the seat and took his own seat behind his desk, while finishing his sandwich. "How can I help you?"

Casero was composed as he sat down and replied, ""I'm on official business. *Military* business. Have you taken any passengers over to the west island today?"

Rob's eyes narrowed. "Do you have credentials?"

Casero waved his hand. "Call RAF Mount Pleasant and tell them that Ben Sign is making official enquiries. They'll vouch for me. Also, tell them that I've warned you that your shipping license will be suspended unless you cooperate with me."

Rob placed his hand on the phone.

"Make the call. I'm sure you have the number. But, if you don't I can recite it for you."

Rob lifted his hand. "What's a London military man doing down here?"

"Something that should be of no concern to you. All I want is a bit of information."

Rob dusted crumbs off his fingers. "I've only made one crossing today. Two men and their jeep. I got back twenty minutes ago."

"Who were the men?"

"Don't know." He picked up his walkie-talkie. "Sally – do you know the names of the blokes I took west earlier today?"

Sally replied, "No. They didn't use a bank card to buy the tickets. Only cash."

"Okay. Thanks." Rob placed the walkie-talkie on his desk and looked at Casero. "No names."

Casero nodded. "What did they look and sound like?"

"They sounded English. One of them had a posh accent. And I can tell you exactly what they looked like. Come around here." Rob was staring at his computer.

Casero peered over his shoulder.

Rob clicked on a file. "My boat has cameras. We have to for insurance reasons, in case there's an accident at sea." He spent a few seconds fast forwarding the video feed from the last crossing before hitting the pause icon. "There we go. That's them, getting out of their car."

Casero memorised the faces of the two men in the image, plus the number plate of their vehicle. "Did they say what business they had on the west island?"

"I didn't speak to them. I've no idea why they wanted to make the crossing on today of all days. The sea conditions were rough enough to make even me a bit queasy."

Casero sat back in the chair, opposite Rob. "Those men are of no interest to me. I know who they are. Like me, they're on official business. But, now I'm here I wouldn't mind visiting the west island. Would you take me?"

Rob looked at the wall clock. "Jesus! I thought I was done for the day."

"I will pay you double and put in a good word to the military base, saying you've been an enormous help."

Rob rubbed his beard. "I can do it, but I won't be able to bring you back today. You'll have to overnight it in Howard. I'll collect you 0900hrs tomorrow and bring you home. If you can't make that time, you're stuffed tomorrow. We're expecting a storm midday. No way am I taking my misses out there when that shit kicks off."

Casero smiled. "0900hrs return is perfect." He stood and held out his hand. "I'll get the tickets from Sally and see you on the boat in a few minutes."

It was one PM when Sign and Knutsen stopped outside a hut in the miniscule Port Howard. Sign pulled down on a rope attached to a bell, outside the front door. A man opened the door. He was in his forties, wiry, medium height, had tousled brown and grey hair, a chest length beard that was tucked into the neck of his blue hemp jumper, and was wearing corduroy brown trousers and boots that were strapped to waterproof calf protectors.

Sign said, "Mr. Oates. Ben Sign. We spoke on the phone. And this is my colleague Tom Knutsen."

Oates gestured for them to come in. The hut wasn't a residential property. It was purely one room and a toilet. The room was crammed with paraphernalia to do with conservation on the west island. There were books about fauna and flora on the island stacked on the floor, maps of the coastline with red pins pierced into various locations, post-it notes with writing stuck next to them, and photos of elephant seals and penguins, all of them with felt pen hand writing at the base of the shots, with the names of the creatures – Pink, Fat Boy, Gorbachev, Cleopatra, Grunt, Boss, and others. There was also a table that was strewn with papers and a bottle of rum. On the floor in the corner of the room was a tea urn. Oates picked up three dirty mugs, washed them in the bathroom sink and poured tea into them. He added a dash of rum to each mug and handed drinks to Sign and Knutsen. He sat on the edge of the table, took a swig of his stewed brew, and asked, "How can I help you."

There were no seats for Sign and Knutsen. So they stood and sipped their drinks. Sign said, "This is the first time we've visited the west island. We're seeking local knowledge and we thought you'd might be able to help."

Oates sniggered. "I'm not a tour guide." He pointed at the photos. "I monitor and sometimes help elephant seals. I also keep an eye on their habitat and feeding grounds."

Knutsen asked, "You work for the government?"

"Nah, mate. I work for a charity, though we do get funding from the Ministry of Agriculture, Fisheries and Food."

Sign said, "We're not looking for a tour guide. Mr. Knutsen and I work for the Ministry of Defence. We're based in London and are down here to do an independent survey of the west coast of the island."

"You mean you want to find out where the Argies would land if they assaulted this island."

"Correct."

"Those types of surveys have been done to death by your pals in Mount Pleasant."

"Yes. But Whitehall wants fresh eyes to analyse the island. So, they sent us. All we're hoping to gain from you is a little local knowledge. We were told that you know the island inside out."

Oates shrugged. "I guess I do. I've been here for eleven years." He placed his mug on the table and crossed his arms. "There's not much to tell you that you can't read in a book. The island's smaller than the east island, but not by much. We've got hills and small mountains on this side of the coast; further west it's flatter. Most people live in Port Howard, but there's not many of us. The last headcount of the island put the total at one hundred and forty one. The majority of adults here are sheep farmers. There's a handful of us who do different stuff."

"What kind of different stuff?"

Oates rolled a cigarette. "We've got a small school, petrol station, airstrips dotted around the island, a shop, one B&B in Howard, one doctor's surgery, and a few ports. They all need servicing and maintaining. We've also got two RAF remote radars – one in the north, one in the south. Sometimes we get RAF blokes out here to check they're working. They stay for days, sometimes weeks. Then they bugger off." He lit his cigarette. "Aside from that it's sheep, sheep, and more bloody sheep."

Sign asked, "What's the road network like here?"

"It's pretty good. It has to be because people rely on it to survive. But, there aren't many roads. All the farmers have quad bikes, or other off-road vehicles, so they can go cross-country when they need to. Think of this place as the Wild West; or more accurately some remote part of the Andes. There's no police or other emergency services here. If anything bad happens, we rely on people flying in from the east island. Trouble is, there are no flights at the moment. We're on our own."

Sign pulled out a piece of paper. It contained five names. Four of them he'd made up. "I have a list of people who may be able to assist Mr. Knutsen and I to analyse the west coast. That said, I concede the list may be wholly out of date or inaccurate. Would you mind taking a look at the list?"

Oates took the paper and looked at the names. "You're right. I've got no idea who four of these blokes are. I know everyone on the island. Either these four were before my time here, or your blokes in Whitehall got it wrong. Maybe they live on the east island." He prodded a finger against the paper. "But this guy, Peter Hunt. Yeah, I know him. He lives near Hill Cove. There's a direct road from Howard that will get you there. It's about a thirty mile drive. You can get there in under an hour."

Sign faked ignorance. "I must apologise. We were sent down here at short notice. We were given no briefing in London. They just told us to get on a plane and do the job. The only thing supplied to us was the list of names."

"And for the most part that was a crock of shite." Oates dragged on his cigarette. "How can Hunt be of interest to your Whitehall people? I know the coastline better than anyone. I can tell you what you want to know."

"But, you're not an islander, are you?"

"No. I'm from Devon. I did my undergraduate degree in Environmental Sciences at the University of Exeter and my PhD at the University of St. Andrews. Then I moved down here."

Though Sign had never been a smoker, he liked the aromatic smell of Oates' cigarette. It reminded him of his father's pipe tobacco. "Therein is the problem. We are required to obtain signed affidavits from a select number of islanders who know the west coast. Only islanders. We need to report back to London with statements about the locations islanders fear would be most vulnerable to an attack. For some strange legal reason, we're not permitted to obtain statements from non-islanders, no matter how expert their testimonies may be."

Oates extinguished his cigarette in his tea. "What kit are you carrying in your jeep? You need to be prepared for anything right now. I can lend you stuff if you need it. I'd drive you over to Hill Cove myself, but I've got a call with our North America office. I'm hoping to reintroduce wolves onto the island. I'd source them from the States. But, it's an uphill struggle because the farmers hate the idea. But, I'm still plugging away with the concept. We used to have wolves here. They became extinct in the nineteenth century. Sorry I can't be of more help today."

Sign smiled. "You've been more than helpful. Our car is carrying a tent, food, a gas stove, flashlights, flares, blankets, maps, knives, an axe, medical kit, spare clothes, tyre chains, tools, and spare fuel. We've come prepared."

"Sounds like you have." Oates rubbed his beard. "My dad was in the army. At one stage I thought about joining the military. But, you know how it is – boys tend to do the opposite of what their fathers want them to do. So, I chose this life."

"And you chose an eminently laudable vocation. If you do succeed in introducing wolves onto the island, I will come back. I've always been fascinated by wolves." Sign shook hands with Oates. "Good luck with your work, sir."

Sign and Knutsen left, got in their car, and drove towards Hill Cove.

It took five minutes for Casero to drive along Port Howard's coast road.. He estimated he had less than one percent chance of spotting their vehicle. Most likely they'd already driven away from the port. If that was the case, it didn't really matter. He knew where they lived. Whatever information they found on the west island could be easily plied out of them back at their cottage in Bluff Cove. But he was curious and persistent. He stopped his car, turned around, and drove back towards the port. That's when he spotted the car. Its headlights and windscreen wipers were on. Casero stopped his car, turned the engine off, and ducked down. He heard the car pass him in the opposite direction. He waited two minutes before sitting upright, engaging the engine, turning his car around, and following the route the vehicle had taken. It was the only route out of Port Howard. He drove close enough to the jeep in front of him, noted its number plate, and slowed down so that there was more distance between him and his quarry. The car belonged to Sign and Knutsen. Casero smiled, though was tense and alert. There was zero room for complacency. He tried calling Sosa and Fontonia but there was no mobile phone signal. He'd gotten used to that. He didn't need the female operatives for back-up. It would take them half a day, at least, to get here. Plus, he was armed with a handgun and an assault rifle with sniper scope. He could handle himself. But, it would have been nice to let the women know that they could stand down from the search of the western part of the east island. He drove onwards, following the road north west, before it bended to face south west. The road changed direction again, heading directly west to Hill Cove and beyond.

Knutsen said, "We've had a car behind us since leaving Howard. It's keeping its distance."

"I know." Sign was squinting to avoid his eyes getting disorientated from the snowfall. He knew it was unusual for two cars to be on the road in these conditions. "It could be innocent, but let's get the measure of the driver. Gun at the ready, if you please. It most likely is a farmer." He stopped the jeep on the side of the road. "Stay here. I don't want him spooked." Sign placed his hand on the jeep's roof and faced the oncoming car. He waved his hand.

The car slowed, flashed its lights, and stopped behind Sign's jeep.

Casero got out. His pistol was hidden in a pocket.

Sign called out, "We're trying to reach the coast. Do we take the left turn a mile ahead, or do we keep going west."

Casero walked up to him. "Which part of the coast are you going to?" His accent was pitch perfect Falkland Islands.

"Roy Cove. This damn snow is playing havoc with my bearings. We've got to get there before night fall. We're instructed to take samples of the seawater to test for levels of salinity."

"Scientist types?"

Sign smiled. "Yes. We're doing a survey. But we're not from here."

Casero pointed up the road. "You're going the right way, mate. Once you hit Hill Cove keep going for a few more miles. Then stop. You'll have to reach Roy Cove on foot. I'm heading that way myself, though not as far as Roy Cove. I'll stick behind you for part of the way. If you get in any trouble, whack your hazard lights on. I've got vehicle maintenance kit in the boot of my car."

Sign called out, "Much obliged. What brings you out here this afternoon?"

Casero rubbed his hands together. "I'm missing a sheep. Her son is pining for her like hell and won't eat. I've got to find mum, put her in my pick-up, and reunite the happy family. I can think of better things to be doing." He turned and headed back to his car. "Take it steady on the road."

Sign got back into his vehicle and drove. "We must be careful. It is possible that I've just met one of the Argentinian assassins."

Casero followed them. He knew they weren't heading to Roy Cove. No one lived there because there was no road access to the coastal location. That meant that instead of turning northwest off the road they were on, passing Roy Cove and heading to the uninhabited West Point Island, they'd stay on the road that led to Hill Cove. Only one person lived there. A mile north of the cove there was another dwelling. Beyond that, the coastal road continued for approximately six miles before stopping. Logically, that meant Sign and Knutsen were going to see one of the two men. He followed Sign's vehicle for fifteen minutes, flashed his lights, and overtook their jeep. He waved his hand while glancing in the rear view mirror and drove at speed. He wanted to be out of sight. He drove close to Hill Cove, but not too close. After driving his vehicle off the road for one hundred yards, he stopped and began covering his car with snow. Sign and Knutsen were at least a mile behind him. And given visibility was appalling, even when they drove past his disguised vehicle they wouldn't be able to see him or his car. He grabbed a holdall containing binoculars and a rifle, and set off on foot.

Peter Hunt was in his house, polishing boots and wiping down waterproof smocks with a wet cloth. He lived alone. He'd never married, and his parents had passed away a few years ago. Mostly, he farmed the adjacent remote land, though money was scant in the winter months. It was only when the lambing season was well and truly over that he was able to slaughter some of the lambs, sheer the older sheep and sell their wool, and have any meaningful income. Before then, running costs remained high. The sheep needed to be housed and fed, his stone cottage was leaky and cold and needed constant repairs, ditto his two barns, and his vehicles were in regular need of new parts due to the strain put on them. So, in the off-season he supplemented his income by doing other things – hunting for game and selling it in Port Howard, catching and smoking river and sea trout and gift wrapping them in string, straw, and wooden boxes, and posting them to delicatessens in England and France, cultivating herbs under LED grow-lamps and selling the crops to anyone that would take them, and getting cash-in-hand for helping other farmers on the island with repairs and supplies.

Hunt was forty one years old, five foot nine, had a weathered face that was tanned all year round, was bald, and had the strength of an ox. Like most farmers, he was a stickler for routine and hygiene. He bathed every day; his clothes were washed after every shift; his other kit and tools were cleaned regularly, and always after usage; and every morning and evening he always smothered Norwegian cream onto his hands and feet to prevent his skin cracking from prolonged exertions and exposure to wet conditions. And yet, there was no mistaking his aroma – he smelled like an animal.

He went into one of the barns. Inside were his beloved sheep. Separated from them, in a pen, was his ram. Perceived wisdom amongst farmers was that one should keep rams and sheep away from each other until breeding season. For the most part that was true. But Hunt had learnt that putting his ram in the same enclosure as the females helped bring a calming influence on the ladies. He didn't know why that was. But he knew it worked. He picked up a handful of nuts from a bowl and held them under the ram's nostrils. The ram had big horns, and was cantankerous, but he never attacked Hunt. His master gave him what he wanted – food, the opportunity to mate with the other sheep, a free reign of a stretch of land in the warmer months, and a cosy home when the weather was dire.

Most people wouldn't have been able to hear the car approaching – the wind was too noisy. But Hunt had an excellent sense of hearing. He had to have that; one survived out here by one's wits and capabilities. He walked back into the house and looked at the road. A jeep was approaching. That was very unusual. Even in the summer, not many people ventured out this far. The last time he'd seen another human being was a week ago, and that wasn't anywhere near here. He started feeling uneasy as he looked through a telescope that was positioned on a window ledge. The car was drawing nearer.

He didn't like this one bit.

He grabbed his daysack. It contained everything he needed if he had to bolt to rescue a sheep or attend to any other emergency. He placed it on his back and looked at his telephone.

Sign stopped his vehicle outside Hunt's cottage. "Let's tread carefully. Hunt will be suspicious of us, simply because he hasn't seen people out here for a long time. He will be exponentially on his guard when we start asking questions."

Sign and Knutsen approached the front door. Sign knocked. There was no answer.

Sign knocked again and called out, "Mr. Hunt?"

The door opened a few inches. Hunt said, "Yes?"

Sign smiled. "My name is Ben Sign. And this is Tom Knutsen. We're from London. We're investigating an incident that took place near Stanley. We're talking to islanders to see if anyone witnessed the incident. May we come in?"

"What incident?"

"Four men fell off a trawler at sea, a mile out from Port Stanley. They drowned. Their names are Eddie Wilson, Rob Taylor, Billy Green, and Mike Jackson. We want to understand what happened that night."

"Who's *we*?"

"Mr. Knutsen and I are accident investigators. We work for a London law firm and represent the interests of Wilson and his friends. There may be an insurance pay out. But, we need further testimonials before we can close the case. Anyone who can help us do that will be financially rewarded."

Hunt tried to look perplexed.

Sign could tell from his expression that it was an act.

Hunt said, "I only go to Stanley about twice a year. I read about the drownings in the paper, but I wasn't anywhere near Stanley when it happened. You should be talking to people in the capital, not people on the west island."

Sign maintained his smile. "We're trying to cover all bases. So far we're not making progress. The men were carrying weapons on the ship when they died. We understand that you're a weapon enthusiast. We are speaking to people like yourself to see if there's anything you might know about the men's state of mind when they sailed out on the night of their deaths. *Please* may we come in? It's dreadfully cold out here."

Hunt didn't buy that Sign and Knutsen were who they said they were. His stomach was in knots. "Okay. Just give me a moment." He shut the door.

Signed snapped at Knutsen. "Cover the back!"

Sign tried to open the door, but it was locked. He kicked the door, near the handle, but it held fast. He heard an engine start up. The sound was coming from the back of the house. He raced as fast as he could to the rear of the property. One hundred yards away was Hunt, driving a red snowmobile. Knutsen was pursuing him on foot, but the vehicle was too fast and was making ground.

Sign shouted, ""Tom. Our jeep. Now!"

Sign ran their car, and drove it a few yards beyond the house. He stopped. Knutsen jumped in.

Knutsen was breathless. "He was on the snowmobile before I could get to him."

Sign drove the jeep as fast as he dared in the slippery conditions. The snowmobile was still visible, driving north along the road. "Where's he heading?"

"As far away from us. Is my guess." Knutsen rubbed his injured arm. "I could have shot him, but what would have been the point in that - shooting a witness?"

"You made the right decision. We need him alive." Sign tried to keep pace with Hunt. "He's scared. We just need him to come to his senses when he realises there's nowhere to go."

Sign was gaining on Hunt. He was one hundred yards behind him. Hunt looked over his shoulder, pulled down fully on the throttle, and drove his snowmobile off the road. He was now on undulating land, travelling at fifty miles per hour.

"No!" shouted Knutsen. "Our jeep won't make it out there. Let me out. I'll go after him on foot."

Sign stopped the car. Both men disembarked and ran along the tracks the snowmobile had carved in the snow. Hunt was at least three hundred yards away. Knutsen was holding his handgun, but the distance was too great to put a shot into the snowmobile to try to immobilise the vehicle.

Sign slowed to a walk and placed his hand on Knutsen's shoulder. "We stand no chance. We know where he lives. He can't escape the inevitable."

They turned to walk back to their jeep.

As they did so they heard a loud bang. It was unmistakably a rifle shot. They spun around. Hunt was motionless on the ground. His snowmobile was careering haphazardly in different directions before it hit a rock, and tumbled in the air before crashing to the ground. Sign and Knutsen ran as fast as the deep snow would allow them to. They were one hundred yards from Hunt when two more shots rang out, bullets hitting Hunt and causing his body to slightly move. Both men threw themselves to the ground.

Knutsen muttered, "The man you met on the road. He *was* an assassin. Somehow he got here before us. We're easy targets."

Sign looked at Knutsen. "You don't have to do this. I can check the body on my own."

"Not a chance." Knutsen got to his feet.

So did Sign.

They trudged through ever-thick snow. It felt like they were wading through waist-height water. When they reached Hunt, there was no doubt he was dead. He had two bullet holes in his chest and one in his head. His killer was an expert marksman. Sign and Knutsen looked around. There wasn't any sign of life, let alone a sniper. Sign checked the body while Knutsen stood guard, his gun in both hands while he scoured any place that might be a good location to lay prone and fire three kill-shots. Sign found nothing in Hunt's clothes. He rolled him over and pulled off Hunt's daysack, the contents of which he poured onto the ground. There was a small blanket, torch, tin of baked beans, flask of water, compass, flare gun, box of matches, and a knife.

"No mobile phone," said Sign.

"He had no idea what he was doing beyond getting away from us. When he lost us, he'd have waited up for a few hours, maybe even overnight, before heading home." Knutsen crouched next to the body. "We got our fifth man, but we got to him too late."

Sign looked at the horizon. "Why hasn't the assassin killed us?"

"What do we do?"

"We notify Richards. There's nothing more to be done here."

They walked back to their jeep, sat in the vehicle, and tried to stay warm while the engine idled and powered the heater.

Knutsen called Richards and notified about what had happened. "We found him. The fifth man. But he's dead. He didn't talk before he died. We've got no evidence." After Richards spoke, Knutsen hung up. "He's sending a helicopter to retrieve Hunt. After it's arrived, we're to drive to Port Howard. Richards is supplying us a boat and crew. They'll transport us and the jeep back to the east island."

Sign bowed his head. Quietly, he said, "So be it."

"Are you okay?"

Sign smiled, though his expression was bitter. "I've always hated failure."

"We could, at least, get the assassin. He's got to get off the west island. Odds are he's going to be on the ferry tomorrow."

"Odds? Yes, what odds are we dealing with?" He looked out of the window. "For the most part the assassins had exactly the same problem as we had – they were searching for a needle in a haystack. Like us they'd have searched Port Stanley. When that didn't throw up any results, they'd have searched a few miles further afield. Then they partially struck lucky – they got Maloney's name. But we came up trumps. We killed Maloney's assassin and we got a deathbed confession from him. We got Peter Hunt's name. Thus, we become the people to pursue because we can lead the assassins to the fifth man. The person I met on the road was not a local farmer. He had an air of command. I have a nose for these things. He's special operations and I would go further to say that he is probably his unit's team leader. He will have wondered where we went today. He has to use his instinct. Collectively, we've exhausted the eastern side of East Island. That leaves the western side of East Island and West Island itself. He'll have deployed his two other assassins – we think they're women – to ground beyond Goose Green. Meanwhile he'll have taken the ferry to Port Howard. Before doing so he'll have spoken to the ferry captain. The boat has cameras; I spotted them when we boarded. No doubt the team leader benignly persuaded the captain to show us images of our faces and our vehicle. That's how he got on to us."

"The case is closed! We tell Richards about the assassination unit. His men take down the sniper at Howard."

"But, then we don't get the whole unit. The women are on east island, I'm sure of that. They'll get off the island by boat, submarine, or light aircraft. The male assassin will never talk. We'll get him, but not the others." Sign looked at his watch. "What time does the helicopter arrive here?"

"Richards estimated about an hour to ninety minutes."

"Then we must move fast." Sign engaged gears and turned the jeep around. He drove to Hunt's cottage. "Stay here." Sign entered the property via the rear door. He knew exactly what he was looking for. In the lounge he found a shotgun. It was loaded with three cartridges. He held it in one hand as he searched the kitchen. He picked up a fish knife – one that had a thin and flexible blade – and tucked it underneath his belt. He went into the upstairs bathroom and opened a cabinet. Alongside many other items, a pair of tweezers were in there. He secreted the tweezers in his pocket, walked downstairs, left the cottage, and opened the passenger door. "We need to go back to the body. Time is of essence."

Knutsen had no idea what was going on as Sign led the way back to Hunt and his crashed snowmobile.

Sign stopped next to the body. "At least two of the assassination team will vanish forever if Richards learns the truth of what happened today. Thus, we must muddy the waters in order to enact absolute retribution. Richards must never know that Hunt was assassinated by Argentinians. I must warn you though – this is going to be messy and will only buy us a day or two. It won't take the coroner in King Edward VII Memorial Hospital long to realise something is amiss. Meanwhile, we must corrupt a crime scene." Sign used the knife and tweezers to dig out the three bullets. He had to cut deep into the head and torso to get them. The wounds looked even more savage as a result of his primitive butchery. He placed the bullets in his pocket. "Your pistol, sir," He held out his hand.

Knutsen gave him his gun. "What on Earth are you doing?"

Sign didn't reply. Instead he fired three shots into Hunt, each in the exact location Hunt had been shot by the sniper. Sign handed the pistol back to Knutsen. He placed the shotgun in Hunt's two hands, curled the dead man's finger around the trigger, and fired the gun into the air. He removed the gun and aimed it at a tree that was one hundred yards away. He walked to the tree. The pellets from the blast had caused no damage to the bark. He walked back to Knutsen and gave him the shotgun. "This thing's useless beyond fifty yards. I'm going to walk back to the tree, cover my face, and you're going to shoot me."

"What?!"

"Just do it." Sign walked to the tree, stood in front of it, and crossed his arms in front of his eyes.

Knutsen was breathing heavily, his arms were shaking. He blinked fast as he raised the gun. No doubt Sign knew exactly what he was doing, but this seemed preposterous.

"Get on with it, Mr. Knutsen," Sign called out.

Knutsen breathed in deeply. He knew Sign was cavalier. But this request was beyond the pale. But, he didn't want to let his friend down. He steadied his legs, leaned forward, and aimed at Sign's chest. One second. Two seconds. Three seconds. Every instinct was telling him not to take the shot.

He pulled the trigger, dropped the gun, and ran to Sign.

Sign was still standing. He withdrew his arms from his face and smiled. "That smarted a bit, But on the plus side I've got pellet holes in my jacket and a number of minor pellet holes in my flesh. It's nothing worse than getting stuck by thirty wasps on a hot summer's day in Hyde Park. Come." They walked back to the body. "Place the gun in his hands. Then we must retire to the warmth of our vehicle and await the arrival of Colonel Richards."

When they were in the car, Knutsen asked, "What the fuck was that all about?"

"Deflection; diversion; call it what you wish. Why is Hunt dead? Because he attacked us with his shotgun. I have damage to my clothes and wounds to prove it. You ran to my rescue. Hunt fired again, but his aim was off. He raised his rifle one last time to kill me. You fired twice into his upper body. He fell to the ground, but was still alive. Hunt pointed his gun at me again. You had no choice other than to take a head shot. In doing so, Hunt flipped onto his side and let off a shot that hit the tree. The forensic analysis of Hunt's hands and forearms will show cordite on his flesh. I am walking wounded, though to be honest I'll pluck pellets out of my chest with Hunt's tweezer. They've only penetrated a couple of millimetres. You killed Hunt to save me. Job done. No need to say anything about an assassin."

"You are mad!"

Sign laughed. "I'm pragmatic." He looked upwards. "Richards is ahead of schedule. Hunt's helicopter has arrived."

They exited the car. When the helicopter landed, Richards and four armed men got out.

Knutsen pointed to the place where Hunt was laying. "He's over there. About three hundred yards."

The men left their commander and went to retrieve the body.

Richards walked to Sign. "What happened?"

"We found your fifth man. Alas, he was somewhat skittish. He fled, we pursued, he opened fire on me," Sign tapped his jacket, "matters escalated, Mr. Knutsen had to shoot him, matters further escalated, Mr. Knutsen had to kill him."

"God damn it!" Richards ran his fingers through his hair. "We wanted him alive!"

"So did I." Sign looked at Richards' men. They were carrying Hunt to the helicopter. "We found the fifth man for you. I would hazard a guess that he was in a state of paranoia. He tried to kill me because he was no longer rational. Do you have an update on when flights will resume to London. Our job is complete."

Richards exhaled slowly. "Two to three days. The high winds will have abated by then."

"Excellent."

Richards looked at Sign's lacerated jacket. "I'll get you to the medical centre in Pleasant."

"No need, dear chap. I've had far worse. This is just a graze; it's not a deep cut."

Richards nodded. "My boat's waiting for you in Port Howard. Try to get there within the next forty minutes. The vessel's high speed and can make the crossing in forty minutes. That should give you enough time to get back to your cottage before nightfall."

"Thank you, colonel."

Richards was about to head to the helicopter, but hesitated. "Is there anything you're not telling me?"

Sign grinned. "Heaven forbid! There are however some loose ends, namely what Hunt's connection was to Wilson and the others."

Richards shrugged. "We won't be bothered to pursue that. Almost certainly he's a mate of a mate of a mate. That's how it works down here."

Sign nodded. "You didn't get your war."

"Not *my* war. An attack on the islands is an attack on Britain. Justice hasn't been obtained."

"We lost a battle. If there's a similar incident in the future, let's hope the outcome is in our favour." Sign walked to the jeep. "Time to go home," he said to Knutsen.

Using binoculars and while prone on the ground, Casero watched the helicopter take off. And he saw Sign and Knutsen drive away from the area where Hunt was shot. When helicopter and car were out of sight, he stood and called Fontonia. "The fifth man's dead. I'll be back on the east island tomorrow. We'll meet at 1400hrs hours at the farm track we parked on this morning. We have one more job to do. Then we'll exfiltrate the islands at 1700hrs. Call Miss S and relay these instructions. There's nothing more we can do today." He picked up his holdall and walked to his car.

Four hours' later Sign and Knutsen were back at Bluff Cove. Sign looked at the drawer he'd opened by a fraction. It was fully closed. "They've been here."

"The Argentinian assassins."

"Yes. But not to worry. Maybe they thawed out and made themselves a nice cuppa."

"Shall I check for bugs?"

Sign reached into the fridge and withdrew a joint of beef brisket. "Yes. I doubt they've planted any because they had to move too fast to search this place plus get on our heels. But one can never be too certain." He diced onions and braised them with the brisket and root vegetables within a casserole pot on the hob, before adding a bay leaf, thyme, pepper, mustard, and red wine into the pan. He placed the dish into the oven, peeled potatoes, and placed them into a pot for par-boiling and roasting nearer to dinner time. He entered the lounge. Knutsen was searching every piece of furniture. Sign said, "Supper will be served in around two hours. Once you've completed your task please get the fire lit. Meanwhile I'm going to have a long bath and extract the pellets some fool shot at me." He smiled and headed upstairs.

When Sign had finished bathing and attending to his wounds, he dressed, came downstairs, placed twenty three ball-bearings on the kitchen counter, turned on a hob to parboil the potatoes, poured two glasses of brandy, and entered the lounge. The fire was lit and Knutsen was sitting in his armchair. Sign handed him a drink and sat opposite him.

Knutsen said, "For an eavesdropping device to work and transmit in these weather conditions and landscape, it would have to be very sophisticated and no smaller than my fist. Certainly it wouldn't be a tiny bug placed under a table or in a lampshade. The logical place to install it would be the ceiling or walls. The walls are stone, and haven't been corrupted. The ceiling could have been corrupted, but it would take at least half a day to open it up, insert a device, and re-plaster and paint the ceiling in the exact colour of the rest of the ceiling. I've looked in and under furniture, in drawers, cupboards et cetera, et cetera. There's no listening device in the cottage."

"Excellent work. You've earned your supper." Sign sipped his drink. "They may come for us tomorrow."

"I know."

"If we tell them something of interest, be under no illusions – they'll kill us."

"Let's make sure that doesn't happen." Knutsen felt weary. "Have you done something like this before?"

"Meaning?"

"Acting as bait? Just waiting?"

Sign smiled. "Like a tethered goat? Yes, many times. But, the point of tethering the goat is to lure in the encroaching tiger or leopard. The predator doesn't know he's walking into a trap. Nearby is a hunter with a gun. It's a tried and tested ploy to kill desperately hungry beasts."

Knutsen rubbed his fatigued face. "If we get out of this alive and make it back to London, the first thing I'm going to do is put shorts and a T-shirt on and sit on a deckchair in a park. I hear southern England's having a heat wave at the moment. I'm sick of the weather down here."

Sign laughed. "By contrast, I shall catch a matinee classical concert at the Barbican or Cadogan Hall. It will take my mind off all matters pertaining to our pursuit of the fifth man."

"Do we have any new cases to work? Anything in our in-tray?"

"Yes. But they're all minor fare – fraud, cheating husbands, vetting of potential employees, and establishing why a woman threw herself onto a train track in Guildford. I could resolve the cases in my sleep and without leaving the comfort of our West Square flat. Still, they pay the bills."

"But, they don't fuel the fire."

Sign's eyes twinkled. "No they don't, Mr. Knutsen. We must hope for a case that is considerably more engaging." He entered the kitchen, drained off the spuds, added them to a metal tray, poured oil over the potatoes, and put the tray into the oven. He returned to the lounge. "As usual, before you sleep make sure you clean your gun We must be on our game tomorrow."

CHAPTER 12

Sign was up and dressed at six AM. He'd barely slept during the night because he'd felt uneasy. That sense was still with him as he placed breakfast food on a chopping board, ready to be cooked when Knutsen emerged, and brewed a pot of coffee. He wondered whether he was making the right decision by staying here until flights resumed. It would be so easy to get accommodation in RAF Mount Pleasant. No one would be able to get to him and Knutsen if they were housed there. But, he still felt a figurative bitter taste in his mouth because matters had not been concluded in the way he would have liked. The only way that could change is if they stayed away from the military base. He and Knutsen had to take their chances. Moreover, there was something that he hadn't told Knutsen. It was a thought that had been nagging him ever since Richards had first visited them in London. The thought wasn't based on any evidence. Rather, it was a question he had; a 'what if', as he liked to call such notions.

He put his fleece on and walked outside. For the first time since he'd been on the islands, the sky was blue. There was still thick snow covering every inch of land, and the temperature was bitterly cold, but a complete lack of wind and no cloud cover showed the islands in a very different light. The landscape around the cottage was stunning, one could see for miles, distant mountains looked like they were only a short walk away whereas they were in fact a long day's walk from Bluff Cove, and all around him was eerily silent.

He stood for a moment, taking in the vista. But, his thoughts weren't on the surrounding beauty. Instead, he tried to imagine where the assassins would come from. Most likely they'd be on foot and would approach from different directions. Was it the right thing to do to put Knutsen in this kind of peril? He didn't know. Knutsen would balk if he told him to leave while he could. Still, he felt a duty of care over his business partner. Plus, he needed him. Knutsen had been in many tight spots during his career as an undercover cop. He was a grownup. He could handle tough situations. That's what Sign kept telling himself. Over and over. But, it was one thing dealing with drug barons and their gangs in London, it was another thing altogether confronting highly trained nefarious types who operated in the secret world. But, there was no one else Sign would rather have by his side. For the most part in his MI6 career he'd worked alone. But, when he'd needed to work with others he'd always applied the same standard in his assessment of them: is this someone you want to stand shoulder-to-shoulder with in the trenches, before the whistle blows and you have to go over the top? Knutsen was that man, without a doubt. It was simple – Knutsen would take a bullet for Sign; Sign would take a bullet for Knutsen. There was no need to overthink that cast iron principal. And yet lesser men and women would never understand that fundamental of sacrifice.

He looked west. He was certain the man he'd met on the road yesterday would be taking the first available ferry out of the island this morning. No way could he have gotten off the island yesterday. And, because he was sure the man was the leader of the assassination team, Sign knew the man would want to be here in person to enact the coup de grâce – the final blow that would put Sign and Knutsen out of their misery. He was coming, Sign was sure of that.

He walked around the perimeter of the house, taking in everything he could see. He and Knutsen were so exposed here. And they only had one gun. They were like chickens in a coop, awaiting three savage foxes to enter. There was nowhere to go; no means of fleeing; no chance of fighting back. That had to change.

He re-entered the cottage.

Knutsen was downstairs, pouring coffee. He was also frying bacon, tomatoes, mushrooms, eggs, and toasting baps. He grinned as he saw Sign. "I thought I'd cook for a change. I'm sick of your shit food."

"Quite right, sir." Sign slumped in a chair. "Visibility is superb today. I wish it wasn't. We are sitting ducks."

Knutsen brought the food through to the lounge and handed Sign a plate of breakfast. "If we're sitting ducks, so are they. We'll spot them before they spot us. What time do you think they'll come here?"

"Early afternoon. I would imagine they want to get off the islands later today. The clock is ticking."

"Eat your food. Drink your coffee."

Sign forced the breakfast and beverage down his neck. He knew he needed the sustenance. But it was a chore to get nutrients and caffeine in to his stomach. "How many rounds do you have left for your Glock 37?"

"Three full magazines. Enough to take down a lot of people."

"Good." Sign put his plate and mug to one side. "Your breakfast has given me a second wind. We must think unconventionally."

"That's what you do."

"Indeed. But, 'amateur improvisation' is probably a more astute term of reference for situations like this. What will the assassins do?"

Knutsen placed his last portion of food into his mouth. "They'll want to overwhelm us, and they'll want to do so up close and personal. There's no advantage to one of them taking a sniper position. We're of no use to them dead. Not until the end, at least. So, they'll come in to the house. They'll shoot us, but not kill us, or they'll physically over power us. They'll tie us up. And that's when the good stuff starts. They'll want to know everything we know about the fifth man. They'll be merciless."

Sign nodded. "I won't tell them a thing." He stared at Knutsen.

Knutsen said, "Nor will I. And the beauty of it is we've genuinely got nothing to say. We got very close to Peter Hunt but not close enough to get him to talk. They can torture us all they like. We never got a confession out of Hunt. So, it's like trying to draw blood out of a stone. They'll get nothing."

"And then they kill us."

"Yep. There's no other outcome."

"I agree with your analysis." Sign stood. "You think I was wrong not to inform Richards about the Argentinian unit. Right now you're probably thinking that I should eat humble pie, call Richards, and get him to send soldiers here."

"The thought had occurred to me."

"Even if I wanted support, it's too late for that now. In all probability, one or both of the women are watching our house. If they see soldiers enter the cottage, the assassins will abort their operation. That would be unacceptable."

"What do you propose?"

Two hours later, Casero boarded the ferry in Port Howard. On this occasion he wasn't the only passenger on the boat. The break in the weather had prompted west islanders to travel to the east island to reconnect with friends and family based there, or to collect supplies in Port Stanley. Casero was glad. He'd been worried that he might be making the journey with Sign and Knutsen. But, Fontonia was watching, from distance, their house in the west island. She'd told Casero that they were both back in Bluff Cove.

From a vending machine, he poured himself a black coffee and strolled on deck. The air was still bitterly cold, but was calm. The sky was azure. For a while, seagulls followed the boat before turning back to land because they sensed they were straying too far from the shore of the west island. Casero sucked in the icy air. He liked the Falklands; they reminded him of the place where he'd grown up in southern Argentina. He had no opinion on whether the islands should belong to Argentina or not. He wasn't interested in politics and power-based land-grabs. His only motivation in life was to do the job in hand. That said, he didn't want to see Argentina and Britain to once again use the Falklands as a battleground. In his view, politicians never understood war. He'd seen too much death to readily embrace a situation where young Argentinian men were told to lay down their lives for a small plot of land. If Sign and Knutsen had learned something from the west islander who'd been shot, they'd take that information to Colonel Richards. They'd have to testify in a British court of law. Then, UK forces would unleash hell on Argentina. Casero's country would be outgunned. It was his duty to get to Sign and Knutsen, make them talk, and then dispatch them.

He walked around the deck for the duration of the journey. When the boat was a few hundred yards from New Haven, he entered his vehicle, checked his weapons, and waited to disembark.

Sign poured coffee in to a flask and handed it to Knutsen. "You're going to need this to stay alert and warm."

Knutsen took the flask and nodded. "Let's do this."

Sign walked out of the house, acutely aware that he was probably being watched by one or more assassins, and got into the jeep. He reversed the car a few yards, and drove it so that it was close to the open front door. The gap between the car and door was only two yards. It would be impossible for anyone with a long range scope to see what was happening in the gap. Knutsen crawled out of the house, entered the rear passenger area, and stayed low. Sign drove the car twenty yards forward, slowed, and said, "Now!"

Knutsen rolled out of the car and dashed into the disused sheep pen outhouse.

Sign leisurely turned the car and drove it close to the front door. He stopped the vehicle and got out. He hoped he was being watched as he leisurely walked around the jeep, pretending to check lights and tyres. He opened the bonnet and leaned forward, looking at the engine. After closing the bonnet, he entered the house, picked up an empty wine bottle, a rubber tube he'd cut off the washing machine, stuffed both in his jacket, exited the house, and crouched by the vehicle's petrol cap. Now, he couldn't be seen. He opened the cap, inserted the tube into the tank, sucked on the other end of the tube, and placed it in the bottle after petrol hit his mouth. While spitting petrol out of his mouth, he waited until the bottle was full. He raised the tube, withdrew it, and screwed the cap back into place. He entered the house, shut the door, placed the bottle on a table, tossed aside the tube, thrust a rag into the bottle so that it was dowsed in the flammable liquid, extracted half of it, and placed a lighter next to the bottle.

Now all he and Knutsen could do was wait.

Casero stopped his car on the farm track, close to the house at Bluff Cove. Sosa and Fontonia were there, standing next to their vehicles. It was two PM. Casero said nothing as he walked to the women. He looked in the direction of Sign and Knutsen's cottage. It wasn't visible, due to the fact that the track was in a hollow and the house was in a dip beyond an elevated stretch of land.

Fontonia said, "They're both in the house, though I haven't seen Knutsen for an hour. Sign, however, is in the lounge. He's pacing backwards and forwards. He's also checked his car. I guess the clear weather has given him an opportunity to ensure everything's in working order. But, he turned the car around to face the road. Presumably they're making a road trip later today."

Casero nodded. "We have no time to waste. Move quickly. Approach the target from the directions we discussed."

They set off on foot, all of them carrying handguns.

Knutsen tried to control his breathing. He was shivering, having been in the tiny sheep pen for two hours. Even the cold-weather attire he was wearing couldn't protect him from the cold. It was the inability to move that was causing him to shake. He had to get control of that physical symptom; had to focus on anything that took his mind of his circumstances. He arched his back to try to relive the muscular tension in his back, got on one knee, raised his pistol, and muttered to himself, "Get your shit together."

Sign walked back and forth in front of the lounge windows. Sometimes he held a phone to his ear, even though he wasn't speaking to anyone; other times he gesticulated with his arms while speaking aloud anything that came into his head. The key objective was for him to appear to a surveillance expert that he was doing stuff. As importantly, he had to be visible.

After all, he was the tethered goat.

Knutsen couldn't see him. And neither of them had mobile phone reception. They were both very alone, their only hope being that they'd stick to their drills and come out on top of the situation. Sign was the most vulnerable, and reliant on Knutsen. But, Knutsen could be shot dead before he got anywhere near his quarry.

Sign kept pacing, even when he got the tiniest glimpse of a person in the snow about eighty yards away. The person was no longer visible.

It was happening.

Sign breathed in deeply. He wasn't scared. That emotion had no purpose in moments like this. And he'd faced death so many times that it now just felt like part of life. But, he was worried about messing this up. He hadn't been able to save Sally, Maloney, and Hunt. If he lost another innocent life he really would be a failure.

He moved to the centre of the room, not caring if he was visible to the assassins. There was no point in playacting anymore. The killers knew he was here. They were coming in to finish the job.

Fontonia slowly approached the cottage from the north. The snow was hampering her progress – it was at least a foot deep. But, she kept her gun held at eye level and focused on the back door.

Sosa walked towards the property from the west. Her job was to incapacitate Sign or Knutsen if they fled the house. It would be a shot to the leg. Then she'd all the injured man into the house so that he could be interrogated. She passed the dilapidated tint sheep pen, got onto one knee, and pointed her gun at the cottage.

Casero reached Sign and Knutsen's jeep. He'd approached the house from the south. He crouched behind the vehicle. The front door of the cottage was only four yards away. He gripped his gun.

Knutsen saw a person walk past his location, stop, and kneel. The person was holding a pistol. It was difficult to tell if the assassin was male or female – a hat, bulky jacket, and other winter clothes hid all indicators of gender. The person had his or her back to Knutsen and was just waiting. Possibly he or she was intending to enter the house through one of the two windows on this side of the cottage. That would be the only way in from the west. More likely, Knutsen decided, she was tasked to shoot Sign if he tried to escape.

He recalled what Sign had said to him earlier in the day.

When they come, don't think like a policeman. Don't call out to them, give them a chance to surrender, attempt to arrest them, or do anything full stop that gives them a second of breathing space. If you give them that second, you're a dead man. They're cold-blooded executioners. The only protocol to be had is to kill them once they're close to the house. No mercy. No hesitation. We can examine our consciences at a later date.

Knutsen aimed his gun at the back of the person's head, pulled the trigger, and watched the head turn into pulp. The person fell forward, blood seeping into the snow.

Sign, Casero, and Sosa heard the shot. All of them reacted.

Sosa raced as fast as she could to the back door. It was unlocked. She pulled it open, ready to storm the building and put her gun in Sign's mouth. But, Sign was standing in the archway between the lounge and kitchen, facing her. He was holding a wine bottle with a flaming rag in its neck. Firebomb. Sosa tried to spin around but she was too late. Sign hurled the bomb at her feet. The bottle smashed. Flames encased her clothes. She dropped her gun, and ran screaming away from the house. She was a ball of orange fire, the colour vivid against the backdrop of the pure white landscape. Sign picked up her gun and shot her in the head. She collapsed to the ground. He put two more shots into her back, knowing that both would have penetrated her lungs. She was dead.

From behind, an arm wrapped itself around his throat. A gun was put against his face.

Casero held him firm. His mouth was close to Sign's ear. "If you wish to live I suggest you do exactly as I say." He dragged him back into the lounge.

Knutsen ran through the snow as quickly as he could. Sign's firebomb hadn't done any damage to the kitchen. He entered the property, breathing fast, his handgun made ready to kill anything that shouldn't be here.

Sign was there, upright. Casero was gripping him tight and using Sign's body as a shield. Aside from the assassins arm, there was barely anything visible of the man holding Knutsen's friend.

Casero said, "Your name is Knutsen. You're holding a Glock. Am I right in thinking it's a 37? That would make it a forty five calibre gun. If you shoot my arm, the bullet will make a mess of my limb. But it will also penetrate Sign's throat. He'll die; I may also die. If you deliberately shoot him in a part of his body where there are no vital organs, the bullet will travel through his body and into mine. But, odds are that both of us will die from shock and blood loss. The only good outcome from this is if you don't pull the trigger. All I want is information."

Despite the cold, Knutsen was sweating. He kept his gun pointing at both men. "You'll kill us when you're done!"

"Maybe I will; maybe I won't. The future is always so terribly uncertain."

Knutsen looked into Sign's eyes. Sign showed no fear.

Knutsen's finger was wrapped around the trigger.

What to do? What to fucking do?

Sign wrenched Casero's arm off his throat and dropped to the floor.

A split second later, Casero opened his mouth.

Knutsen shot him in the chest.

Casero fell back onto the floor.

Sign got to his feet and picked up Casero's discarded gun.

Casero was wheezing, his face screwed up in agony.

Sign crouched beside him and examined the wound. "You have no friends to help you. They're dead. Mr. Knutsen's bullet has made an awful mess of you. I suspect you've got one minute to live. I regret to inform you that I can't repatriate your body to your homeland. You were never here; we were never here; and no one can know why we weren't here. But, I will ensure your body is treated with respect."

Casero was struggling to breathe.

Sign leaned in closer. "You and I don't want war. We're professionals. I'm asking you to do one last thing – be a professional to the end. Will you do that for me? Will you do that for yourself?"

Casero's eyes were wide. Blood was coming out of his mouth.

"You killed a man. His name was Peter Hunt. He supplied military grade weapons. You saw us go to his house. You shot him."

"I... I... saw him die. I didn't do that."

"Oh come on! You were there. You wanted him dead. It was the sole reason you and your colleagues were on the islands."

"It... It was an incredible shot. Whoever killed the fifth man is an expert shooter. But I can't take credit for the kill. Nor can my colleagues – they were on the east island."

"Well, if you didn't pull the trigger, who did?"

"Don't... don't know. Didn't see a shooter." Casero's back arched. "Ask yourself – where was Hunt going when you tried to speak to him?"

"When he got onto his snow mobile and headed north? I've already asked myself that question." Sign stood. "Do you know the answer?"

"No... No." Casero's eyes were screwed tight. "I thought Hunt may have spoken to you. That's... that's why we came here. Information."

Sign glanced at Knutsen. His colleague was no longer pointing his weapon at Casero. Sign returned his attention to the assassin. "Men like you and me walk in the shadows. And we die in the shadows. We don't get medals; recognition; meaningful relationships; peace; or a hero's funeral. But we do get solitude. And that's not a bad thing. After all, how many people can move around the world amid billions of people who don't the slightest inkling of who we are?" He gripped Casero's hand. "It is a rare occasion where men like us bump into each other. We know in a shot that we are one and the same, even though we also know that we can never be kindred spirits. That is our nature – to be alone. You've served your country. This is your hero's funeral." He released Casero's hand.

Casero exhaled one last time. He died.

Sign said to Knutsen, "We need to hide the bodies in the sheep pen. They can be properly dealt with later. Tomorrow, we have a final job to do."

CHAPTER 13

At six AM, Sign and Knutsen left the Bluff Cove cottage. They'd never return. In the boot of the car were their bags containing all their belongings. Knutsen was driving. He'd reasoned that if he was strong enough to help Sign carry three bodies into the outhouse, he was strong enough to turn a steering wheel. In any case, his arm barely hurt now.

It was funny. When Knutsen had first arrived here he'd felt like a fish out of water. Most of his police career had been spent operating in urban environments. The Falklands was as far removed from that as possible. Even Port Stanley was nothing more than a large village. And yet, during his stay on the islands he'd become enamoured with the climate and harsh but spectacular terrain. And as brutal as conditions could be in winter, he found the islanders' way of life endearing and effective. They lived a simple life, were happy, always accommodating, helped each other out at the drop of a hat, were hardworking, and wouldn't swap their circumstances for any others in the world. And they were a peaceful bunch. The only people they hated were Argentinian politicians and generals. They just wanted to be left alone.

As Knutsen drove the jeep onto the road, he said, "I presume we're going to RAF Mount Pleasant?"

Sign answered, "We are but not just yet. I want to have another peek at the west island. After that, we go back to London."

Knutsen frowned. "We didn't achieve our task, but most certainly our business on the islands is concluded. Why go back to Hunt's house. We'll find nothing there that can change the fact that the fifth man is dead."

In a distant voice, Sign said, "I want to know how he died."

Knutsen slapped the steering wheel. "He was shot in the head! A bullet in the brain doesn't tend to help people live a longer life!"

Sign ignored Knutsen's sarcasm and frustration. "New Haven, if you please." He checked his watch. "If we make good speed we should be able to board the nine AM ferry."

At eleven AM they disembarked the ferry, in Port Howard. Knutsen had barely spoken to Sign during the journey. As far as he was concerned, this was a waste of time. Sign, he believed, was trying to salvage his reputation. No doubt he was hoping to find something in Hunt's house that explained why Sign and Knutsen had never stood a chance of speaking in depth to Hunt before the Argentinian assassin killed him. It was a folly. Sign and Knutsen had unwittingly led the assassin to Hunt. The fifth man had panicked and fled. The Argentinian took the incredible shot. Hunt was dead.

Sign said, "I called Oates yesterday evening. He's expecting us. Or rather, he's expecting me. Please take me to his hut."

Two minutes later Knutsen parked outside the conservationist's workplace.

Sign said, "The only reason I want to see him alone is because he's more likely to help if the meeting is one-to-one. But, if you want to come in you have my blessing. I don't want you to feel that I'm excluding you."

Knutsen huffed. "You *are* excluding me! I've no idea why we're here."

Sign touched him on the arm. "I have to protect your reputation. I'm here on a hunch. If I'm wrong, I might as well firebomb myself, just as I did to that poor woman yesterday. I'll go out in a ball of flames. You, however could get another job; your dignity intact."

Knutsen looked at Oates' hut. He breathed deeply. "Is there any danger in there?"

Sign smiled, his expression warm. "No, dear chap. I'll be safe."

Knutsen looked at the dashboard and nodded. "Okay. I'll wait here."

Sign got out of the car and knocked on the door.

Oates opened the entrance.

Sign said, "Mr. Oates. So good of you to see me at short notice."

Oates moved aside, let Sign in, and closed the door behind him. He rolled a cigarette, placed it in his mouth, poured two cups of tea, and sat on his desk. "How can I help? Did you get any joy out of Hunt?"

"He was most helpful. Alas, he's a busy man and could only give us thirty minutes of his time. Our survey of the west coast needs input from others." He walked to a map of the island on Oates' wall and placed a finger on Hill Cove, where Hunt lived. "The road from Hunt's place goes north for another few miles. That would suggest someone else lives at the end of the road. Unfortunately, when we were interviewing Hunt the weather was drawing in. We had to return to the east island. I wonder if you could shed any light on who might be worth talking to in this sector." He placed his finger on the end of the road.

Oates peered at the map. "Yeah, I know who lives there. Harry Monk. He'll be happy to help you out."

"What does Monk do?"

Oates shrugged. "Farmer, like most people here."

"He's a local?"

"Yes. I knew his parents better than I know Monk. They used to let me use some of their farming equipment to restore sea defences. They're dead now. Monk lives on his own. From what little I've seen of him, he's a nice enough bloke. But, I don't use the equipment he inherited from his parents. He had to sell a lot of it. Six months ago he lost a lot of money. I heard it was because he'd invested in a business venture in the east island. He had to pare his farm back to the bone."

"Does he live alone?"

Oates frowned. "What's with all the questions? Just go and see him. He should be useful."

Sign sipped his coffee. "I'm a busy man. Any statements I obtain from islanders who know the west coast of this island must be taken from credible witnesses. Such credibility doesn't just pertain to their knowledge of the island; it also pertains to their character. For example, I've been told not to speak to anyone whose property, or parents' property, was damaged in the Falklands War. They would hold a grudge against Argentina. Their statements would be biased, driven by anger."

Oates sucked on his cigarette. "Pope lives alone." He looked away. "I'm trying to remember; give me a minute." He looked at Sign. "Yeah, I remember. His dad once told me that they had a fishing business on the east island. It was back in the late seventies and early eighties. Dad would work there Monday to Friday, then come home to work the farm at weekends. But, it didn't work out. The farm was too high maintenance and needed him here fulltime. Plus, he said the fishing business wasn't doing so well. He moved back to the west island."

"How old is Pope junior?"

Oates shrugged. "I've never asked him. At a guess I'd say mid-forties."

"Thank you. From what you've said I don't see any reason not to speak to him. May I use your name by way of introduction?"

"Sure."

Sign was about to leave, but hesitated. "Do you happen to know who he was trying to do business with on the east island – the venture that lost him so much money?"

"I do actually." He walked to a filing cabinet, opened a drawer, and rifled through files. "Monk was investing in four trawlers. His idea was to create a fleet that could dominate fishing catches off of Port Stanley. He came to me because he wanted to pick my brains on sea beds, fish migration, and ultimately the best locations for his new trawlers to set up anchor and drop nets. Part of my job as a conservationist is to know shit like that. I was happy to help. Four trawlers ain't going to make much of a dent in sea life. If anything, it's useful. Too many fish in the waters means elephant seals start breeding like crazy. We need a balanced ecosystem here. If the seal population gets too big, I have to cull some of them. I'm the only person on the island authorized to do so. And I fucking hate that part of my job." He pulled out a file. "Here we go." He opened the file. "To give Monk the information he needed I had to go through formal channels. Technically, the charity I work for can't demand money for information. We're not a business. But we can request financial donations. That's what we did with Monk. I asked him to donate five thousand pounds. I drew up a contract. The money paid to us was signed by the investors in the trawler business. Alongside Monk, there were four others." He handed Sign the file. "At the bottom of the first page you'll see their names and signatures."

Sign looked at the paper and handed the file back to Oates.

Oates looked Sign in the eye. "Four of the men in that document recently drowned. I know that from the local rag. You knew it anyway. You're not here to analyse the west coast, looking for points of vulnerability to attack, are you? You're here to investigate the deaths of the four men."

Sign was silent for a few seconds. "On the night they drowned, there is evidence to suggest that there was a fifth man on board the trawler. The fifth man witnessed the deaths of Eddie Wilson, Rob Taylor, Billy Green, and Mike Jackson. He panicked, got into a dinghy, and paddled to shore. Since then, he's gone to ground. I'm working an angle. It is possible that an Argentinian vessel cut across the bow of Wilson's boat. It caused him to urgently change course. After that, I don't know. What I do know is that four men washed ashore, dead. The fifth man can help me fill in the gaps as to what happened that night."

"You think Pope is the fifth man?"

"No. I've already identified the fifth man. But, I haven't interviewed him yet. I need to tread very delicately. He's understandably scared and confused. He may clam up; he may run; he may blame himself for what happened; he may do any number of things. I must treat him with the utmost respect and kindness. Just knocking on his door and introducing myself won't do. I must speak to someone who knows him. I'd like that person to come with me to the fifth man's house and tell him that I'm not a threat and will do nothing to him. I am a stranger from London. I need a local by my side. Someone the fifth man trusts."

Oates looked at the wall-map. "I'm not stupid. You've not spoken to Hunt because you can't do so yet. Hunt is the fifth man. And you're hoping Pope, his nearest neighbour, is the man to calm Hunt down."

Sign didn't answer him fully. "Mr. Oates. I'm dealing with some very deep waters. A man of your intellect can probably estimate just how deep those waters are and why they are dangerous. Can I rely on you to keep our conversation private?"

Oates turned to face him. "I don't want to know how far this goes."

"And I'm not going to tell you. But I would ask that you don't call Hunt and Pope and tell them that I'm driving to see them this morning. To do otherwise would not be in their interest, your interest, or my interest. Between us, we have an island to protect."

Oates stubbed out his cigarette. "We're conservationists." He laughed for a few seconds. "Sure, I won't call them."

"Thank you. Does your charity have a website?"

"Of course."

"I get paid by results. If matters come to a successful conclusion I will transfer ten thousand pounds to your charity and I will express a desire that the funds are funnelled into the research and animal welfare work you're doing on the west island." He walked to the door. "Good day to you, sir."

When Sign was in the car, Knutsen asked, "Where to?"

"We drive west to Hunt's house, but we don't stop there. Instead we follow the road north for a few miles. There'll be a farmstead at the end of the route. Its owner is a man called Harry Pope. I want to talk to him."

Sixty four minutes later they stopped outside Pope's property. As well as a cottage, there were outhouses, a barn, and a paddock in the ranch. A Hilux pickup truck was parked outside the cottage. There was the sound of a chainsaw coming from the rear of the complex.

Sign said to Knutsen, "Whatever happens, don't take your eyes off Pope. And keep your gun close to you at all times."

Both men exited their jeep. Sign knocked on the door. There was no answer. He waved his hand to gesture to Knutsen that they should walk to the back of the house. They did so. A man was there. He was hunched over a tree trunk that was resting on a saw bench, using a chainsaw to slice chunks off the wood. He was wearing a face mask and goggles. Knutsen stopped in a spot where the man couldn't see him, ten yards from the saw bench. Sign walked ahead, sticking close to the cottage's wall, and stopped in a place where he was visible to the man.

Sign smiled and held up his hand. He called out, "Mr. Pope?"

The man turned off his saw and removed his face attire. "Who wants to know?"

Knutsen gripped his handgun, hidden underneath his jacket.

Sign said, "My name is Ben Sign. I work for the military. I wanted to speak to you about one of the islanders. It's a private matter. But, don't worry – this doesn't involve you. May we speak inside?"

The man rested his chainsaw on the bench and loaded the cut wood into a wheelbarrow. He looked annoyed. "What's this about? I'm busy."

"I assure you this won't take up much of your time. Are you Harry Pope?"

"Yep, that's me." The man wheeled the barrow to a nearby woodshed. In doing so he caught sight of Knutsen. "Who's he?"

"That's Tom Knutsen. He works with me."

Pope tipped out the logs into the shed and shut the door. "Why's he flanking me? Is he armed?"

Sign's smile broadened. "Heaven forbid, no. We just didn't want to surprise you. Are the logs for your cottage's fire?"

"Of course they damn well are," said Pope as he walked past Sign, removed his gloves, and opened the kitchen door. "Come in, but make it quick. I've got a shit ton of jobs to do before the sun goes down."

Sign and Knutsen followed him in to the house.

Pope put the kettle on, washed his hands, and turned to them. "So, tell me."

Sign replied, "You obviously know Peter Hunt, just down the road?"

"Yes." Pope's expression was suspicious.

"Tom and I work for the Royal Military Police. There's been an accident involving Mr. Hunt. We've been tasked to investigate the incident."

"Accident? What kind of accident? And why aren't the local old bill looking in to it?"

Sign took a step closer to him. "It's a delicate matter. Hunt was shot. We're exploring the possibility that he was attacked by an Argentinian reconnaissance unit. Possibly they were compromised by Hunt. They shot him and fled. Thus far, this is a military matter, not a civilian police investigation."

Pope frowned. "Is he alright?"

"Yes, yes. He'll need a week or so in hospital, but it's nothing serious. He's conscious and is recovering. We've interviewed him but unfortunately he didn't know who his assailants were. But, we know they were Argentinian. The bullet extracted from his chest was Argentinian. We wondered if you'd seen any unusual activity on your stretch of the coast? Perhaps four men; a boat?"

Pope relaxed. "Can't say I have, but then again would I spot them if they were nearby? I don't know anything about military stuff, but I'm guessing blokes rocking up here in the middle of the night, or whenever, must be Special Forces or something. Why would they be doing a reconnaissance of the coast?"

"To examine potential beach heads for a sea-born assault by thousands of troops. It's a tricky business. They'd have been taking samples of the sand on the beach, checking water levels in the coast, seeing whether armoured vehicles would become bogged down when they drove off landing craft, and many other things." Sign walked out of the kitchen. "Let's sit in the lounge. It will be far more comfortable."

"It's messy in there. Don't…"

"Nonsense." Sign stood in the centre of the lounge, looked around, and called out, "Mr. Knutsen!"

Knutsen put his pistol against Pope's head. "Get in there. Don't try anything. I'm good at this stuff." He pushed Pope into the room.

Sign said, "Sit in that chair and put your hands on your forehead. Don't do anything silly. My colleague is an excellent shot."

Pope did as he was told. "What the fuck's going on?!"

Sign remained standing. "That rifle leaning in the corner of this room is an FLFAL 50.61. The FAL was originally designed in Belgium, but it was subsequently manufactured in Argentina and used in the Falklands War. It is a highly effective assault rifle. It is illegal for a civilian to possess one."

Pope glanced at the gun. "It… it doesn't work. It's just an antique. My dad found it after the war."

Sign picked up the weapon and examined its workings. "It's been regularly cleaned; there are bullets in the magazine; a sight has been attached; modern shock absorbers have been fitted onto the stock. This gun is most certainly on active duty." He placed the gun down. "You used this weapon to kill Peter Hunt."

"What?!"

"It's okay. We don't need amateur dramatics." Sign sat down. Knutsen remained standing, his pistol pointing at Pope's head. Sign said, "Let me tell you what you already know. In the late seventies and early eighties, your father worked in the east island. The war happenèd in ninety eighty two. It was brief and chaotic. Guns, bullets, landmines, and other munitions were left on battlefields. Your father fancied himself as a trophy hunter. He picked up guns and bullets – British and Argentinian – and brought them back here. I don't know whether he did that during the war or after. Either way he'd collected himself an arsenal. It wasn't unusual. The war was brutally short. Most British forces buggered off after their victory. Largely, it was left to islanders to clean up the mess. I'm sure some of them kept trophies as well. From time to time we all bend rules. But your father's trophies must have been fascinating to you. You were only a young kid at the time of the war. When your parents recently passed away you wanted to use the weapons. You enrolled your friend Peter Hunt, because he had access to Terry Maloney's shooting range in Goose Green. You and Hunt would spend quality time there, firing at targets. It was illegal but it didn't warrant anything more than a slap on the wrist by police."

Pope's eyes were venomous. "Fuck you!"

Sign was unperturbed. "Using military-grade guns for target practice is one thing; using guns to kill people is another thing altogether. You entered into a business arrangement with Eddie Wilson, Rob Taylor, Billy Green, and Mike Jackson. You invested, with them, in the purchase of four trawlers, to be based in the east island. But, the business deal went sour. You lost money. That would have hurt. But you kept your mouth shut and did nothing. You were waiting for the right moment. That moment presented itself when Wilson and his pals decided to take on an Argentinian spy ship that had been lurking around the islands. Wilson knew you had British guns. He called you, asking to borrow them. You complied, with the stipulation that you had to be with them on that fateful voyage. Wilson thought nothing of that demand. He assumed that you just wanted to ensure that your guns were kept in good order. But, he didn't foresee the real reason you had to be on the boat that night. When Wilson and his friends got close to the Argentinian trawler, they opened fire on the vessel with the British guns you'd given them. Most likely it was amateur hour. Wilson and his men were drunk and probably didn't want to kill anyone. They just wanted the boat to go away. But, things then got serious. You shot Wilson, Taylor, Green, and Jackson, with one of your Argentinian war trophy guns. By this time, the spy ship was sailing fast away, fearing it had been compromised. And no doubt it was damaged by gunfire. You didn't care. You dumped the bodies in to the sea, left the British guns on board, and took your Argentinian weapon to the emergency dinghy and headed back to shore. It was all a set-up. Everyone in the know would assume that Wilson and his pals had been killed by Argentinians. You knew where that could lead, but you never knew it would lead back to you. And you did all of this because you wanted revenge. Wilson and his friends never paid you back after your silly investment. You wanted them dead. However, there is one thing I'm not entirely sure about – why did Hunt flee his house when Knutsen and I went to see him? And why did you kill him?"

Pope bowed his head. "He... he knew. I told him. He'd leant me the money to invest in Wilson's project. He hated Wilson and his friends as much as I did." He looked up and removed his hands from his head.

Knutsen stepped forward, tightly gripping his gun.

Pope smiled. "It's a tough life out here." He looked at Knutsen. "Take the shot. Go on. I confess to the murders. Your friend is right about everything. Take the shot."

Sign said in a firm voice, "That won't be necessary unless you do anything stupid." He used his mobile to call RAF Mount Pleasant. "I need to speak to Colonel Richards."

The switchboard operator told him that Richards had worked a night shift and was currently sleeping.

"Wake him up! Tell him I have the fifth man in custody and he needs to get to the west island right now! This is where he and his men need to land their helicopter." He gave the operator details of their location.

One hour later, Richards and four men were in Pope's house. Sign told the colonel what had happened. Pope was placed into hand and ankle cuffs and put on the chopper.

When Richards was alone with Sign in the lounge, he said, "So this was a local murder enquiry all along?"

Sign nodded. "When you first came to see me in London, I wondered if that might be the case. You thought it was the Argentinians who killed the men. But your insight that there was a fifth man on the boat rang alarm bells with me. I wondered if he'd cleverly staged their murders to look like a foreign power had killed them." He smiled. "When investigating matters like this, sometimes the obvious is not so obvious."

Richards nodded. "Pope will be kept in a secure wing in Pleasant. He'll be flown to London on one of my military jets. He'll stand trial and will get life imprisonment. He's killed five men. There'll be no chance of parole."

"Good." Sign smiled. "Oh, and talking of killing people, there is a somewhat delicate matter I need to impart to you. The man I shot at Maloney's place was an Argentinian assassin. He belonged to a four person unit who were here to kill the fifth man. The other three are dead. Their bodies are in the sheep pen at the Bluff Cove cottage. It would be terribly kind of you if you could arrange for the discrete disposal of the bodies."

Richards' eyes widened. "An Argentinian assassin unit?! You killed them?! Why didn't you tell me about them?"

"I didn't want to bother you with such matters." Sign checked his watch. "I believe you've lifted the ban on flights. Knutsen and I will be on the first flight out tomorrow. Meanwhile, tonight we're staying in Port Howard. There's a lovely B&B there. And the owner is a charming host. For dinner she's going to cook us lobster, fried seaweed, mash potato, and roasted lemons, served with a mustard pickle relish on the side. Hopefully she'll also throw in a nice bottle of dry white wine to accompany the dish." He held out his hand. "The case is closed. You owe me and Mr. Knutsen fifty thousand pounds. Goodbye Mr. Richards."

Richards shook his hand. "Thank you. Thank you both very much. Have a safe journey home."

As Sign walked out of the house he called out, "And I hope you have a lovely retirement. Avoid military reunions. They are so tiresome."

CHAPTER 14

Two days later, Sign and Knutsen were back in London. Despite having lived and worked in the capital for the majority of his adult life, it was the first time Knutsen noticed how frenetic and crowded the city was. As they sat in a cab, taking them from Paddington Station to West Square, he looked out of the window and thought his senses were going to overload. His eyes were wide as he looked at cars, people walking along streets, shops, buses, government buildings, high rise commercial properties, and boats as they drove over Lambeth Bridge to cross the Thames. His passenger window was open, because London was enduring a heatwave and the cab was stifling. The aperture enabled him to gain a variety of smells as they made their journey – petrol, diesel, food, overheated tarmac, coffee, perfume, and other scents. The noise was incredible – cars, horns, men using equipment on roadworks, helicopters, emergency vehicle sirens, music, voices, and shouting. It felt like the antithesis of the islands. He was relieved when they pulled up in the quiet retreat of the Edwardian and regal West Square. Sign paid the cabby. Both men entered the communal apartment block.

When inside their flat, Sign dumped his luggage on his bed and called out to Knutsen, "One hour for showering and changing. After that, I suggest we take a stroll."

An hour later, Knutsen emerged into the lounge. Sign was on his laptop, reading an email. He looked at Knutsen. "What on Earth are you wearing?"

Knutsen was in knee-length shorts, a T-shirt that had a picture of a surfboard emblazoned on its front, sandals, and had polarized wrap-around black sunglasses on his forehead. "It's hot out there."

By contrast, Sign was wearing immaculately pressed trousers, a striped shirt, and brogues. He'd shaved. Knutsen hadn't. He looked like a gentleman cricketer, about to partake of cucumber sandwiches and glass of Pimm's in the VIP stand at Lords. Knutsen looked like he was about to have a bottle of beer with some slacker dudes on a beach in Bali.

Sign said, "We need to adjust to the robust entanglement of our home's surroundings. We must mingle with the masses and recalibrate our bodies' tempo. I have the perfect solution. Chop chop. We have a walk to do."

It was late afternoon when they entered Borough Market. The venue was one of the largest and oldest markets in London, dating back to the twelfth century, and possibly even earlier. It sold fine speciality foods, was overlooked by Southwark Cathedral, and was nearby to the southern end of London Bridge. The sprawling venue was busy, in large part because discerning customers knew that at the end of the day they'd get discounted prices on produce.

Sign placed his hand on Knutsen's shoulder. "Follow me, Mr. Knutsen, and ignore the hustle and bustle. I know exactly where to go to fetch some delicious items for our supper." He stopped in front of a fruit and veg counter and addressed a thin man working the stall. "Good day to you Rick. What do you have for me today?"

Rick beamed and said in a London accent, "Mr. Sign. Good to see you sir. It's been a while. What are you cooking?"

"Most likely fish."

Rick patted some of the veg. "In that case, take a look at these beauties. Lemons from Spain. They're in season. Got some lovely parsley if you're hankering after a nice white sauce. Green beans are from a farmer in Berkshire. He knows his stuff. Spuds are the best I've seen in a couple of seasons – you can mash 'em, boil 'em, or roast 'em. And the carrots – blimey, sir. They hold their shape, ain't too sweet, and can be cooked whole or, as I prefer them, cut into slithers on one of them mandolin things. Just watch your fingers if you use that damn thing though."

Sign nodded approvingly. "Excellent, Rick. We'll take them all. Please bag up enough of each to satiate the appetite of two hungry men who've had to endure airplane food for the last fourteen hours." He looked at a basket of chillies. They were different shapes and sizes, some red, others green and yellow. He picked up a red chilli and held it to his nose. "Where did you source these?"

As Rick was placing Sign's order into brown paper bags, he replied, "There's a bloke I know. He's got a loft above his house in North London." He winked. "He grows all sorts of stuff up there, under lamps. These lovelies will be perfect for a few days. After that they'll dry out. But, you can still use them when they're dry."

"I'll take a small bag of them. A mix, if you please."

"Will you be looking to have a pudding? These strawberries are from East Kent. And these are from the Isle of Wight. I can't split them apart in terms of taste. They're the best in the world. Nice dollop of cream on them and you'll be job done."

"Why not."

After paying Rick, they walked to one of fifteen fishmonger stalls.

Sign spoke to a ruddy-faced proprietor. "Larry. How's your beautiful lady? Is she still working the flower stall?"

Larry grinned. "You bet she is. She keeps an eye on me. Stops me from chatting up the women-folk."

Sign laughed. "Quite right." He peered at the array of fresh fishing resting on ice. "I'm interested in this fella. Where was it caught and when?"

The fish was a two foot porbeagle shark. Wearing plastic gloves, Larry picked it up. "Caught off Dorset yesterday. Came in this morning with a load of other stuff. Fresh as a daisy."

"I'll take it. There's no need to clean the fish. I'll do that myself. Do you recommend steaming it in a foil parcel with butter, white wine, lemon, and herbs?"

"Bang on, sir. It should take about forty five minutes in the oven, but you can't go wrong with steaming it for an hour."

Sign and Knutsen walked back to West Square. Sign prepared the food, ready to be cooked an hour before they wanted to eat. He poured two glasses of Calvados and entered the lounge. He gave one of the glasses to Knutsen. Sign sat in his armchair. Knutsen was facing him, in his armchair. Sign raised his glass. "To the successful conclusion of the fifth man case."

Knutsen chinked his glass against Sign's glass. "How did you know that the fifth man was the murderer?"

Sign sipped his drink. "I didn't know for sure. It was a hypothesis. Throughout the investigation, I wanted to prove myself right or wrong. It transpired I was right, but it could have gone the other way. Regardless, we must be bold in our deductive processes. Poor Sally gave us no valuable information, simply because she didn't know what was valuable. It was only when she was under extreme duress by one of the assassins that she blurted out a nugget of valuable intelligence, from her memory vault. The name of Maloney. Thankfully for us, Richards gave us the heads up on Richards, though he imparted that data too late. Maloney was shot by an assassin; we killed the assassin; Maloney told us about Hunt; Hunt bolted when we tried to speak to him; and in doing so he inadvertently told us that he was running to a place of safety. Little did he know that the opposite was true. He called Pope when he saw us. Pope mobilised with a rifle. He shot Hunt before we could catch up with him. When I questioned Oates about whether someone lived near Hunt, I was wondering if someone could get to Hunt quick enough to kill him. Distance was key, as was the fact that the road north of Hunt abruptly ends after a few miles. Oates told me about Pope. I ascertained that Pope had motive to kill Wilson, Hunt, Taylor, Green, and Jackson. He became my prime suspect."

"But, we had to get rid of the assassins first."

Sign waved his hand dismissively. "They were nothing more than pit bulls, trying to latch their jaws onto our heels. Still, they wouldn't have stopped unless we stopped them first."

Knutsen smiled. "You followed an audit trail to Pope. But, when you were speaking to him, you said stuff that you couldn't possibly have known."

Sign looked out of the window. "I knew some things; other things I said were filling in gaps; and there is the most important component – imagination and bluff."

Knutsen laughed. "In my neck of the woods we'd call it the ability to *bullshit*."

Sign looked at Knutsen. "When a man is terrified, the correct use of bullshit will chill him to the bone." His expression softened. "I will cook dinner in a moment. But, I must warn you that while I'm doing so you must shave and change into a suit and tie. I too will adorn a suit. We have a guest who will be joining us for dinner. We must look the part. She's our next client."

Knutsen frowned. "What's the job?"

"She's head of MI6's Russia Department. That means she's
ry high ranking and tipped to be the next chief of service. But
e's hit a roadblock. She wishes to know why her prize foreign
ent no longer wishes to spy for her. She also has a personal matter
at she wishes us to look into. She has a twin sister. But they were
parated at birth. She wants us to find her sister." Sign stood. "Mr.
utsen – up and at 'em; onwards! We must be on point. I fear this
xt case may be our toughest yet. Remember – nothing will be what
seems. The case won't be merely about a person who's lost their
rve, or a mundane missing person investigation. It will take us into
bowels of national security. And we journeymen will have to
low that path, no matter what the cost to our lives."

THE END